"Get up," Mac ordered succinctly.

Maggie was still lying in bed when Mac marched into her room and yanked the blanket off her. "You're coming back to the station with me."

"I'm doing no such thing. You have no right to be here!" she exclaimed.

"*You* have no right to be here, either. You're supposed to be working. So get dressed. I'll give you two minutes."

"Just admit how much you need me, Mac, and then maybe I'll reconsider my position."

"I'll reconsider it for you, honey," he said, and with one quick movement he picked her up, flung her over his shoulder and headed for the door.

She objected to his manhandling, but she was smiling. Obviously, he needed her, whether he wanted to admit it or not.

Dear Reader,

This month Silhouette **Special Edition** brings you the third (though not necessarily the last) volume of Lindsay McKenna's powerful **LOVE AND GLORY** miniseries, and we'd love to know if the *Return of a Hero* moves you as much as it did our Silhouette editors. Many of you write in requesting sequels or tie-in books—now we'd like to hear how you enjoyed our response!

Many of you also urge us to publish more books by your favorite Silhouette authors, and with this month's lively selection of novels by Jo Ann Algermissen, Carole Halston, Bevlyn Marshall, Natalie Bishop and Maggi Charles, we hope we've satisfied that craving, as well.

Each and every month our Silhouette **Special Edition** authors and editors strive to bring you the ultimate in satisfying romance reading. Although we cannot answer your every letter, we do take your comments and requests to heart. So, many thanks for your help—we hope you'll keep coming back to Silhouette **Special Edition** to savor the results!

From all the authors and editors of Silhouette **Special Edition**,

Warmest wishes,

Leslie Kazanjian, Senior Editor
Silhouette Books
300 East 42nd Street
New York, N.Y. 10017

BEVLYN MARSHALL
Radio Daze

Silhouette Special Edition

Published by Silhouette Books New York

America's Publisher of Contemporary Romance

SILHOUETTE BOOKS
300 East 42nd St., New York, N.Y. 10017

ISBN: 0-373-09544-9

First Silhouette Books printing August 1989

Printed in the U.S.A.

Books by Bevlyn Marshall

Silhouette Special Edition

Lonely at the Top #407
The Pride of His Life #441
Grady's Lady #506
Radio Daze #544

BEVLYN MARSHALL,

a Connecticut resident, has had a varied career in fashion, public relations and marketing but finds writing the most challenging and satisfying occupation. When she's not at her typewriter, she enjoys tennis, needlepoint, long walks with her husband and toy spaniel, and reading. She believes that people who read are rarely bored or lonely because "the private pleasure of a good book is one of life's most rewarding pastimes."

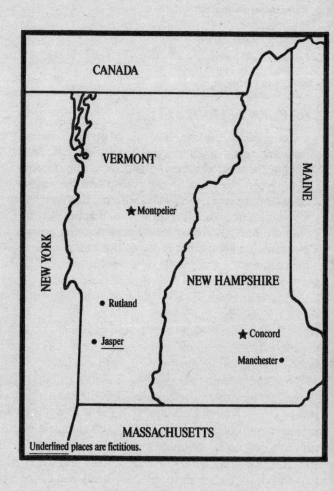

CANADA

NEW YORK

VERMONT

★ Montpelier

● Rutland

● Jasper

MAINE

NEW HAMPSHIRE

★ Concord

Manchester ●

MASSACHUSETTS

Underlined places are fictitious.

would have shocked her dear mother to the core. Then she reviewed her options.

She could start walking with the hope of finding help, but it was a frail hope. She hadn't passed a house, a gas station, or any sign of civilization for the past twenty miles she'd traveled on this Vermont country road.

Or she could wait in the car until some passing motorist came along. It went against Maggie's grain to take such a passive course of action, but since it seemed the wisest one she opted for it. She would have appreciated a radio to help pass the time, but the one in this lemon of a car she'd rented didn't work. Maggie sorely regretted the lost opportunity to check out station WPEU before her interview. But more importantly, her chances of making that interview on time were growing dimmer with each passing moment.

A few minutes later she glimpsed a truck approaching in her rearview mirror. Sure that her streak of bad luck had ended, Maggie got out and hailed it, arms flailing, smile wide. All she got for her trouble were some hoots from the three short-necked men who were wedged shoulder to shoulder in the cab. The driver saluted her by raising his beer can as the truck rattled past without slowing down.

"Damn Yankees!" Maggie shouted, shaking her fist at them as they receded into the distance.

But she was more relieved than disappointed that they'd passed her by. The idea of being at the mercy of such a rough-looking trio made her shudder. It also made her appreciate what a precarious position she was in—stranded in a strange and lonely place. Perhaps she should have listened to her mother's dire warnings and never left home for parts unknown. Refusing to give in to such bleak thoughts, Maggie concentrated on the positive. It was a beautiful September afternoon, and surely some kind, lovely soul would come along at any moment to help her out.

* * *

Driving a little too fast, Madison MacNair navigated his old Jaguar convertible along the twisting country road. She was performing well, he thought with satisfaction. He'd spent a lot of time and energy rebuilding the engine during the past year or so. Precious time. But that was all behind him now. He had said his goodbyes. Now it was time to get on with his life.

He fiddled with the radio dial until he tuned in station WPEU. His expression became more and more disdainful as he listened to the disc jockey drone out a list of birthday greetings, then introduce an insipid rendition of a great Beatles classic. Mac snapped off the radio, unable to stomach one of his favorite songs turned into elevator music. There was no doubt about it—WPEU was the pits, he decided, feeling a little depressed. He popped a Bruce Springsteen cassette into the tape deck, and pretty soon Mac was thumping his hand against the steering wheel and singing along with "the Boss." His spirits lifted as the wind ripped through his thick, shaggy hair.

He would soon be back on top again, he assured himself, even if it meant starting all over at some third-rate station in Rutland. He figured it would take him less than a year to reestablish his reputation as the best disc jockey in the business. Then goodbye Vermont, hello Manhattan!

He sped on to his destination, paying scant attention to the woodland and meadows glowing in the September sunlight. But as his car sailed over the crest of a hill, the scenery ahead suddenly became a lot more interesting. Mac shifted gears and slowed down to appreciate the sight of a pretty blonde dressed head to toe in peach, leaning against a dark blue sedan. He gave her a long, steady appraisal. Her tire may have been flat but *she* certainly wasn't. He pulled over, cut his engine and got out.

"Looks like you're in trouble," he said, ambling toward her.

Was she? Maggie eyed him warily as he approached. Although he seemed a big improvement over the three yahoos in the pickup truck, she still found his appearance intimidating. He was taller than average, broad shouldered, with wild dark hair. The mirrored lenses of his aviator sunglasses hid his eyes completely. Maybe he wore them to keep from going blind at the sight of his own shirt, Maggie thought sardonically. It was his shirt that really put her off—a Hawaiian print in loud, clashing colors. She would have trusted a man dressed more conservatively.

Observing the apprehension in her wide golden eyes, Mac sympathized with her. Here she was, a defenseless young woman at the mercy of anyone who came along. The last thing Mac ever claimed to be was a gentleman, but he supposed he was as much a sucker for a lovely damsel in distress as any man.

"This shouldn't take long. I'm a fast worker," he told her, quickly unbuttoning his shirt. Her face registered absolute horror when he bared his chest. Since he had no lewd tattoo etched upon it, Mac couldn't understand her reaction.

And then he did. "I'm about to change your tire, not attack you, lady. But if you don't mind, I'd just as soon keep my shirt clean. It's hand painted and set me back five hundred bucks." He took off the costly silk garment, tossed it to her, and stomped to the rear of her car, miffed that she'd so badly misinterpreted his good intentions.

Relief flooded over Maggie, replacing the adrenaline shooting through her system. She'd been fully prepared to put all the karate moves she'd learned in her self-defense class into practice.

"Give me the key to your trunk," Mac demanded in a gruff, injured tone. "And if you don't stop clutching my shirt like that you're going to get it all wrinkled."

"Oh, sorry." She smoothed out the material with her palm to make amends. But she still didn't trust him. What sort of man would pay five hundred dollars for a shirt depicting gaudy hula girls and pineapples? "I appreciate your offer to help, but there's no spare in the trunk, I'm afraid." She handed back his shirt.

Mac slung it over his shoulder and sighed wearily. "No spare? How typically female."

"My gender has nothing to do with it, sir. This car is a rental. And if the person who's supposed to check out those things had done *his* job, I would have changed the tire myself and been on my merry way by now." Having made that clear, Maggie rolled down her sleeves and began buttoning up the cuffs.

Mac observed her hands as she worked the tiny pearl buttons. They were small and delicate, with perfectly manicured fingernails. Not the kind of hands he could easily picture jacking up a car and loosening tight bolts. He snorted his disbelief at her claim. "Changing a tire is a man's job, honey. There's no way you could have managed it on your own."

If he'd started thumping his chest right then Maggie wouldn't have been a bit surprised. He certainly looked fit enough to take on the Tarzan role. He seemed to have just the right ape-man mentality for it, too.

She batted her eyes at him in her best southern belle manner. "Well, there's no sense arguing about it, is there, sir?"

Mac guessed that although she'd addressed him as "sir," she'd really meant *idiot*. He'd definitely picked up a note of condescension in that sugary drawl of hers. It made him disinclined to offer his help again, especially after she'd been so quick to misjudge his altruistic motives the first time.

"Then I guess I'll be on my way," he said. But instead of going on his way, he draped one long arm across the hood of her car and waited. If she wanted a lift, she was going to have to ask for it.

So now he's going to make me beg for a ride, Maggie thought irritably. Everything about the man bothered her. She wished he would put on his shirt and stop showing off. She couldn't help but watch in fascination as his muscles rippled when he shifted his pose, stretched and hooked a thumb in the band of his low-riding jeans.

"Yeah, I guess I'll be on my way," Mac said again. From the way she was gnawing at that plump bottom lip of hers, he could tell she was reluctant to ask a simple favor. "Unless I can be of some further use to you," he added to prod her along.

Maggie cleared her throat. If he wasn't going to put on his shirt, she wished he would at least take off his mirrored sunglasses. She found it rather difficult to ask a favor from a half naked man without first seeing his eyes. "Are you by any chance going in the direction of Rutland?"

Mac gave her his best deadpan look. "Could be."

"Well, are you or aren't you?" Maggie asked, impatience getting the better of her. "You must have known where you were headed when you got into your car. I'm sure you didn't drive off without a destination in mind."

Then it occurred to her that maybe he had done just that. Maybe he was the sort of man who had nothing better to do with his time than put on a silly hula-girl shirt, jump into his old, dented sports car, turn on loud music and just *drive*.

Her impatient attitude annoyed Mac. He didn't much care for that frilly getup of hers, either. As far as he was concerned, her taste in clothes rated zero. But the body wearing them was surely a ten and so he relented.

"In fact, I *am* headed for Rutland. And you're welcome to come along." He put on his shirt at last and Maggie decided that his bare, golden chest had been a much more pleasing sight.

"I'd appreciate knowing your name before I accept your offer," she said. "My mother always warned me never to get into a car with a stranger."

Mac flashed a dangerous grin. "You want to see my driver's license?"

"Well, now that you mention it, some sort of identification *would* be appreciated. Please don't take this personally, but a woman can't be too careful nowadays."

She was pretty demanding, Mac thought, considering he was the one about to do *her* a favor. Who did she think she was, anyway? Scarlett O'Hara? He extracted a card from the back pocket of his jeans. "Allow me to present my calling card," he said with a bow as he offered it to her.

Maggie examined the card and it gave her no reassurance whatsoever. The bold print proclaimed the bearer to be Mad Dog MacNair. There was no address nor telephone number, only a drawing of a snarling dog beneath the name.

"Mad Dog. What a charming name," she said wryly. What bothered Maggie most was that his name had a familiar ring to it. Was he some notorious criminal she'd read about? But surely notorious criminals didn't go around handing out business cards.

"Actually that's my professional handle," Mac explained, disappointed that an explanation was necessary. Fame was indeed fleeting, he reminded himself.

Then it hit Maggie. Of course! Mad Dog MacNair—that "bad boy" northern disc jockey everybody in the business had been talking about a few years ago. Predictions at the conservative Birmingham station where Maggie had worked were that he would burn himself out with his own outrageousness—if Federal Communications Commission regulations didn't shut him up first. And then Mad Dog had disappeared from the airwaves as suddenly as he'd set them on fire. There had been rumors of payola, of drugs, of an emotional breakdown to account for his unexplained absence. Remembering these dark rumors gave Maggie little comfort now.

She folded her fingers over his card. "It just dawned on me who you are, Mr. MacNair. We happen to be in the same profession."

"You mean you're a radio jockette?"

She bristled at the belittling term. "Yes, I'm a disc jockey."

"With your looks you'd be better off trying to sell your wares on television."

"Sell my wares! You have a rather crass way of expressing yourself, Mr. MacNair."

He pushed his sunglasses up the bridge of his long, straight nose and smiled. He'd been accused of a lot worse than that. "Hey, don't take offense. I was just trying to give you a little free advice. Radio is a tough business for women to break into." Although he had to admit she had a good voice for it. Her southern accent was pure honey, with an underlying huskiness cutting through the sweetness.

"I've managed to get along just fine without your advice," she told him. "I produced and hosted my own show in Birmingham for the past three years. And now I'm being considered for a deejay job in Rutland."

"Not the morning slot at WPEU, I hope?"

She replied with a noncommittal stare but Mac read the answer in her narrowed gold eyes.

"That's too bad, honey. I'm going to take over that show. Better luck next time." Mac gave her a consoling pat on the head.

"Hold on a minute." Maggie tossed back her head, not appreciating his patronizing pat. "Mr. Stanmore, the station manager, called me yesterday to ask me to fly up from Birmingham to talk about it. Why would he do that if he'd already hired you?"

"Because he didn't know I was going to accept his offer yesterday," Mac explained with great patience. "He still doesn't. I'm on my way to give him the good news personally."

"Then nothing's been officially settled yet."

Mac shrugged. "It will be as soon as I walk into Stanmore's office. It's not every day a two-bit station like PEU gets the chance to have someone like me boost its sagging ratings."

"Or someone like me," Maggie declared. "Don't be so quick to count me out, Mr. MacNair. The way I see it, I still stand a chance for that job."

He chuckled softly. Poor kid—she wasn't even savvy enough to appreciate who she was up against. "What's your name, anyway. Maybe I've heard of you."

"Margaret Bloomer," she replied, doubting he had.

Mac feigned amazement. "Not *the* Margaret Bloomers!" he cried, enjoying the image of lacy turn-of-the-century unmentionables that had popped into his mind.

"It's Bloomer. Singular," Maggie stressed.

The irritation in her voice spurred Mac on to tease her further. "How do I know that's your real name, lady?"

"Don't be absurd. Why would I lie about it?"

"Please don't take this personally, but a man can't be too careful nowadays," he said, not only repeating her words but mimicking her accent, too. He held out his hand, palm up. "Any form of identification will do, ma'am."

Maggie glared down at his open palm, tempted to slap it. "I don't find this the least bit amusing."

Well, *he* did. Containing a smile, he folded his arms across his chest. "I'm not driving you anywhere until you prove you're who you claim to be."

Maggie was sure he wouldn't budge unless she went along with him. Muttering under her breath, she marched over to her car and got her purse. She took our her wallet and threw it at him.

Mac caught it as it bounced off his chest. "Thank you," he said with the utmost politeness, then began to peruse its contents. "Well, I see you've managed to acquire a lot of Margaret Bloomer's charge cards."

"Those are *my* charge cards," she muttered, wondering how long he would continue his stupid game.

"Who's this?" he asked, taking out a picture of an attractive blond man in tennis whites.

"My fiancé, Lamar Bleaker," she stated flatly.

Her reply caused Mac to experience an irrational flicker of jealousy. "Looks like a stuffy jackass to me."

Maggie gave him a haughty glare. "Don't judge your betters, Mr. MacNair."

"Gee, have I just been shot down?" Unconcerned, Mac went back to studying the photograph. There was something about the guy that really irritated him. "I bet your precious Lamar is a real dud in the sack. I can tell by that stiff pose of his, that self-satisfied smirk. Hell, I bet he even wears monogrammed boxer shorts."

Maggie would have taken great pleasure in wringing MacNair's neck. It infuriated her that he'd guessed right about the boxer shorts! And...other things, too. "Please put back the picture," she requested frostily. "You're way out of line."

More like right on target, Mac surmised from the way her face had flushed. He slid the photo back into its plastic holder, but purposely upside down, then took out Maggie's driver's license. "Let's see. Five feet six. A hundred and ten pounds." He slowly took her in from head to toe. "Well, that doesn't fit. You're obviously taller."

"I'm wearing high heels, you nincompoop."

"No name-calling, please. Just turn around, if you don't mind, so I can verify your weight from behind."

"I most certainly *do* mind! And I'm plumb fed up with your tomfoolery."

Her drawl got much thicker when she was angry, Mac noted. "Temper, temper," he cautioned without looking up. "Date of birth—June 15, 1963." He paused a moment, making a big display of counting on his fingers. "That makes you thirty-six years old," he pronounced.

"*Twenty*-six!" Maggie corrected sharply.

"Whatever you say, honey. It's a woman's prerogative to lie about her age."

He handed back her wallet and Maggie clutched it so tightly her knuckles turned white. He was making it so easy for her to loathe him. So very, very easy. "If you're quite through with your idiotic interrogation, perhaps we can proceed to Rutland," she said.

He didn't budge. "I'm still not sure I can trust you to act like a lady while you're sitting beside me."

"Surely you jest, Mr. MacNair."

Mac maintained a straight face. "I saw the lust in your eyes when I took off my shirt, Miss Bloomer. So there's no sense in denying it. You've got the hots for me."

Maggie rolled her eyes and groaned. He was going to tease her to death, she was sure. It would be a slow, excruciating torture, and then she would expire, relieved to be put out of her misery. Hell was not fire and brimstone, after all. True hell was asking a man called Mad Dog MacNair for a ride to Rutland. She took a deep breath and decided she would manage to hold on a little longer.

"I promise you that I won't get fresh with you during our trip together," she said through clenched teeth. "Now *please*. Let's go!"

"But how can I be sure you'll have enough self-control to keep that promise?" Mac persisted. "While my hands are on the wheel, who knows where yours will be, Miss Bloomer. Caressing my knee, perhaps?" His voice became low and insinuating. "Slowly creeping up my thigh? Then playing with my belt buc—"

"Enough!" Maggie shouted. "You're insulting and odious and rude and crude, MacNair. Why, I wouldn't touch the likes of you with a ten-foot pole!"

His smile was slow and lazy. "Careful, honey. Or I may take offense and drive off without you."

Maggie gave him a challenging look. "You wouldn't dare leave me stranded."

"Hey, from the way you just described me, it sounds like I'm capable of anything."

"Don't try to bluff me, MacNair. You can't refuse to drive me to my interview. Think how bad that would make you look when I turned up at the station and told everyone what a low-down thing you did to get the job."

Mac took a pack of gum out of his shirt pocket, slowly unwrapped a stick, then chewed on it awhile, as if contemplating his dilemma. "You seem to be under the false impression that I give a damn about what anyone thinks of me," he finally said. "But I stopped doing that a long time ago. See you later, honey." He blew a kiss her way. "If you ever *do* make it to Rutland, make sure to tune me in on PEU.'' He began walking away.

Maggie was stunned for a moment, unable to move or speak. Then suddenly a thought occurred to her. Surely no one, not even Mad Dog MacNair, could be that despicable. He was just taunting her again and would turn around any second now to beckon her to his car. But he didn't. He got in, started the car, and rock and roll blared through the quiet countryside once more.

"Waaaait!" Maggie wailed over the music, running toward his convertible as it started to pull away. "Please, stop!"

When she realized that he wasn't going to, she took off her shoe and threw it at him in a rage that gave her toss both power and accuracy. The shoe glanced off the side of Mac's head and landed in the passenger seat as he drove on.

Maggie watched him disappear, amazed at her own capacity to hate another human being so instantly and intensely. Not that a low-down creature like Mad Dog MacNair was actually *human*, she told herself, hobbling back to her car. She kicked off her other shoe, and the sight of it lying on the road—so forlorn and useless now—made her want to weep. Better yet, it made her want to swear. Since no one was around to hear her, she shouted curses at the top of her lungs, spewing out her frustration and anger, then took a deep breath.

"Having a bad day, dearie?"

Maggie swiveled around to see a tiny, silver-haired old lady leaning on an ebony walking stick, calmly observing her.

Chapter Two

I beg your pardon, ma'am." Maggie attempted an apologetic smile. "I wasn't aware of your presence."

"I've heard worse in my time," she replied mildly, smiling back. She was wearing a kelly-green jacket and slacks and looked a bit like an elf.

No, a mischievous pixie, Maggie decided, catching the twinkle in the old lady's deep-set blue eyes. "Where did you come from?" she asked.

"The woods yonder." She waved her ebony cane toward a thick stand of spruce. "I spotted two yellow-bellied sapsuckers today."

"That's nice," Maggie said, having no better response.

The tiny woman shrugged her frail shoulders. "They're hardly rare in these parts." Her eyes skimmed Maggie's disabled car and rested on the New York license plates. "Your timing's a good month off if you're a leaf peeker."

Maggie was unfamiliar with the term, but it sounded a little sordid to her. "I'm no such thing," she assured the woman. "I'm on my way to Rutland on business. Or I was before my tire gave out. There's no spare in the trunk and no one has passed this way for ages."

Gray eyebrows were raised in disbelief. "But didn't I observe a young man drive away as I came out of the woods? In fact, I saw you throw your shoe at him."

"Oh, *him*," Maggie said with heated contempt. "He left me stranded, that low-down..." She held her tongue. There was no need to assault this little old lady's ears again. "Suffice it to say he was *no* gentleman."

"Well, it's a good thing you're not on the isle of Zerbonia right now or you'd be officially engaged to him. Throwing a shoe at a man—more precisely a jute sandal— is a girl's formal declaration of affections there."

"How interesting," Maggie said politely, although she had little use for that particular piece of information at the moment. And little use for the shoe she'd left lying in the middle of the road, either, since its mate was accompanying MacNair to Rutland. She chastised herself for letting her temper get the best of her like that. She hadn't packed a spare pair in her overnight bag. Oh, well, she would figure out something. She always did.

"Do you happen to live nearby, ma'am?" Surely, at her age, she couldn't have hiked a great distance. "I'd really appreciate the use of your phone. Perhaps you can suggest a local service station I could call for help. I have to get to Rutland as soon as possible." If Mad Dog MacNair thought he'd left his competition in the dust, he was badly mistaken.

"I'll be happy to get you to Rutland, dearie."

How? Maggie wondered. By waving her magical cane and clicking her heels? Nothing would have surprised Maggie at this stage. MacNair's desertion had shaken her up more than she wanted to admit. No man had ever treated her with such total disregard.

The wrinkled little pixie didn't wave her cane, though. She put two fingers between her lips and gave a shrill, piercing whistle. Maggie half expected a unicorn to come prancing out of the woods in response, but a long, black Rolls-Royce appeared over the crest of the hill instead. The chauffeur stopped beside them, got out and opened the back door.

"We're going to take this young lady to Rutland, Ralph."

"Okeydokey, Miss Jasper." The chauffeur tipped his baseball cap to her. His livery was as casual as his attitude and headgear—a plaid flannel shirt and baggy work pants. "You want me to continue on this road, or should I turn around and take the shortcut?"

"The shortcut, but mind the ruts." Miss Jasper hopped into the car with an agility that belied her age and beckoned Maggie to join her. "Ralph will get you there in no time flat," she assured Maggie.

"Please, don't even say that word!" Maggie said, settling into the plush back seat as Ralph made a U-turn. She gave her companion a grateful smile. "I almost believe I conjured you up through wishful thinking."

"What a fanciful thought, dearie. Next thing you'll be claiming is that I'm your fairy godmother."

"Only if you happen to have a pair of glass slippers handy. I don't relish walking into an important interview barefoot."

"I'll be happy to lend you my shoes." She raised one sneaker-shod foot for Maggie's inspection. "Size five and a half."

"Close enough," Maggie said, suppressing the urge to give her a big hug. She offered her hand instead. "Thank you, Miss Jasper. My name is Margaret Bloomer."

"But of course I already know your name and everything about you, Margaret, being that I'm magical." She tittered over Maggie's wide-eyed look of amazement. "Just joking, dearie. Just joking."

Mac tapped Maggie's shoe against the dashboard in time with the music, grinning broadly. She wasn't going to get too far without it, was she? He considered the possibility that he'd gone too far with his teasing and then discarded the thought. She was one feisty female; she could take it—and dish it out, too, he reminded himself, rubbing the side of his head. Luckily the toe of her shoe had hit its mark instead of the sharp high heel.

He stopped a few miles down the road and turned around, looking forward to seeing the relief and joy on her face when he came back for her. "Hop in, honey," he would say casually. And hop she would have to, with only one shoe. Mac threw back his curly dark head and laughed.

His glee quickly faded, though, when he reached her car and discovered that she was gone. No vehicle had passed his way from either direction, so he couldn't figure out how she'd managed to disappear like that. He spotted her other shoe in the middle of the road and his stomach knotted with apprehension as he got out to investigate. Had she kicked it off in order to flee from danger? From someone on foot? Mac looked toward the woods, cursing himself for driving off and leaving her alone for even a few minutes. A beautiful young woman had vanished into thin air and he felt totally responsible.

He had no choice but to search for her. As Mac headed into the woods he considered the possibility that she was playing a joke of her own by hiding behind a clump of trees. He couldn't picture her dashing through the prickly undergrowth barefoot, though, catching her ruffled dress and

tearing her hose. No, that didn't fit his image of dainty
Margaret Bloomer. He plunged onward, calling out for her,
becoming more and more anxious to find his lost lady.

Less than an hour later Maggie was sitting across the desk
from Stanton Lovell Stanmore, Jr., WPEU's station manager. He was a vague sort of man in his late thirties, with
long, thinning red hair. He wore wire-framed glasses, over-
alls and a constant, lopsided grin. He appeared to be an
anachronism to Maggie, a laid-back hippie from the sixties.

"I'm sorry I arrived a little late for our interview," she
told him. "I had a flat tire on the way."

And was left in the lurch by a low-down weasel, she added
silently. She'd expected to find Mad Dog MacNair in Stanmore's office and had been looking forward to confronting
him. She refrained from bringing up his name, though, deciding to let sleeping dogs lie for the time being.

Stanmore waved away her apology. "So you're a little
late, Maggie. No big deal. I don't have any hang-ups about
time. My old man always says time is money, which drives
me up a wall. His corporation owns this radio station, by the
way. Dear old Dad has given me six months to make a success of it. He expects me to fail, of course. Like I have in
everything else."

Maggie didn't know quite how to respond to that bleak
pronouncement. "You can always prove your father
wrong," she suggested, certainly hoping he would if she
became an employee.

"That's been my life's dream," he replied wistfully. "And
maybe you can help me achieve it, Maggie. When I heard
your audition tape, it like really knocked me out."

"Thank you, Mr. Stanmore. Of course, I had to telescope my show down to five minutes, but I hope I managed to get across the—"

"Hey, cool this mister stuff and call me Stan," he interrupted. "I don't have any hang-ups about formality, either. That's my old man's bag, not mine." His easygoing manner became more intense. "If my father could get away with it, he'd have everyone call him King Stanmore, supreme ruler of the corporate world and all galactic subsidiaries!" Stan took a deep breath after stating this, closed his eyes and chanted something inaudible. "My mantra," he explained to Maggie, his smile returning. "It calms me down. Now what were we talking about?"

"My audition tape, Stan," she reminded him patiently. "As I was saying, it only gives a tiny flavor of the type of show I hosted. I tried to make it as innovative and interesting as possible with special features and interviews. For instance, I created a segment called—"

"Hey, with a voice like yours, I bet people would tune in to hear you read the phone directory," he interrupted again.

Maggie sighed with frustration. She'd been trying to get across the opposite point.

"Why'd you leave your deejay gig in Birmingham, Maggie?"

"The station changed ownership after I'd worked there five years," she explained. "Now it specializes in religious programming and there was a complete staff change."

"What a bummer for you," Stan said sympathetically.

"Oh, well. You've got to learn to roll with the punches in this business."

Maggie's pragmatic tone gave no hint of the initial blow it had been to her. She'd started at her hometown station right out of college, working her way up from programming assistant to traffic reporter to entertainment reviewer, and eventually reaching her goal as a full-fledged disc jockey with her own show. She'd wanted a career in radio ever since she was twelve or so, pretending her hairbrush was a microphone and her row of Barbie dolls her avid listeners. But now she would have to relocate if she wanted to continue in the field. Opportunities didn't come to you in radio—you went to them. So here she was in Rutland, hoping some aging hippie would give her a chance behind the mike at WPEU.

Meanwhile, a mad dog was hot on her heels in pursuit of the same job. Maggie restrained herself from glancing over her shoulder. What was keeping MacNair, anyway? Surely he should have made it here by now. Of course, she'd had the advantage of Ralph's shortcut over a bumpy dirt road. That must have saved more time than she'd supposed, and she had no intention of wasting it. She was going to do her best to wrangle a job offer out of Stanmore before MacNair arrived on the scene. Oh, what a coup that would be!

"Alabama's loss could be Vermont's gain, Stan," she said, disregarding another of her mother's many dictums— *A lady never toots her own horn*. She was a long way from home now, after all, with no one to toot it for her. "I built up quite a following with my show. Ratings doubled within two years after I took over the morning slot, and I'm confident I could do the same at PEU." At least she hoped she *sounded* confident.

"Could you start right away?"

Maggie's heart picked up a few beats. "Immediately."

"That's cool."

Did that mean he was going to hire her? It was hard to tell with ambiguous Stan. Maggie held her breath and waited, but all he did was stare at the ceiling for a while, saying nothing. She shifted in her chair impatiently. Finally he looked back at her.

"I want to be up-front with you, Maggie. You're not exactly the type of deejay that I originally wanted for the morning show. You're . . . well, you're a *lady*, you know?"

"I certainly always try to be one," she replied stiffly. But she knew what he really meant. "Listen, Stan, this prejudice against female disc jockeys on radio is really outdated. Women have been accepted in every other communication medium."

"Hey, I'm no male chauvinist pig," he objected in a mild voice. "No way, Maggie. I remember back in '64—no, maybe it was '66. Yeah, I'd transferred from Columbia to Berkeley. Or the other way around. Anyway, I was a staunch supporter of women's liberation, Maggie. I was right there at the bra burnings. If they wanted to go around without upper supports, hey, it was okay with me."

"You're obviously a truly enlightened man," Maggie drawled. Remain patient, she cautioned herself. You need this job.

"So it's not that I object to hiring a woman deejay," he continued. "It's just that I envisioned the new morning show to be sort of wild and crazy and, like, a little raunchy."

"I'm *certainly* not raunchy," Maggie declared. A part of her yearned to be a little more wild and crazy, though.

"Oh, I could tell that right off from your audition tape," he assured her. "You've got a lot of class, Maggie. And it made me begin to rethink my original concept."

Maggie arched an eyebrow. It was difficult enough to imagine Stan thinking, let alone *re*thinking. "Do you have a new concept now?"

"Well, it's not completely worked out yet, but I figure that if I hired you for the six-to-ten slot you could give the listeners a little sugar with their morning coffee, Maggie—

instead of the jolt they would have gotten from Mad Dog MacNair.''

Hearing his name certainly gave Maggie a jolt but she didn't mention her encounter with Mad Dog to Stan.

"No doubt you've heard of him," Stan went on. "He was the hottest jock on radio a few years back. But then he dropped out for some reason." He lifted his narrow shoulders. "Anyway, I tracked Mad Dog down a few weeks ago and asked him to take over the morning show. Actually I begged him to."

"Then why did you ask me to come all the way up here for an interview if you want *him*?" she asked, not trying to hide how put out she was.

Stan sighed. "Because Mad Dog never got back to me about my offer. I didn't want to settle for a pale imitation of him, so I decided to go in the opposite direction. And there can't be any disc jockey more opposite in style than you, Maggie."

Maggie had long ago given up trying to follow Stan's convoluted reasoning, but she understood one thing clearly. "You mean I'm your second choice, don't you, Stan."

"No, no, no. You're my first choice *after* Mad Dog. And since he's obviously not interested in working for a small station like PEU, there's no contest." Stan slowly got to his feet and put out his hand. "Welcome aboard, Maggie."

Maggie rose, too, but didn't shake hands. How could she accept his offer in good conscience after he'd made his preference so clear? "It really kills me to tell you this," she said and she wasn't exaggerating that much. "But I happen to know that MacNair wants this job so much he'd do almost anything to get it." She was tempted to relate his lowdown tactics to Stan, but decided against it. A face-to-face confrontation with that snake in the grass was one thing, but talking behind his spineless back was another. It simply wasn't Maggie's style.

"You know this for a fact?" Stan's pale eyes widened and he withdrew his proffered hand. "But how? Do you actually know Mad Dog personally?" There was a tinge of awe in his voice.

"Not *that* personally," Maggie stressed. "We met briefly on the road to Rutland. The last I saw MacNair, he was on his merry way here to accept your offer. I can't imagine what's keeping him."

"I've been looking for you, that's what, honey," a deep, droll voice broke in.

A shiver ran up Maggie's spine when she heard it and she spun around. MacNair was leaning against the open office doorway, twirling his sunglasses between his fingers. His wide grin was just as maddening as Maggie remembered it, his shirt just as loud, but there was something different about his appearance now. Of course. His eyes. It was the first time she'd seen his eyes.

And they surprised her. She'd assumed they would be small and narrow and mean. But actually they were large and luminous, brimming with humor. And there seemed to be more than humor in their deep brown depths. Sensitivity, perhaps? Maggie shook her head. No way. Only a man with the sensitivity of a rock would leave a woman stranded on a desolate road to beat her out of a job.

"You really had me worried," he continued. "My last hope was finding you here."

His false sincerity didn't fool her one bit.

"How can you even look me in the face after what you did to me?" she asked in a voice trembling with righteous rage. What made his effrontery even more galling was that his dark, glinting eyes were drinking in every part of her anatomy and not just her face.

"After what I did to *you*?" He laughed and rubbed the side of his head. "You're the one who resorted to physical violence, honey. By the way, I really like your sneakers. Definitely a less lethal form of footwear."

"I only wish I'd had a shotgun handy when you left me in the lurch like that, you skunk. I would have happily blown out your..." Maggie paused. Even in the throes of her outrage, she couldn't bring herself to complete such a murderous proclamation.

"My brains?" Mac finished for her with a gleeful grin.

"As if you had any! No, your tires."

"Then it's lucky for me that you didn't have a gun handy. I'm very fond of that car. But enough of these pleasantries, Miss Bloomer. Let's get down to the one burning question that's been on my mind for the past two hours or so. How did you manage to disappear on me like that? Were you hiding in the trunk of your car when I came back to get you?"

"You came back to get me? Oh, that's a good one!" Maggie wasn't smiling, though.

"Of course I came back. What do you take me for? Some kind of creep?"

"Of the lowest order," she replied. But as much as Maggie believed that to be true, she couldn't help herself from finding him physically attractive. She wished she didn't and turned her back on him. "I assume our interview is over, Stan," she told the station manager. "You won't be needing me to take over the morning show now that your first choice is here." Her tone was bitter but resigned.

"I can't believe it's true." Stan just stood there, looking stunned. "I can't believe Mad Dog MacNair is here in person."

Mac gave him a quick once-over. "Are you Stanmore? The one who called me a few weeks ago?"

Stan managed a nod.

"I've got some unfinished business to settle with this lady first and then we'll talk, okay?"

"Anything to oblige, Mad Dog. I'll be as quiet as a mouse."

"Better yet, you could leave Miss Bloomer and me alone for a few minutes," Mac suggested.

"No problem, man." Stan started tiptoeing out of his own office.

"Stay right where you are, Stan," Maggie commanded, unable to bear his toadying a moment longer. "I have no desire to be left alone with *him*." She nodded her head in the direction of MacNair without deigning to look at him, then snatched her purse and headed for the door, intent on making an abrupt but dignified exit.

But Mac blocked her way. "Trying to give me the slip again, honey?"

"This time forever, I hope."

She pushed against him but he didn't budge. She pressed her shoulder harder against the muscled wall of his chest and he pressed back gently.

"We seem to have reached an impasse," Mac said softly.

His solid warmth disturbed her and she took a step back. "I'm not going to play games with you, MacNair."

"Too bad. I bet you'd enjoy playing with me, Miss Bloomer."

"I doubt it. Mother always cautioned me to avoid scalawags who cheat."

"You should have stopped listening to your mamma years ago, honey," Mac advised, picking up her drawl. "Does she actually call people scalawags?"

"Leave my mother out of this, MacNair."

"Well, you brought her up." He leaned against the door-jamb and showed his bright, strong teeth in a smile. "And by the way, I don't cheat."

Maggie managed a choked laugh. "Oh, spare me! What do you call driving off and leaving your competition behind? I call it foul play."

"But I didn't leave you behind." A hint of irritation crept into Mac's voice. "Listen, lady, I don't know how you pulled off that cute vanishing act of yours, but you caused me a lot of aggravation. I actually went searching through the woods for you, then realized how futile that was. So I went straight to the local police and reported you missing."

"Is that what you did?" Maggie shook her head in disbelief. "Goodness me! You should be awarded a good citizen medal for sure."

"Cool the sarcasm, will you? I got enough from those yokel cops. They started grilling me like *I* was some kind of criminal."

"Which is exactly what you are, MacNair. Not that I believe your cock-and-bull story. You left me high and dry without a qualm and now you're trying to worm your way out of it."

"That's not the way I operate. You'd realize that if you knew me better."

"That's the last thing I want to do! I already know too well how you operate from our brief encounter. But if you're trying to save face in front of Stan, you needn't be concerned. He's going to hire you over me no matter what."

Mac continued to gaze at Maggie, not bothering to even glance in the hovering station manager's direction. "I'm sorry about that, honey. I really am. Like I told you before, radio's a hard business for women."

"Spare me your phony sympathy routine," she shot back. She wouldn't tolerate that from him!

Mac's eyes darkened. "You talk pretty tough for a refined southern belle, Bloomers."

"It's Bloomer, singular," she corrected him once again. "At least get my name straight, Crazed Cur."

"My friends call me Mac," he said, ignoring her mockery.

Maggie turned up her pert nose in an effort to look down at him, which wasn't easy, considering his height. "Who could possibly survive being friends with you? Or is it just strangers you stab in the back?"

"You're really testing my patience now," he warned, but his deep voice was cool and smooth.

"And *you* have failed every test to qualify yourself as a decent human being in my book, MacNair."

Mac pressed his hand against the area of his heart, covering up the vivid depiction of a swaying hula girl. "That really hurt, Miss Bloomer. Why, I bet that book of yours is just filled with the names of fine gentlemen. And no doubt Lamar Bleaker is on top of the list."

It surprised Maggie that he'd remembered the name. "That's right," she agreed stiffly. "Lamar is number one on my list."

"Then why don't you forget the radio business, go back to Alabama and settle down with that prissy-looking fiancé of yours, honey?" Mac suggested. "You can pick cotton or sip mint juleps or do whatever you do for entertainment down there on the old plantation."

Maggie let Mac's satire of southern life roll off her back. It was too off base to even bother getting angry about. Her "plantation" was a modern ranch house in the suburbs of Birmingham. She wouldn't know a cotton plant from a tobacco one. "Mint juleps" were what she assumed people at the Kentucky Derby drank. And she hadn't seen Lamar

Bleaker for over a year. Not that she didn't still care for him.
As memory served her, she did. Sort of.

"Oh, I'm not about to quit radio just yet, MacNair," she
replied with determination. "I know I've got what it takes
to make it."

He considered her a long moment. "Maybe you do,
honey. Maybe you do. I wish you all the luck in the world,
believe me."

His lucid eyes glowed warm and sincere but Maggie
wasn't going to let herself be fooled by them. She always
tried to be fair and objective when judging a fellow human
being. But judge she did; it was her major flaw. And she'd
already slammed the gavel on MacNair—guilty as proved by
past actions!

"I wish you luck, too, Maggie," Stan piped up. "I hope
you find a spot on another station real soon. And I'm sure
you will."

Breaking free from Mac's intense stare, Maggie directed
her own heated gaze upon the station manager. "How kind
of you. It was worth the long trip up here just to hear you
wish me well."

"Hey, you sound a little upset, Maggie." Stan shuffled his
sandal-shod feet.

"Oh, more than a little upset," she assured him.
"Goodbye, *Mr.* Stanmore. Thanks for wasting my time."

She intended that as her exit line, but MacNair's big, solid
frame still blocked her way out.

"You can't leave yet," he told her. "Not until you get
reimbursed." He looked over her head toward the station
manager. "Isn't that right, Stanmore? You're going to
reimburse Miss Bloomer for her traveling expenses? And
time, of course."

"Yeah, right. I almost forgot. I'll write you a check right
now, Maggie."

"Very well." She saw no reason to refuse what was so obviously due her and only wished she had thought of asking for it herself.

Stan hurried to his desk and sifted through the disorganized rubble of papers atop it. "Now where's my checkbook?" he mumbled, then slapped his palm against his high forehead. "Now I remember. My accountant has it."

"How convenient," Maggie said, tapping her foot.

"No. Really. I'm not trying to put one over on you, Maggie. I'll send you a check, I promise."

That didn't sound too promising to Maggie. She didn't doubt Stan's sincerity in stating his good intentions as much as she did his ability to follow through on them.

"Are you flying back to Birmingham tonight?" Mac asked her.

"No, tomorrow." The tone implied that it was none of his damn business.

Mac wasn't put off by it. "Where are you spending the night?"

"At the home of a friend."

"Where does this friend of yours live?"

"Nearby."

Mac smiled at her reticence. "Nearby? Is that the name of a town?"

"What's this sudden concern about where I spend the night, MacNair? When you left me on that deserted road, I could have ended up spending it in my car for all you cared!"

"Back to that, are we? Okay, believe what you want about me, lady. I'm not going to waste my breath trying to convince you otherwise. But I do have a suggestion to make. Give Stanmore your friend's address and his accountant can send your check there by messenger later today."

"Well, sure," Stan said. "I could arrange that if you really want the money before you leave, Maggie."

She really did, sensing she would never get it from Stan otherwise. She extracted a notebook and pen from her purse, jotted down her expenses and Miss Jasper's address, ripped out the page and handed it to the station manager. "Thank you," she told him, knowing full well it was MacNair she should be thanking. But she couldn't bring herself to do that.

"I'm really sorry things didn't work out," Stan reiterated, timidly offering his hand.

Maggie accepted it. How could she refuse not to? He was only doing what he thought best for his station and she had nothing against him personally.

But she ignored Mad Dog MacNair's hand when he extended it. She had plenty against *him* personally and he couldn't begin to make amends. She gave him a long, withering stare but rather than shrivel from it, he winked back at her. The insufferable wise guy! She shoved hard against him and this time he made way for her. She stomped out of the office without looking back.

Chapter Three

Mac watched Maggie march down the hall to the elevator. She'd been heavy on his mind ever since he'd lost her on that country road and even now, knowing no harm had come to her, he still felt a vague sense of guilt.

He disregarded it as the elevator doors closed off his last view of her. He had enough to feel guilty about in his life without adding Margaret Bloomer to his list of regrets. She was nothing to him—a complete stranger—and he wasn't going to worry about her anymore. Besides, he sensed that she was a woman who could take care of herself.

Mac did feel a tinge of regret, though, that their paths had crossed so briefly. He would have enjoyed the challenge of breaking down her barricade of dislike for him. Ah, well. The world was filled with interesting challenges and he wasn't going to dwell on lost opportunities. He turned back to Stanmore.

"You make sure she gets that expense check," he said.

"My word's as good as gold," Stan assured him. "It's too bad Maggie came all this way for nothing, but her southern accent probably wouldn't have worked up here, anyway."

"On the contrary. My instincts tell me she would have been a big hit. People like to hear a soft, melting voice like hers early in the morning. It soothes the nerves."

"Yeah, but you jangle them, Mad Dog. You get folks riled up. And that's just what PEU needs right now to boost the ratings, man." Stan put his arm around Mac's shoulder.

Mac shrugged it off and strolled across the office to the window behind Stan's desk. He didn't like the way Stanmore had treated Maggie. He didn't like it one bit. One minute he was about to hire her, in the next he was giving her the brush-off. Mac had seen the disappointment in Maggie's eyes. For all her bravado, she couldn't hide it. And what disturbed him most was that he was to blame for it. He looked out the window to the street five stories below, waiting.

"I used to be one of your biggest fans back in New York, Mad Dog," Stan went on. "I was living in the East Village then and everybody in the neighborhood was talking up your show. You were like our morning fix, dig? I remember that routine of yours, the Subway Superman . . ."

Mac stopped listening. He'd just spotted the top of Maggie's burnished gold head as she left the building. She crossed the street and hopped into a waiting limousine. Whose? Mac wondered as he watched it glide away. He forced his attention back to Stanmore.

"Right, I remember that bit," Mac said in a bored tone. He'd gotten bored with all his routines after a while. But it had been difficult to come up with fresh, funny, irreverent material every day. It had consumed all his time and energy and he'd promised himself never to allow that to happen

again. "I don't think jokes about the New York transit system would go over too big in Rutland, Stanmore."

"Well, all your other material will, Mad Dog. I want you
to know that you'll have free reign to be as wild as you want
on my station. Just like you were back in New York."

"No, it wouldn't work here," Mac told him. "This is a
different market, a different audience." Obviously Stanmore didn't know the first damn thing about radio. "How'd
you get to manage a station anyway?" he asked bluntly.

"The easy way. Nepotism."

Mac laughed, warming up to Stanmore a little. "Well, at
least you're honest about it." He made himself comfortable in Stan's swivel chair. "And I'll be honest with you,
too, man. If I used the same material I got away with in New
York, the folks in Rutland would run me out of town on a
rail. They don't want to listen to some wisecracking city
slicker make fun of all they hold near and dear. I'm telling
you, Stanmore, I'd go over like a lead balloon here. You'd
be a fool to hire me on that basis."

Stan looked stunned. "What are you talking about?
You're the best there is. Didn't you come here to accept my
offer?"

"You mean you still *want* me to? After what I just told
you?"

"Of course I do. You're like my idol, Mad Dog."

Mac sighed. Stanmore was hopeless. But so was his own
situation at the moment, he reminded himself. None of the
big stations would touch him until he proved he was reli-
able. He'd managed to shatter his reputation in the business by breaking his contract. All the rumors about why
he'd done that were false, but what did that matter if the
people in power believed them? Hell, the only station manager willing to take a chance on him now was this spaced-

out, middle-aged hippie who didn't even know what he was doing.

"I don't understand," Stan said, pacing in front of his desk. "Maggie told me you really wanted this job."

"Is that what Maggie said?" Mac leaned back and put his feet up.

Maggie. Mac let the name roll around in his head for a moment and decided it didn't suit her. Too plain. Too ordinary. He tried Margaret. Better, but not quite right. Didn't southern belles usually have more romantic names? Like Scarlett or something? What kind of flower grew in the south? Azalea? Nah, that wouldn't work. Honeysuckle? Too cloying. Magnolia? Hmm. Magnolia Bloomer. No... Magnolia *Blossom*. Mad Dog and Magnolia Blossom.

"Bingo!" Mac slammed his fist on the desk, then smiled at the startled station manager. "I just got an idea how to make your morning show work, Stanmore." He paused. "It's going to cost you a little more money, though."

Stan moaned. "But I already offered you double what I have any other deejay, Mad Dog."

Mac's smile didn't waver. "We'll negotiate. And if we reach an agreement, you can call me Mac."

He was pretty sure he could convince Stanmore of almost anything. But Margaret Bloomer? Well, she would be more difficult. *Whose* limousine did she drive off in? Mac wondered again. It bugged him more than he cared to admit.

After Maggie called the rental company about the abandoned car, she joined Miss Jasper in her parlor for a glass of sherry. "You don't know how much I appreciate your kindness to me, ma'am," she told the elfin lady.

Miss Jasper waved away her remark with a fluttering hand. "Think nothing of it, Margaret. If you catch us on a good day, we Yankees are as hospitable as you folks down south."

Maggie smiled at the perfect image of "catching" Miss Jasper, as one would an elusive leprechaun. Even now, sitting beside her on the overstuffed sofa in a room crowded with bulky furniture and memorabilia, Maggie could still easily imagine Miss Jasper the denizen of some magical forest.

"Besides, I enjoy your company," Miss Jasper continued. "This big old house can get pretty lonely at times." She patted Maggie's hand. "I only wish you could stay longer than one night. It's a pity you didn't get that radio job."

"The pity is losing out to someone as contemptible as Mad Dog MacNair!" Maggie spat out his name.

Miss Jasper clicked her tongue softly. Maggie had apprised her of MacNair's chicanery in detail. "He sounds like the devil incarnate."

"Well, not quite that horrible," Maggie had to admit. "Although his taste in clothes is certainly hellish enough." She wouldn't be surprised if she had nightmares about that Hawaiian shirt of his for weeks to come.

"The devil has never been known for his good taste, dearie," Miss Jasper remarked. "Nonetheless, he's supposed to be quite a dashing figure." She gave a long sigh and her expression became winsome. "The devil who broke my heart was, anyway. But I won't bore you with that sad remnant of my past."

"No, please, tell me about him," Maggie was eager to turn the conversation away from MacNair. The sooner she forgot about him, the better.

"Well, if you insist," Miss Jasper said, needing no further urging. She picked up the sherry decanter and topped both their delicate glasses before proceeding. "I was twenty years old when Slade Berrymore came to work at the bank in Jasper. This town was named after my great-grandfather, by the way. But that's another story." She took a birdlike sip from her glass, cleared her throat and continued. "Slade always wore a spanking white linen suit and a diamond tie clip. My father warned me never to trust a man who sported a diamond, but of course I didn't listen." Miss Jasper shook her head and laughed. "I handed Slade my heart on a silver platter, but somehow he misplaced it, along with a large sum of money he embezzled from the bank. He left Jasper in the middle of the night without saying goodbye, and I've never trusted a man since."

"Never?" Maggie couldn't imagine letting any man who had disappointed her affect the rest of her life. When Lamar Bleaker had broken their engagement she'd recovered in a matter of weeks. She was still fond of Lamar and considered him as close as a brother, or at least a first cousin.

"Oh, well, things work out for the best," Miss Jasper said with chirpy resignation. "If I'd married Slade, or any man after him, perhaps I wouldn't have been so intent on pursuing my career in anthropology and would have missed so many exciting experiences. Why, I've traveled to places you probably never heard of, Margaret."

Maggie recalled her quaint story about women throwing their sandals at the men they wanted to claim. "Like Zerbonia?"

"Ah, Zerbonia!" Miss Jasper clasped her hands together and smiled blissfully. "I lived in that paradise for over twenty years and long to return. Yes, indeed, my dear—I've had a wonderful life. And I'm glad that devil Slade Berrymore was a part of it, too. As Tennyson said, 'Tis better to have loved and lost/Than never to have loved at all.'"

"Why, Miss Jasper, you are a dyed-in-the-wool romantic if there ever was one."

"And you aren't, Margaret?"

"No, I don't believe I am. The last thing I want to do is get swept away by passion. My career is important to me, too, and if and when I do marry, it will be a sensible arrangement, based on respect and friendship and mutual goals."

Miss Jasper raised a hand to her mouth to cover a yawn. "Yes, that *is* sensible, Margaret," she said. She stood and stretched her small frame. "Now if you'll excuse me, I'll get dinner started."

"Please let me help."

"That's hardly necessary. I'm just going to pop two frozen dinners in the oven. I've never been much of a cook and see no reason to employ one for only myself. Which would you prefer? Lasagna or turkey?"

"Oh, surprise me," Maggie told her.

"What a keen sense of adventure you have, dearie," Miss Jasper commented dryly as she left the room.

Maggie sensed that she had somehow disappointed Miss Jasper with her practical remarks about passion and marriage. Well, that's the way she was—practical, and rather proud of it. She'd been taught to be both by her mother. Mrs. Bloomer, widowed young, had raised five daughters on a meager music teacher's salary and had even managed to give each of them a successful if modest debut into Birmingham society. All four of Maggie's sisters had married well and seemed relatively happy. Maggie, the youngest, was sure that she would have been happy, too, if she'd married Lamar Bleaker. But she wasn't unhappy that she *hadn't*, either.

No, she certainly was no great romantic like poor Miss Jasper, Maggie decided, pushing herself out of the deep

velvet sofa. And thank goodness for that! She began to
roam the large parlor for want of anything better to do,
working her way around the fine examples of antique furniture that crowded it, now and then pausing at a table or
shelf to examine a bibelot or silver-framed photograph. She
was vaguely hoping to come across a picture of Slade
Berrymore, but none of the dour images of frowning men,
some beside equally dour women, seemed to fit the image of
the dashing cad that Miss Jasper had instilled in her mind.

And then she spotted him on the mantelpiece, a small,
candid photograph of a man squinting yet smiling deter-
minedly into the sun. It was framed in gold, not silver, and
Maggie picked it up to look at it more closely. Slade's rum-
pled linen suit shone white and bright, and she could discern the glint of the diamond in his tie clasp. He was a
handsome devil, for sure, Maggie acknowledged. Yet she
was disappointed. For some reason she had expected Slade
Berrymore to look exactly like . . . Mad Dog MacNair.

The front doorbell rang, and Maggie jumped at the unexpected sound of it in the quiet house. She carefully replaced Berrymore's picture on the mantel, in the exact
position she had found it, and waited for Miss Jasper to
come out of the kitchen. The bell rang twice more before
Maggie decided that it was up to her to open the door to
Miss Jasper's visitor. She hurried to the foyer and did just
that, a polite smile of greeting on her face. It faded immediately at the sight of a hula girl depicted on top of a pine-
apple.

"You!" she gasped, raising her eyes to meet her neme-
sis's dark, sparkling ones.

"Hello, Maggie. Don't look so surprised. Surely you
didn't think you'd seen the last of me."

"What are you doing here, MacNair?"

"Oh, I was just passing by and thought I'd stop for a little chat," Mac replied blithely. "I want to get to know you better, honey."

"Forget it. I wish I'd never met you in the first place."

"Granted we got off to a bad start," he acknowledged. "But that doesn't mean we can't work things out and become friends."

"I'd just as soon make friends with a rattlesnake!"

"Does that mean you're not going to invite me in?"

"That's right. Get lost."

"Wow, you southern gals really *do* have gracious charm," he replied, unperturbed. "And here I thought it was all a myth until you proved me wrong, Miss Bloomer."

"I'm fixing to graciously slam this door in your face," she warned.

Mac put his shoulder against it. "Let's not be hasty, Miss Bloomer. Surely you're a mite curious about why I've come a callin' on you."

Maggie wasn't going to get into another shoving match with him, knowing she would lose. And she *was* curious. She let go of the door handle and stepped aside. "Come in and state your business, MacNair. But drop your awful attempt at a southern accent, will you? It makes my flesh crawl."

Mac laughed. "It was intended to, honey."

"And stop calling me *honey*," she ordered, turning her back to him and leading the way to the front parlor. "I don't much like that, either."

"There's not much you do like about me, is there?"

She turned abruptly, not realizing he was so close behind her because his voice had been so soft. She smashed right into his hard chest and ricocheted back, losing her balance. He caught her waist with both hands to steady her. Quickly regaining her equilibrium, she twisted away from his grasp.

"I have every reason to despise you," she reminded him. Despite that—despite herself—she'd enjoyed the pressure of his strong hands around her waist. The brief intimacy of it had sparked something deep within her, something new and exciting.

He latched his dark eyes on her. "No, you don't. But for some reason you've wanted to believe the worst about me from the first moment we met. That's okay with me, lady. It'll work to my advantage in the end."

Mac had both of Maggie's shoes in his car to prove that he'd come back for her. Better yet, he had the name of the police officer who'd taken down his report and laughed it off as a lover's quarrel when Mac had declared her missing. But Mac didn't want Maggie to like or trust him. He wanted her exactly as she was—insulting and downright hostile. It would make good radio. So he said nothing to defend himself. He only smiled.

"You will never have me at your advantage again, you dog," she told him evenly. "How did you track me down here?"

"You left this address with Stanmore, remember?" He glanced around the room and let out a low whistle. "Wow, some place. Whose old mansion is this, anyway?"

"Mine, young man," Miss Jasper informed him from the parlor doorway. "Excuse me, Margaret. I didn't realize you had a visitor."

"He'll be leaving shortly, Miss Jasper," Maggie said, then remembered her manners. "May I introduce you to Mad—"

"Madison MacNair," Mac interrupted, crossing the room to shake her hand. "You have a beautiful home, Miss Jasper. One of the finest examples of Victorian Gothic in New England, in my humble opinion."

Maggie gave him a suspicious look. Since when was Mad Dog MacNair humble about anything? And was his first name really *Madison*?

"Oh, it's just a big old white elephant of a place," Miss Jasper replied modestly, but she smiled with pleasure at Mac. "Are you interested in architecture, young man?"

"I admire anything that's well built." His eyes roamed over Maggie before lighting on a corner chair. "Like that Queen Anne piece, for instance. Lovely curves."

"Indeed." Miss Jasper arched a gray eyebrow and gave Mac a close examination. Apparently he passed it. "Would you care to stay for dinner, Madison?"

"No, he has other plans," Maggie hurriedly answered for him. She gave him a hard, determined look. "Don't you, Madison?" She couldn't help the little quiver of a smile that was edging her lips. Madison! How...decorous.

Mac shook his head and turned soulful eyes on Miss Jasper. "I hate eating alone but I'd certainly never dream of imposing."

"It's no imposition whatsoever," she insisted. "I'll just heat up another frozen dinner. What's your preference, Madison? Turkey or lasagna?"

"One of each would be great."

Miss Jasper laughed and snapped her fingers. "Done!"

Maggie followed her out to the kitchen, hoping MacNair wouldn't steal anything while left alone in the parlor.

"Miss Jasper, how could you? How could you ask that horrible man to dinner? Don't you realize who he is?"

"Of course I do, dearie." Miss Jasper opened her freezer and took out two more entrées. "And I find it rather exciting to be entertaining such a rapscallion. Admit it, Margaret. So do you."

"I most certainly do not."

"Then why are your cheeks all flushed and your eyes sparkling?"

"Because I'm angry, that's why. It isn't my place to tell you who you may or may not invite into your own home, of course, but frankly, Miss Jasper, I can't understand why you're putting me through this torture."

"Come, come, don't exaggerate the situation, my dear. I'm sure Madison has come here to explain himself or apologize to you. Now go back to the parlor and hear him out. I'll leave you two alone for a while."

"I don't *want* to be alone with him."

Miss Jasper gave her a gentle shove toward the door. "He isn't going to eat you up, dearie. So stop acting like he's the big bad wolf. You can handle him just fine, I'm sure."

Some fairy godmother *she'd* turned out to be, Maggie thought, feeling betrayed by her elfin hostess. She returned to the parlor to find MacNair, his back to her, toying with an antique silver snuffer. She waited a moment, watching him, half expecting him to pocket it. But he put it down on an end table and turned to her.

"Trying to catch me in the act of pilfering from a sweet old lady, Maggie?"

"I wouldn't put it past you."

He let out a sharp laugh. "No, I guess you wouldn't. Couldn't you convince Miss Jasper to send me away?"

"I tried, but she wouldn't listen to reason. She's under the impression that you're here to apologize to me."

He took a few steps closer and lowered his voice. "Actually, I've come to proposition you, honey."

"Why do you go out of your way to be offensive, MacNair? It really is overkill. Your mere presence is offensive enough."

"Am I really all that repugnant to you?" He moved closer still, until the space that separated them was less than a foot.

Maggie held her ground. She wasn't going to let him intimidate her, or at least let him *know* that he did. But he was really too close for comfort now. Every detail of his face seemed magnified to her—the dark shading of beard along his lean cheeks, the strong, aquiline nose, the wide, sharply etched mouth and thick, fierce eyebrows that were as dark as a raven's wings. It was an uncompromisingly masculine face, and would have been almost cruel except for his eyes. Again she found their dark depths strangely compelling. She broke the gaze he'd caught her in and stared at his forehead instead. Curls of his unruly black hair spilled across it and she had a crazy impulse to tenderly brush them aside. She laughed at her own foolish inclination, but pretended she was laughing at him.

"Back off, MacNair. You're crowding my space."

He surprised her by obeying her sharp order. "Sorry, Magnolia Blossom. I didn't realize you were wearing an invisible hoop skirt."

"Magnolia Blossom?" Maggie drawled out the name, rather liking the sound of it.

"Yeah, I came up with that name for you for our radio show. Mad Dog and Magnolia Blossom. Catchy, huh? Stanmore bought the idea, anyway. That's the proposition I was referring to before you took me the wrong way, as usual, and jumped down my throat."

"What's the joke, MacNair? I don't get it."

"I'm serious, Maggie. I'm here to offer you a job. We start working together bright and early Monday morning."

She didn't know what he was up to but he'd piqued her interest. "You mean you want me to be your partner on the show?"

"Well, more like my sidekick, actually."

Maggie sniffed. "Forget it. I'm not going to be the bru[n]t of your wisecracks and put-downs, Mad Dog. I'm not th[at] desperate for a job. Go find yourself another patsy."

He threw her a challenging smile. "Don't you think yo[u] can hold your own with me, Maggie?"

"Any day, anytime," she declared, placing her hands o[n] her hips.

"Then you're on, honey. Every day of the week from si[x] to ten. We'll be the biggest hit since Burns and Allen."

She wasn't buying it. "You made your reputation on ra[-] dio as a solo act, MacNair. Since when does that inflated eg[o] of yours need to be propped up by someone else?"

Mac hesitated, wondering if he should level with her. H[e] instinctively knew that his brash style of humor wasn[']t suited for the Vermont area and she could temper it with he[r] softer one. He needed Maggie, at least temporarily. Mac[']s agent had assured him that a big-market station would pic[k] him up within a few months and he could say goodbye t[o] Rutland forever.

Meanwhile, he wanted to make his show on WPEU work[.] He wanted it to be the biggest hit in Vermont since map[le] syrup. And Maggie, with her sexy voice, could help him d[o] that. She was physically appealing to boot and that woul[d] make his sentence in Rutland seem a lot less like punis[h]ment.

But Mac kept his thoughts to himself. The last time he'[d] shown a chink in his armor to a woman, she'd hammered a[t] it relentlessly. No, he wasn't going to let Maggie get the u[p]per hand on him the way his ex-wife had. All she had t[o] know and appreciate was that he was doing her a favor—[a] big one.

"This is the chance of a lifetime for you, honey. An o[p]portunity to work with one of the biggest names in radio."

"If you're referring to yourself, perhaps you should speak in the past tense," Maggie suggested. "Hasn't the name Mad Dog MacNair been dead air for the past year or more?"

She coated the barb with her sugar-coated drawl but that didn't make it any easier for Mac to swallow. Anger sparked in his dark eyes. He quelled it by reminding himself that those sugary slights were exactly what he wanted from Maggie on the show. It would make the audience side with *him* in the end.

"Thank you for reminding me of that, Magnolia Blossom." He bowed like a gentlemen. "But at least I have a show of my own again, while you, angel face, remain unemployed." He lowered his voice to a more persuasive level, a deep, resonant one that had worked for him time and time again with women. "Unless you agree to share the mike with me, that is. Come on, Maggie. Don't pass up this chance because you don't like me. That nose of yours is really so adorable. Don't cut it off to spite your own face."

Despite all her misgivings, he was tempting her. What did she have to lose in the end? She had no other prospects at the moment, and working with Mad Dog MacNair really would be an invaluable experience. At the same time, she found the idea of being cooped up with him in the close, intimate quarters of a radio studio every day more than a little disquieting. She just didn't trust the man.

"We'll have a strictly business relationship, nothing more, of course," he said, as if reading her mind. "Why not at least give it a try, Maggie? Where's your sense of adventure?"

"The poor dear has none," Miss Jasper piped up. Her slippered feet had made no sound as she'd entered the parlor.

What an unsettling way she has of simply appearing out of nowhere, Maggie thought, still a little put out with Miss Jasper for inviting MacNair to dinner. She was relieved the old lady had interrupted them, though, and smiled at her.

"What I have plenty of is common sense, Miss Jasper."

"Then prove it by accepting my offer," Mac said.

She turned back to him. "I'll think about it and give you an answer tomorrow."

Impatience flickered in his brown eyes. "You'll have to think faster than that, honey. I'll give you exactly one hour to realize what a great opportunity this is."

"We might as well sit down and eat while Margaret is mulling over your offer, Madison." Miss Jasper beckoned them to follow her into the dining room across the wide front hall. "And I shall do my best to quench my burning curiosity and not ask either of you what this offer happens to be."

"I'll be happy to tell you, dear lady," Mac said, pulling out her chair for her at the head of the table. "I have an idea for a radio show and I'd value your opinion."

He's not a total boor after all, Maggie thought, noting his deference toward Miss Jasper. Seating herself before he had a chance to help her, too, she took in the elaborately set table. Each piece of silverware was monogrammed with family initials, as were the place mats and napkins of heavy white linen. The tall candles in the glass candelabra were lit and there was an arrangement of freshly cut chrysanthemums—gold and violet—in a silver vase at the center of the glossy mahogany table. And on each gold-rimmed china plate lay an aluminum container of piping hot processed food.

"How nice of you to go through all this trouble for us," she said, appreciating that Miss Jasper *had* gone through a

ot of trouble with her flowers and china and silver. The
ood was secondary.

"My pleasure, dearie. It isn't often I have the chance to
hare dinner with such a charming couple."

Maggie found such a description of herself and MacNair
disconcerting and exchanged a brief glance with him across
he table. He winked back at her.

"We're not a couple yet," he said. "But we *will* be if
Maggie is willing to give us a try." He snapped open his
napkin and smiled expansively. "Now let me tell you all
about this idea I've come up with, Miss Jasper. You know
he folks in this area better than I do. Do you think this will
appeal to them?"

And Mac proceeded to more or less monopolize the conversation for the next half hour or so, much to the obvious
delight of Miss Jasper, who encouraged him with nods and
silvery peals of laughter. He was amusing enough, Maggie
had to grudgingly admit, unable to contain her own occa-
sional spurts of laughter. He was a master at working an
audience, there was no doubt about it. Maggie had never
heard Mad Dog MacNair on the air, but she'd assumed,
from his reputation, that his humor would be rather coarse
and offensive. It wasn't that evening, though. He had a
gentle, sly way of tickling an old lady's funny bone.

And a young one's, too. As he explained the concept of
The Mad Dog and Magnolia Show, enacting bits he made
up as he went along in both his own voice and a southern
drawl meant to be hers, Maggie found herself wiping tears
of glee from her eyes with her napkin. Yes, it could work,
she decided. They could play off each other just fine.

"Well, perhaps I've talked too much and bored you lovely
ladies." He paused to take a sip of water.

But Maggie observed how his dark eyes glowed with sat isfaction in the candlelight. He knew damn well he hadn' bored them for one second.

"Of course, the bits will be even funnier with sound ef fects," he said. "So what about it, Maggie. Are we on?" H looked her directly in the eye, waiting.

She hated to give in to him but the bait was too temptin, to pass up. She swallowed hard. "You said we start o Monday?"

Mac kept his face expressionless, not even giving her th small satisfaction of seeing his own. "Right, Maggie. Tha gives you the rest of the week to relocate."

"That's not very much time!" Her head started spin ning. This was all happening too fast for her.

"You can stay right here with me," Miss Jasper said.

"Oh, I can't accept such a generous offer, Miss Jasper. I will be way too much an imposition and—"

"Time for dessert!" the old lady announced, refusing t listen to Maggie's objections. "I'll go put some blueberr, turnovers in the oven while you entertain our guest in th parlor, Margaret."

Alone there with Mac, Maggie had renewed misgivings "Why do I get the impression that I've been completel, bamboozled by you?" she asked him.

"Oh, stop looking so worried, Maggie. It'll all work ou just fine, believe me." The smile he gave her was sly. "Cal me when you get back from Alabama. And don't let tha fiancé of yours stop you from coming back."

She was glad she had instinctively lied to him abou Lamar still being her fiancé. She wanted Mac to think sh was off-limits. At the same time, she felt an unexpecte twang of disappointment as he headed for the door. Sh followed him. "Aren't you staying for dessert?"

"No. Please give my regrets to Miss Jasper." He paused and let his eyes roam along the soft curves of Maggie's upturned face. "On second thought, I will have dessert."

He encircled his long arm around Maggie's waist, pulled her to him and pressed his lips against hers. It was a brief kiss, an almost impersonal one.

"Why did you do that?" she asked when he released her, too surprised to be angry.

He shrugged. "Just to get it over with. It won't happen again so don't worry about it. Goodnight, Magnolia Blossom."

She leaned against the door after he made his abrupt exit. However she looked at it, Maggie had every reason to worry.

Chapter Four

Let's get one thing straight right away, honey. I'm the one who's going to be in charge around here."

That was the first thing Mac said to Maggie when he walked into the studio before dawn Monday morning and found her reviewing the control panel with Clyde Cobb, WPEU's midnight-to-six disc jockey.

Startled, Maggie looked up from the rows of switches and dials and knobs that operated the microphones, tape recorders, cartridge machines and turntables. She hadn't seen MacNair since she'd returned from Birmingham and would have appreciated a civil greeting from him before he jumped down her throat.

"I'm sure I can run a board as well as you," she said. "I've had plenty of training."

"I don't care if you've had training as an air-traffic controller. No one can run a board like I can. And I want complete command of this prehistoric version when we're on the air.'' He gave a disdainful glance at the console.

Or at her. Maggie wasn't quite sure, since she was sitting behind it. She stood, immediately defensive. ''Listen, MacNair, you'd better change your attitude if we're going to work to—''

Clyde Cobb hushed her and gestured to the blinking red light above the big clock on the wall. ''Thirty seconds before I'm on again,'' he reminded her. ''Why don't you two kids take this discussion outside?''

Clyde called himself the ''Wild and Crazy Night Owl'' but during the hour Maggie had gotten acquainted with him, she could discern nothing crazy or the least bit wild about the elderly, mild-mannered deejay. She couldn't help but think that he did indeed look like an owl, though.

''We were just leaving,'' she told him.

''Didn't mean to trespass on your territory like that,'' Mac added.

Clyde raised his heavy-lidded eyes to the clock. ''It'll be all yours in twenty-five minutes, Mac. And I'll be happy to let you take over, believe me.'' He plopped into the chair Maggie had vacated, put on his headphones and spoke wearily into the mike. ''That was the mellow voice of Perry Como, folks. A special request from Mrs. Duffy in Arlington. Hope you enjoyed it, Mrs. Duffy. The time is now...''

He picked up a cowbell and as he was ringing it, Maggie and Mac left the small studio.

Mac moaned as he headed for the coffee machine at the end of the dingy hall. ''How did this happen to me? How did I end up at a station like PEU?'' He poured some coffee into a Styrofoam cup and made a face of disgust after tasting it. ''Maybe I'm dead. Yeah, that's it. I died in some tragic accident or something, and now I'm in hell.''

Maggie poured her own cup of coffee and took a tentative sip. It wasn't *that* bad. "You probably deserve to end up there, mister, but I don't think I do," she informed Mac tartly.

"Then you must be the angel sent to save me from my misery, honey."

His remark, so gently stated, caught Maggie off guard and she felt a soft melting for him. But only for a moment. She wasn't going to allow herself to get all sappy because Mad Dog MacNair had unexpectedly said something nice to her for a change. She blamed her momentary weakness on her jittery nerves. And she blamed him for her tenseness. In less than an hour they were going on the air, totally unprepared, and it was all his fault.

"This angel's about ready to fly the coop," she said in a testy tone. "I didn't appreciate the way you snapped at me in the studio, MacNair."

"That was wrong of me and I apologize."

He touched her hand, the one clutching the coffee cup, and his touch felt warmer to her than the heat from the cup. Not trusting the sincerity of his apology, Maggie jerked back her hand and coffee sloshed over the rim and onto her skirt.

"Look what you made me do!" she cried, dabbing at the stain with a paper napkin.

"Calm down," Mac said soothingly, but he made no move to touch her again.

Maggie glowered at him. "How can you possibly expect me to be calm when we haven't had a chance to rehearse the show, thanks to you?"

"Rehearse?" He made it sound like a dirty word. "That would ruin the spontaneity. We'll be a lot funnier if we play it by ear." He gave her an unconcerned smile. "Trust me."

"I wouldn't trust you as far as I could throw a piano, honey chil'," she replied in a slow, seething drawl.

"Perfect," Mac pronounced. "All you have to do is keep that melting voice of yours dripping with disdain for me, Magnolia Blossom. Now that shouldn't be too hard."

No, it sounded far, far too easy, Maggie thought, narrowing her eyes as she studied MacNair. He was wearing a rather conservative striped shirt and tweed sport jacket, which Maggie considered a huge improvement over his loud Hawaiian shirt. But he was in need of a shave and the shading of dark bristles across his lean cheeks and angular jaw gave him a slightly disreputable mien. As did his bloodshot eyes.

"Have you been on a wild bender all weekend?" she asked him bluntly, feeling she had the right to know.

Mac laughed. "That's not my style, Maggie. I was in Phoenix helping out a friend." He rubbed his tired eyes, and then his rough jaw. "I traveled all night to make it here in time for the show."

"You were cutting it pretty close."

"I made it, didn't I?" Mac said, with an obvious lack of concern.

She didn't appreciate his cavalier attitude. "Listen, MacNair, I rushed back from Birmingham in order to spend some time with you over the weekend."

"Aw, Maggie, how sweet. I didn't know you cared."

"I don't! Not about you, anyway. But I *do* care if the show bombs."

"It won't. We'll slide into it slow and easy this first week and get a feel for working together. Meanwhile, we've got at least twenty minutes to get our act together for today."

"Twenty minutes!" Maggie wailed. She twisted the paper napkin she was grasping, wishing it were MacNair's neck. "That's not nearly enough time!" Her eyes darted toward the elevator doors down the hall as she contemplated a quick escape.

Noting her wayward glance, Mac captured her by the arm and kept a firm but gentle grip on it. "Let's go into Stanmore's office and spend a little quiet time together before we go on the air, honey."

Maggie had the warring inclination to yank away from Mac's hold and to lean against his solid frame. She did neither. He released her when they entered the office and she immediately began pacing, still wringing the napkin.

"Sit down," Mac ordered.

"I can't. And I can't go through with this, either."

Mac raised his thick eyebrows. "You're not bailing out on me, are you, buddy?"

"Don't you buddy me, MacNair. It's your fault we're not prepared, not mine. So why shouldn't I bail out and let you crash by yourself?"

"Gee, you're a real little trooper, Maggie Bloomer," Mac said sarcastically. "I misjudged you, honey. I thought you were a gutsy pro and could ad-lib your way through anything. That's what it takes to be a good disc jockey. But you're obviously just a humdrum grind with a pleasant voice who can read copy into a mike without stuttering."

"I can do more than read copy," Maggie objected. "I'll have you know I can improvise with the best of them."

"Then prove it. Since we don't have anything much planned—"

"Hah! Now there's an understatement!"

"I thought we'd invite the listeners to call in," Mac continued calmly. "And ask anything they want about us, no matter how personal."

Maggie circled around him. "I don't much care for that idea. I'm a very private person."

"Maybe Maggie Bloomer is, but on the air you'll be the extroverted Magnolia Blossom. Just stay in character and say any outlandish thing that comes to mind."

"Anything?" The idea had a certain appeal to Maggie. She could be as outrageous and daring as she'd always wanted to be because it would be Magnolia talking, not herself. Her golden eyes began to sparkle mischievously. Did she have the gumption, she wondered, to test her own mettle? She figured this was as good a time as any to find out. "Okay, MacNair, I'll give it a shot," she said.

"So you really *are* a trooper." Mac didn't sound the least bit surprised. He chucked her chin, tilting it up, and looked into her eyes. "All you have to remember during the show is that your dislike for me is part of the act, honey."

"It won't be an act, I assure you," Maggie replied, but she immediately looked away from him. It was difficult to dislike a man with such beautiful eyes.

Maggie was relieved that the station manager chose that moment to stumble into his office and bid them both a sleepy good morning. "Oh, man, getting up this early is for the birds."

"Birds and morning deejays," Mac said. "But there's no reason for you to come in so early, Stan."

"Sure there is. The Mad Dog and Magnolia Show may become a legend in its own time, and I wanna be able to say I was present for the launching."

Stan's great expectations rekindled Maggie's nervousness. She checked her watch. Less than five minutes to go. Taking a deep, calming breath, she looked out the window. Dawn was just breaking and thin shards of light cut through the dark sky. As she was saying a silent prayer, Mac touched the back of her neck. She jumped, as if electrified.

"Sorry, honey. I didn't mean to startle you," he said in his softest, most soothing voice. "But it's time to go to the studio."

Maggie gulped down her fear and followed Mac down the long hall, as if bravely marching to her own execution.

"Good luck, kids," Clyde the Night Owl said before turning the studio over to them.

Maggie managed to give him a wan smile and it stayed frozen on her face as she looked at Mac. But he was paying scant attention to her. He'd taken the seat in front of the control panel and was busy checking the transmitter meters.

Maggie sat down at the desk facing him, which was equipped with a microphone and headphones. It rankled her that MacNair had taken over the board, but with only minutes to go before airtime, she let it go, promising herself that she would fight him on it at a more opportune time. She put on her headphones. The newscaster was in the smaller, adjoining studio, reporting on local events. Half listening, Maggie looked over her copy of the program log but found it impossible to concentrate. She had never been this unprepared to go on the air before. It was a horrible feeling, akin to falling from a great height.

Meanwhile, Mac was selecting music cartridges from the stacks lining one wall. "All we've got is Top 40 dreck and moldy oldies to work with," he said in a tone of disgust. "We'll have to do something about that." Scowling, he glanced around the room. "Now where the hell is my collection of sound effects? Damn! I left them in Stanmore's office. I'll be right back."

"No!" Maggie cried. "There isn't time. Don't you dare step out of this studio, MacNair."

"Honey, honey, honey," he murmured, shaking his head. "You should know better than to dare me by now. The last time you did, I drove off without you. Remember?" Not waiting for her reply, he was out the door.

"Hurry!" she shouted after him.

He looked back at her through the large soundproof window and gave her a jaunty wave. Her answering gesture was less friendly. And then she turned her eyes up to the clock, where they remained riveted as the red hand paused at each passing second. Before it had made a full circle Mac returned with a bulky cartridge rack. He set it up beside the control board and gave Maggie an easy smile.

"See, no problem. We've got seconds to spare."

"You play too close to the edge for my taste, MacNair."

"You'll acquire a taste for it, honey."

"Oh, I doubt that very mu—" Maggie's words broke off as she noticed the red light above the clock begin to flash. Her heart leaped into her throat and she was unable to swallow—or move. She sat rigid, and as pale as a ghost. In thirty seconds she was going to be expected to speak, but her mind was a complete blank.

Mac put on his own headphones. "Okay Magnolia Blossom. I'll start with a quick intro, then you do your bit," he said, and opened his mike.

It all seemed like a bad dream to Maggie. She could see Mac's mouth moving but was unable to hear his words as blood pounded against her eardrums. And then she saw him looking at her expectantly, then pointing at her with a jabbing finger. She opened her mouth. Nothing came out. I will wake up any moment now, she told herself. Mac began to speak again. Now she could just manage to hear his voice over the thumping of her heart.

"Well, isn't that just like Magnolia Blossom, folks," he was saying breezily, not missing a beat. "She got bored waiting around for me to introduce her to you and now she's flirting with the Wild and Crazy Night Owl." As Mac spoke he popped one of his sound effect tapes into the cart machine and punched the start button. A female's shrieking giggles assaulted Maggie's ears. "Now leave poor Clyde alone, Magnolia!" Mac shouted over it. "I better stop her before she goes too far, folks. Be right back."

Mac had another tape ready to go on an upper deck, punched it up and a Madonna song filled the airwaves. Staring hard at Maggie, he slowly removed his headphones, walked over to her desk, grabbed her upper arms and pulled her out of her chair. And then he kissed her.

He kissed her fully, deeply, without restraint, forcing her head back with the power of his demand, crushing her to him. She gasped, shocked and indignant and...thrilled to the core. A rush of desire jolted through her, and then a sweet, pleasurable melting. Her wide eyes fluttered closed and she swayed against him. She could feel the scratch of his rough beard against her tender skin, feel the strain of his hard muscled body against her soft one. He kissed with abandon, as if he had every right to take this liberty with her. And he *did* have the right because she was giving it to him without the slightest protest.

And then, just as suddenly as he'd kissed her, he broke their intimate connection and pushed himself back. She almost lost her balance when he released her.

"Why did you do that?" she demanded.

"It was the quickest way I knew to warm up your cold feet, honey."

"Cold feet?" It wasn't the most romantic reply he could have come up with.

"Yeah. You were frozen with fear a minute ago and I figured you needed thawing out." He studied her flushed face for a moment, his dark eyes gleaming with satisfaction. "Looks like my remedy worked."

"Don't flatter yourself. And don't you ever try to kiss me again." Her objection, she realized, came a little too late and made her all the more indignant.

"Then don't freeze up on me again." Mac pointed to the light above the clock. It was flashing again. "You think you can talk now?"

"Circles around you," she replied. Her stage fright had dwindled away in the heat of all the charged emotions he had pulled to the surface. Now she was seething, and raring to go.

Smiling to himself, Mac returned to his seat behind the board and opened his mike as Madonna's song faded out. "Here she is, folks. Rutland's very own material girl," he announced. "I heard you taught Madonna everything she knows, Magnolia."

Maggie leaned toward her mike. "But not everything *I* know, sugah. I reckon that's too much knowledge for any gal to handle ... exceptin' me."

Mac pushed the cart button and produced a drumroll sound effect.

"But I don't want our listeners thinking I'm materialistic, Mad Dog," Maggie continued.

"Hah! Didn't you say you wouldn't go out with me because I wasn't rich enough, honey?"

"I believe I said you weren't *good* enough."

"Why don't you give me a chance to prove otherwise, Magnolia?"

"Don't hold your breath. I hate to see a grown man turn blue in the face."

And so *The Mad Dog and Magnolia Show* commenced.

Not bad, Mac thought at one past ten, pulling off his headphones and unplugging them. Not bad at all considering it was the first day they'd worked together. He stood, lazily stretched his long frame and went to Maggie's desk to give her a pat on the back. She shrugged it off without so much as looking up at him.

She was still ticked off about the kiss, Mac guessed. Ah, well. It was the only thing he could think to do to shake her out of her attack of nerves. The trouble was it had really shaken him up, too. He hadn't counted on that. There was no room in a small control room for high-voltage passion. That would cause too much static and interfere with the flow of the show. And so Mac decided that the best thing to do was act as if nothing had happened between them. Nothing much at all.

John "Fat Man" Spratt, the ten-to-three disc jockey, waddled into the studio and waved to Maggie and Mac.

"Welcome aboard the WPEU Enterprise," he said in a resonant bass voice. He placed a box of doughnuts on the console and took out a chocolate-coated one. "We'll chat later. Right now I got five minutes to eat breakfast before I'm on the air." He bit into the doughnut. "People write in and complain when I talk with my mouth full," he said with his mouth full.

Mac and Maggie left Fat Man Spratt alone with his baker's dozen. Stan was waiting for them in the hall, his lopsided grin even wider than usual.

"Hey, man. Like wow! Groovy show," he told Mac.

"I didn't do it alone, Stan. Maggie did her bit, too."

She sniffed at that, feeling she'd done a lot more than her *bit*. But she let it go, not wanting to quibble. At least MacNair hadn't taken full credit for pulling it off.

"Oh, yeah, Mag. You were great, too," Stan allowed.

Maggie thanked him in a hollow voice. She was exhausted. MacNair's nonstop intensity while they were on the air together had drained her. It wasn't easy keeping up with all his wisecracks and double entendres and leading questions. It was as if he'd kept throwing firecrackers at her and the only way to survive was to toss them right back. All she wanted now was some time alone and couldn't wait to get back to Miss Jasper's peaceful home to sort out her chaotic emotions.

But Mac had other plans. "Let's have a meeting to discuss the show," he said, leading the way to Stan's office. The station manager followed like a puppy dog. Not about to be left out of any decisions, Maggie poured herself another cup of coffee and joined them.

"The first thing we need is our own office," Mac demanded, making himself comfortable in Stan's desk chair again.

"You can use this one any time you want," Stan offered.

Mac shook his head. "No, Maggie and I want a place where we can be alone together, without interruptions. Isn't that right, honey?" He gave her a guileless smile.

"Not really," she replied flatly. She wasn't coy Magnolia Blossom now. She was tired and peevish Maggie Bloomer, with the beginnings of a nasty headache gathering force at the base of her neck.

"You mean you just want to wing it every day like we did today?" Mac raised his thick eyebrows in mock surprise.

"Lord no!" Maggie said with more energy.

"Then we need an office where we can work on new material and plan at least part of our show every day. Okay, Stan?"

"I'll see what I can do. But space is really limited. None of the other deejay's have their own offices, you know."

Mac waved away that point. "So what? We're special. A good morning show becomes the flagship of a radio station, Stanmore. You know that."

Stan nodded, looking pained that he couldn't immediately meet Mac's demand. "I'll see what I can do," he said again.

We're special. Maggie liked the sound of that. After surviving this first day's baptism of fire, she was beginning to believe she and MacNair really could make a good team. On the air, that was. Not off it. He was a selfish egotist who'd

deserted her, proven himself unreliable and played with her
very deep, private emotions when he'd kissed her. Not exactly the sort of man she wanted to get involved with.

She allowed that he did have a few good traits, however.
He was dynamic and creative and extremely good at what he
did. And if she were completely honest with herself, which
she always tried to be, she would have to admit that he'd
helped her look good, too. She was beginning to believe that
he wasn't all bluff and bravado and really was the best in the
business.

"Now getting on to the next matter," Mac continued as
Maggie watched and listened to him carefully. "This station has got to get its programming act together. Every deejay working here uses a different format, from easy listening
to Top 40. Personally I think we should stick with adult
contemporary 'round the clock, but maybe you'd like to get
your program director in here to be part of this discussion."

Stan gave out a sad little laugh. "You're looking at him.
I'm also the news, sports and public affairs director. When
Dad's corporation took over this station, the first order of
the day was to cut staff. He almost hit the roof when he
heard what I was paying you, Mac."

Maggie's ears perked up. She'd assumed, of course, that
MacNair was making more than her. But how much more?
she wondered. She observed him give Stan a stern, caution-
ary look. A lot more, she decided.

"Let's stick to the subject at hand," Mac suggested
coolly. "You mean to tell me, Stan, that you just let your
announcers use any format they want to?"

"Hey, man, I'm no dictator. *Laissez-faire*, that's my bag.
Besides, that's been the tradition at PEU. Clyde Cobb has
been the Night Owl for over twenty years, and his fans dig
the oldies sound. Fat Man Spratt leans toward country. And

if you want to go with adult contemporary, that's cool, too, Mac.''

Mac groaned at Stan's casual approach to programming. No wonder WPEU was in the ratings pits.

"How are you ever going to attract a sizable enough share of the audience to satisfy your advertisers if you don't have a solid format?" Maggie asked the station manager.

Mac gave her a nod of approval. "That's a damn good question."

Stan shrugged. "Maybe I should call Lola in to answer it for you." He shuffled out of his office, apparently to get her.

Lola? Mac and Maggie shared a questioning look. And then Mac beamed a smile at her. "You were terrific this morning," he said. "And I really mean that, honey. You may have held back for a minute or two, but then you got right into the swing of things."

Maggie blushed, partly because his praise warmed her, partly because she was embarrassed about his allusion to her initial attack of nerves—and how he'd cured her. "Well, it's no wonder I choked at first, considering how ill prepared we were," she blurted out defensively. "It was downright unprofessional of you to go away for the weekend."

"Would you stop harping on that?" Mac asked, not bothering to hide his irritation. "Why is it that every time I try to be nice to you, you respond with a reproach?"

Did she? Maggie wondered. "Well, maybe that's all you deserve," she told him.

Mac gave her a long hard look. "Listen, honey," he finally said. "I don't mind you putting me down on the air because it's part of the act. But I'm not going to put up with it in our private conversations. And I'm not going to explain my actions to you, either. I go where I please whenever I please and if the show suffers for it, that's my problem, not yours.''

"I beg to differ! It's my show, too. I'm cohost, after all.''

"Wrong.'' Mac was implacable. "I told you once and I'll tell you again—you're my sidekick, Magnolia Blossom. I created your name, I created the concept and I created your job. Just remember that and we'll get along a lot better, okay?''

It was *not* okay and Maggie was sorely tempted to tell MacNair where he could go with the job. But at the same time, she didn't want to give it up. What would she do then? Go back to Birmingham and pine away until another opportunity in radio came along? She knew how rare they were, and appreciated how lucky she was to be working behind a mike at all—even if it meant working with an impossible bully like Mad Dog MacNair. Besides, it was only off the air that he was impossible. While they were doing the show they'd been on the same wavelength, in perfect symbiosis, and Maggie had experienced a natural high that was too exhilarating to give up just yet.

"Oh, very well. I'll accept that you're top dog around here if you stop barking at me,'' she replied huffily.

Mac laughed. "You'll always try to get in the last word, won't you, Maggie?''

But before she could get in another, Stan returned with an attractive, elegantly dressed woman. Maggie quickly estimated her age to be around thirty, and her sleek black suit to be around eight hundred. Her dark hair was also sleek and beautifully coiffured, and her makeup was flawless. Her perfection in grooming was starkly set off as she stood next to disheveled Stan.

"This is Lola Medesa, our new sales manager,'' he announced.

Mac immediately stood and crossed the room to shake her hand. "What's a classy dame like you doing in this neck of the woods?" he asked.

Lola smiled and her perfect white teeth looked even whiter against the bright red of her lipstick. Maggie immediately decided that they were capped.

"And what's a superjock like you doing at a small market station like this?" Lola countered. She continued to grip his hand. Or MacNair continued to grip hers. Maggie wasn't quite sure.

"Ah, well, that's a long story," he said.

"I can make time to hear it, Mad Dog."

"Call me Mac, Ms. Medesa. All my friends do."

She fluttered thick eyelashes. Maggie was sure they were false. "And you call me Lola, Mac. I think I'm going to like being your friend."

"May I call you Lola, too?" Maggie piped up. "Then we could *all* be friends."

Lola gave Maggie a quick once-over and her smile tightened. "Why, of course." Her eyes latched back on Mac. "Are you free for lunch at noon? We can go over some ideas I have for a promotion campaign to get new advertisers for your show."

"Well, I'm free," Mac said. "But are you, Maggie?"

Maggie appreciated his effort to include her despite Lola's obvious intent not to. "Free as a bird," she chirped.

Stan tapped Lola's padded shoulder. "So am I, in case anybody's interested."

"Then I'll make reservations for four," Lola said, not sounding especially pleased about it. "Now if you'll excuse me, I have to get back to my desk. I'm expecting a call from New York headquarters."

Stan let out a deep, soulful sigh after she exited. "Lola is one of my father's up-and-coming execut̶i̶ here to keep an eye on me and increase PEU's ad revenues. She thinks I'm a jerk." Stan sighed again. "And I think she's outta sight and dynamite."

Maggie felt a little sorry for him; she was sure an outdated hippie like Stan didn't stand a chance with a fashionable yuppie like Lola Medesa. During lunch at a homey local restaurant she was even more certain. Lola ignored Stan completely. She ignored Maggie, too, and beamed all her attention and intense energy in Mac's direction. She talked shop with him, quoting unit costs and rating points and frequency formulas. Whenever Maggie tried to put in her two cents worth Lola made it clear that that was exactly how much she felt Maggie's opinion was worth.

"If anyone can put PEU on the right track, it's you," Lola told Mac, resting her elbows on the table to lean closer toward him.

Maggie wondered if she was playing footsie with him under the table. Not that she cared, of course, she reminded herself quickly.

"I'm inclined to agree with you, Lola," Mac replied, never one to be self-effacing. "But we've got to target a younger audience. The listeners who phoned in today to ask Maggie and me questions sounded pretty ancient. One old gent actually called me a smart aleck whippersnapper."

Maggie smiled, remembering how nice Mac had been to the crusty old coot. "And what about that dear old lady who shared her recipe for pickled pigs' feet over the air?"

"Those callers must have been Uncle Wilbur's fans," Stan said. "He had the morning slot at PEU for as long as people around here can remember. He used to read the *Farmers' Almanac* over the air, and have a recipe exchange and limerick contests, stuff like that."

"Sounds like a tough act to follow," Mac commented dryly. "What happened to Uncle Wilbur?"

"I hope he wasn't fired," Maggie said.

Lola laughed harshly. "Of course not. Stan's such a marshmallow he couldn't fire anybody."

"It's bad karma," Stan explained softly.

Lola tossed the station manager a disparaging look. "Luckily Uncle Wilbur decided to retire. No one ever listened to him, anyway." She gave Mac her bright, hard smile. "They'll listen to Mad Dog MacNair, though. I'm counting on you to pull in new advertisers. And not only on the local level. I've contracted a major rep firm to pitch PEU to national agency media buyers."

"Did you?" Mac asked politely, but Maggie noted with a small degree of satisfaction that he was studying the list of desserts on the blackboard behind Lola rather than giving her his full attention.

Lola didn't seem aware of this. "I'd like you to come to New York with me next Saturday, Mac. We'll meet with some agency people and discuss station promotions centering around you. And if time allows, we'll get in some fun while we're at it."

Mac turned away from her and looked at Maggie. "Would Saturday be okay with you?"

"With me?" It was quite clear to Maggie that Lola hadn't included her in the invitation.

"There's no sense meeting with these promo people if you can't make it," Mac said. "After all, Magnolia Blossom is a big part of the show. Isn't that right, Lola?"

Rather than answer, the sales manager carefully examined her coffee spoon. And then she waved the waitress over to the table and told her to replace the spoon with a clean one. They all gave their dessert orders while she was there and Lola never did agree with Mac about Maggie's importance to the show.

Although she noted it, Maggie didn't much care. What mattered to her was that Mac had included and supported her. All the many faults she perceived he had dwindled in importance for the moment and she offered him a warm, friendly smile across the table. He raised his water glass to her.

"Here's to *The Mad Dog and Magnolia Show*," he said. "We may have gotten off to a rocky start but I have a feeling it's going to be smooth sailing from here on in."

Maggie wanted to believe him. But deep down she sensed that there was no such thing as smooth sailing in the company of Madison MacNair. He was too unpredictable, too unreliable, and storms were sure to erupt between them. They were total opposites, but she was quite confident that she could handle him if she kept a cool head. She silently raised her own glass in response, promising herself that that was exactly what she would do.

just as she had when Mac had come up with that suggestion.

"How many times do I have to assure you that you're *not* imposing, Margaret? I want you to consider this your home, too." She fluttered around the cluttered room, adjusting a picture here, a knickknack there. "Are your living quarters satisfactory?"

"More than satisfactory. Perfect." Miss Jasper had given her a suite on the east wing of the rambling Victorian house consisting of a bedroom with its own fireplace, a small sitting room and a large, marble-tiled bathroom.

"Good. And if there's anything I can do to make you more comfortable here, please tell me."

"Actually there is one thing that you could do," Maggie responded. "And that's let me pay rent."

"Nonsense," Miss Jasper frowned, as she had every time Maggie brought this up. "Your company is payment enough, dearie. My only concern is that you feel some kind of obligation to stay here with me rather than get an apartment in Rutland. I certainly don't want to cramp your style."

Maggie laughed at the elderly lady's colloquialism. Cramp her style, indeed! For twenty-six years she'd lived at home with her formidable mother. During her college days it had been for economic reasons, and after getting her first job it had been for convenience, since the radio station was only five miles from Mamma's house. Besides, she'd been engaged to Lamar Bleaker at the time and it seemed silly to move into a place of her own, only to move again once they married. They'd never gotten around to doing that, and Maggie had never gotten around to leaving home. Until now. She couldn't quite believe how drastically her life had changed in less than a week. She'd relocated to Vermont, of all places, and agreed to work with Mad Dog MacNair, of

ll people—one of the most disreputable personalities in
adio. She required no further disruptions in her life at the
noment and living with a kindly old lady suited her just
ine.

"My style is rather simple and quiet," she told Miss Jas-
ser. "I'm very happy here, and only hope you don't find my
·ompany too dull."

"Only a tad dull, my dear."

Maggie laughed again, although she wasn't sure Miss
Jasper was joking. "Maybe if I play Magnolia Blossom long
·nough, some of her audacity will rub off on me."

"But of course you *are* Magnolia Blossom and she is you,
Margaret. I found the show quite amusing this morning, by
he way. You and Madison sounded so natural and sponta-
leous together."

"We were spontaneous all right! We had to make the
·how up as we went along because MacNair took off for the
veekend." Her temper automatically rose, as it usually did
vhen she talked or even thought about him. "That man is
mpossible, Miss Jasper. A totally disreputable character."

Miss Jasper stopped her fluttering and alighted at the edge
·f the sofa. "You mustn't judge him too harshly, Marga-
·et."

"Have you forgotten how you and I met?" Maggie tried
·o keep the exasperation out of her voice. "You found me
·tranded because that snake deserted me in order to beat me
·ut of a job."

"But then he offered you a job." Miss Jasper shook her
·ilvery-gray head. "That doesn't make sense."

"Yes, it does. Once he got what he wanted, he wanted
·omething else. Men like him usually do. He never misses a
·hance to remind me that he's top banana and I'm just his
·idekick on the show. If he hadn't shown up *I* would have
·een the starring deejay."

"Why did you agree to work with him if you feel tha(t) bitter about it?" Miss Jasper asked.

"Oh, I'm not bitter. You have to roll with the punches i(n) this business." Maggie always tried to sound tough when sh(e) was discussing her career. "I accepted his offer because frankly, it was the only one I've had since the station I use(d) to work for was sold. At least I'm working behind a mik(e) again."

"That's a very sensible, pragmatic attitude, dearie."

"My relationship with MacNair is strictly professional," Maggie added unnecessarily, since Miss Jasper hadn't s(o) much as made the slightest hint that it was otherwise.

The elderly woman smiled impishly. "Whatever you say dearie." The doorbell rang and she jumped up from th(e) sofa, quick as a pixie. "I'm off to my study. I'll be im(-) mersed in writing my Zerbonia memoir all night. Do sa(y) hello to Madison for me." And with that she fluttered ou(t) of the room and down the hall.

Maggie rushed to the gilt-framed convex mirror above th(e) mantel to check how she looked, at the same time tellin(g) herself that she didn't really care how she looked t(o) MacNair. She had dressed with deliberate simplicity—a gol(d) turtleneck and beige gabardine slacks. The color of th(e) sweater did happen to bring out the rich gold of her hair an(d) eyes, though. But so what? She certainly wasn't going to g(o) out of her way to look unattractive, either.

She opened the front door to him, determined to b(e) brusque and businesslike. This wasn't a social call, after all He'd come to go over plans for tomorrow's show with her But he caught her off guard once again by giving her a brie(f) kiss on the cheek in greeting and then presenting her with (a) shoe box.

"For me?"

"Well, I just gave it to you, didn't I?" His smile was teasing.

She examined the front end of the box. "Size twelve Nikes? Sorry, Mac, but I don't think they'll fit me."

"That's the only box I had. I'm positive that what's inside will fit you."

"Oh, I get it." She marched into the parlor and tossed the box on the sofa. "The shoe I threw at you is in there, right?"

"Aw, Maggie, you're just too smart for me." He made himself comfortable on the sofa and placed the box in his lap. "I thought you'd like to have it back."

She purposely sat in the chair farthest away from him. His dumb joke irritated her. She saw no point in him bringing her this useless shoe and reminding her of how badly he'd behaved that afternoon they'd first met. Unless the point *was* to irritate her. Well, he'd succeeded. "What good is one shoe going to do me?" she asked in a scornful voice.

"One?" He looked surprised. "What happened to its mate? I don't recall you throwing two shoes at me when I drove off and left you in the dust."

Why was he insisting on going into the sorry details of his shoddy behavior? Maggie wondered. Surely the incident was best forgotten if they were going to work together. Not that she intended to ever forget it—but she was perfectly willing to ignore it in order to have a tolerable working relationship with him. He was making that impossible, though. He provoked her even more by drumming his fingers on the top of the box.

"I kicked the other shoe off and left it in the middle of the road," she admitted reluctantly.

Mac clicked his tongue. "Such impetuous, childish behavior."

That did it. Maggie leaped to her feet and strode across the room to glare down at him, fire in her eyes. "How dare you criticize my behavior that day when yours was so disgraceful?" He only smiled in response, fueling her anger. "Do you consider what you did amusing? Maybe you'd like me to tell the radio audience how you abandoned a fellow traveler in need."

Mac laughed at her threat. "'A fellow traveler in need.' I like that. Try to remember that phrase tomorrow when you describe our first meeting on the air."

"Surely you don't want people to know how rotten you acted." She was sure he was bluffing.

"Hell, it'll make good radio," he replied in an uncaring tone.

"Don't you give a hoot about what others think of you?"

"No. That's always been my biggest asset. I don't give a damn if people like me, just as long as they listen to me. Life isn't a popularity contest, honey."

"Oh, you're impossible," Maggie pronounced, turning away from him to return to her chair.

He reached up and encircled her delicate wrist with his long, strong fingers. "Sit here beside me," he commanded, tugging her arm.

Rather than make an issue of his simple request, she complied. His big, solid frame took up three quarters of the plush velvet sofa and once she was seated her thigh grazed his. She moved a few subtle inches away from him but could still feel the heat radiating from his body and smell his clean, masculine scent. He was wearing a light, lemony after-shave and she found herself wondering if he'd worn it especially for her. She had refrained from spraying herself with scent that evening, not wanting him to get the wrong idea. And now his heady nearness was giving *her* all sorts of wrong ideas. She wished, not for the first time, that she didn't find him so attractive. It upset her that she did because he was all wrong for her. She didn't trust him or even like him that much. Well, sometimes she liked him. But not at this moment.

"Would you stop drumming your fingers on that dumb box," she told him irritably. "Just get rid of it and let's get down to work."

"But I want you to open it." He transferred the box to her lap.

"Why should I?" She really couldn't understand why he insisted on teasing her about the shoe. "I already guessed what was in it, didn't I?"

"Not quite." He shifted his wide shoulders so that he could look her full in the face. Whenever he did that his eyes captured hers completely. Just another of his little tricks, she thought. "And I wasn't being totally honest with you a moment ago," he continued.

"Hah! So what else is new?"

"That's not fair, Maggie. When have I ever lied to you?"

"Just a moment ago, apparently," she parried.

He heaved a weary sigh. "I wonder if I'll ever manage to break down your defenses, honey. You've been prejudiced against me ever since you first laid eyes on me. Why?"

It was a difficult question for Maggie to answer without giving away too much of herself. It was true that she'd distrusted him from the moment he'd appeared over the crest of the hill, his arrival announced by blaring rock music rather than trumpets. She'd been hoping for a knight in shining armor to rescue her, not some wild man in a souped-up sports car. And when he'd gotten out and walked toward her, his long stride so bold yet easy, she'd sensed an implicit danger in him that she really couldn't pin down. It hadn't been his manner, exactly, although his absolute self-assurance had been troubling enough. It had been the effect his very presence had had on her equilibrium that she'd found so disturbing. And still did. But she wasn't going to tell him *that*.

"It was your shirt," she said. "I took an instant dislike to that tacky hula-girl shirt you were wearing."

"Tacky?" He pretended to look upset but his deep, dark eyes sparkled with humor. "I think it's pretty spiffy myself. But I guess there's no accounting for taste. Besides, didn't your mother ever teach you never to judge a book by its cover?"

In fact, Maggie's mother, intensely concerned with appearances and social status, had taught her just the opposite. "Oh, forget I ever mentioned it," she said.

But he wouldn't. "What about the shirt I'm wearing now? I'll be happy to take it off if you find it as offensive."

She recalled that he needed little or no encouragement to strip down to his bare chest. "That won't be necessary," she said quickly. "It's not as bad." It was a very acceptable rugby shirt, striped emerald, blue and red. The vivid colors suited his dark hair and eyes.

"Whew! That's a relief." Mac drew the back of his hand across his forehead dramatically. "I wouldn't want to offend your delicate sensibilities, Miss Bloomer. Now getting back to the shoe box."

Maggie groaned. "I've a mind to throw it across the room this very instant."

"Before you do that, let me finish what I started to say. I wasn't completely straight with you—" he held up his finger to prevent another interruption "—when I claimed I didn't give a damn what anybody thought of me. It's true enough about people in general, but I *do* care what you think about me, Maggie."

"Really?" She raised her eyebrows, wondering what he was up to now. She was sure a punch line was coming.

"Yes, really," he replied, looking about as serious as she'd ever seen him. "I don't want you to go on believing the worst about me. At first I didn't mind. I even thought it would give a sharper edge to our radio dialogues. But now I want to convince you that I'm really not the louse you think I am."

"Actions speak louder than words, MacNair. But I'm willing to let bygones be bygones for the sake of the show."

"You are one obstinate, close-minded woman," he declared, standing. "And I don't know why I'm so determined to make you realize that you're wrong about me." He really did look puzzled as he gazed down at her, thumbs hooked into the belt loops of his low-riding jeans. Then he smiled at her and shook his head. "But I am. Listen to me, Maggie. I had no intention of leaving you stranded on that country road. It was just a little joke."

"And I bet you laughed all the way to Rutland."

"No! I came back for you a few minutes later. Now will you open that damn box before I run out of patience?"

Maggie tried to imagine Mac with his patience on empty and decided it wouldn't be a pretty sight. Although she'd only seen the tiniest flicker of it, she sensed he had a red-hot temper when riled. Sort of like disturbing a hibernating grizzly. So she complied and took the cover off the box, expecting a little peace offering, chocolates or something, along with the shoe. But there was no conciliatory gift in the box. All it contained was a pair of her shoes. A pair!

She looked up at him, eyes wide. "But how in the world did you . . . ?"

"Like I said, I came back for you, honey. And there's the proof."

Yes, there it was. Maggie quickly looked down at the shoes again as tears of relief sprang to her eyes. She chided herself for overreacting. Maybe he wasn't the complete cad she'd assumed he was but that hardly made him a prince among men.

"Thank you for returning them," she said stiffly.

"That's all I get? A cold little thank-you?"

"What did you expect? A medal for behaving halfway decent?"

"An apology would be nice. Tell me you're sorry for misjudging me, Maggie."

"But I'm not sure I have."

"God, you're stubborn."

Maybe she was. A little. It was a character trait she wasn't proud of. Relenting, she stood and offered her hand. "Let's start fresh. Without preconceived notions on either side," she suggested.

"Sounds good to me."

They shook on it.

"But there is one other thing that's been bothering me," Maggie said, then hesitated.

Why was this so difficult? It was a simple matter really. She took a deep breath and plunged into the heart of it. "I don't want you to kiss me again, Mac. You were wrong to do that this morning. You took advantage of the situation."

"As I recall, I *saved* the situation. You missed your cue and blanked out, honey. What did you want me to do about it? Shake you? Throw water in your face? I figured a kiss was a more pleasant form of shock treatment." His wide lips stretched slowly into a knowing smile. "And it worked just fine, didn't it? Admit it, Maggie. We both enjoyed that kiss a little too much."

Unable to deny it, she turned her back on Mac and began examining the collection of framed photographs on Miss Jasper's mantel with intense interest. Not that she actually saw the images.

"Well, I don't want it to happen again," she said feebly.

"It won't."

His assurance came so easily that Maggie found herself wishing that he'd at least shown some regret. Hadn't he just admitted that he'd enjoyed it, too?

"I certainly hope it won't," she said, attempting to make her voice sound more adamant than petulant. She glanced over her shoulder, expecting him to be sneering or leering or smirking at her. She was relieved to see that he wasn't and turned to face him again. "If we're going to be stuck together in that studio day in, day out, we can't let messy emotions take over."

"Or even neat ones," Mac added, maintaining a straight face. "We're in complete agreement, Maggie. It would be a big mistake to get sexually involved. We'd still have to work closely together after the affair ended, and that could be a little uncomfortable. Women especially find that sort of situation difficult."

Again his response disappointed her although she knew it was an irrational reaction. But why did he so easily assume that *if* they had an affair, it would eventually end rather than progress into deeper feelings? Because he's incapable of deeper feelings, Maggie concluded to assuage her own ego.

"Well, I'm glad that's settled," she said, returning to the sofa.

"Is there anything else bothering you?"

He took the chair across the room, surprising her a little. She really wouldn't have minded him sitting close to her again. She wasn't a prig, after all. "Actually there is," she said.

He slouched in his seat, looking like a cross between a restless little boy and a condemned criminal. "Out with it then," he said.

"I think I deserve a better explanation of why you found it necessary to leave Vermont for the weekend rather than work on the show with me."

"It couldn't be helped," Mac replied tersely.

"That's not an explanation."

"I had to host a charity telethon in Phoenix," he mumbled.

Maggie wasn't sure she'd heard him correctly. "A what?"

"A forty-eight hour telethon to raise money for the Leukemia Society."

"Oh."

"Don't look so astounded, honey. Mad Dog MacNair's favorite charity may be himself, but he occasionally weakens and does something unselfish. Don't let it get around, though. It'll ruin my rep."

"Mum's the word." As Maggie once again adjusted her opinion of him, her expression and attitude softened. "I wish you had told me about the telethon before you left, Mac. I would have offered to go with you and help in some way."

"Really?" Mac's own face softened as he studied her across the room. "Well, it was a last minute thing. An old pal of mine from my early days in radio was supposed to emcee the show, but he had an accident and ended up in traction. So I flew out to replace him. No big deal. I did try reaching you in Birmingham, though. I had quite a little chat with your mother when I called. Talk about South Mouth! She's got an accent you could cut with a knife."

Maggie rolled her eyes. "Mamma usually lays it on extra thick when she's conversing with a Yankee."

"I figured as much. She didn't sound too pleased about you relocating up north. She made Vermont sound like the other side of the moon."

"That's Mamma all right. She wants all her chickies to roost close to home." But Maggie didn't want to discuss her mother with Mac. If never the twain should meet, she was sure those two wouldn't. "Well, now that everything's cleared up between us," she said in a brighter tone. "Why don't we get down to work and plan out tomorrow's show?"

"Hold on a minute." Mac sat up straighter. "Has it ever occurred to you that I have a few grievances of my own?"

Maggie blinked. "Why, no."

"You think you're just perfect, don't you?"

"No, my four older sisters used up all the perfection in the Bloomer family, I'm afraid." That's what Mamma always told her, anyway. She tossed back her hair. "But I always try to do my best, if that's what you mean, Mac."

"I bet you were on the honor roll in school."

"Most of the time." Not often enough to please dear Mother, though, she silently added.

"And you were a cheerleader, too," Mac conjectured.

"As a matter of fact I was." It was still a sore point in her memory because unlike her sister, she'd never been elected team captain.

"And no doubt you belonged to a sorority like Kappa Gamma Globulin or something in college."

"Kappa Kappa Gamma," Maggie corrected tersely. How could she *not* have joined, when her sisters and mother were Kappas? Mac's little guessing game was becoming irritating.

"You know what you are, Maggie?" he asked.

"What?" She braced herself for the expected insult.

"The quintessential southern beauty queen."

She laughed. "I never entered a beauty contest in my life," she happily declared to prove him wrong.

But that fact didn't seem to make the slightest difference to Mac. "I can see you on a float gliding through the center of town," he said, framing the imaginary scene with his hands. "Throwing kisses to the crowd as you clutch a bunch of long-stemmed roses to your ruffled bosom."

"I do believe you're confusing me with Magnolia Blossom. You of all people should know better than that, Madison. You wouldn't want people to think you're as much a reprobate as your Mad Dog character, now would you?" She'd been one of those people, Maggie reminded herself. But she was beginning to see that Mac had deeper dimensions.

"Actually Mad Dog used to be my alter ego," he readily admitted. "I developed that persona years before I went into radio. Just to drive my father crazy, I suppose."

She leaned forward and rested her chin in her palm, interested. "I bet you were quite a rebel as a teenager."

"Yeah. I left home at sixteen." Mac got up and began roaming the room with his casual, loose-limbed grace. Maggie watched him closely. If there was one thing about him she could never object to, it was the way he moved.

"That was pretty young to leave home," she said, deciding right then and there never to let Mac know that she'd waited until she was twenty-six.

"I cleared out rather than continue being a constant embarrassment to my father. He was the high-school principal and I was close to being a juvenile delinquent. Needless to say, we never got along."

"But how did you manage to get by on your own at that age?"

Mac shrugged. "Odd jobs. Picking fruit. Pumping gas. Stuff like that. After a couple of years I got fed up with that kind of hand-to-mouth existence and joined the army."

"You? In a uniform? Following orders?" Maggie couldn't quite picture it.

"Hey, it was the smartest thing I ever did." Mac paused at a parquetry side table and picked up a heavy bronze figure of a naked Amazon holding aloft a torch. "I got training in electronics and a first class radio-telephone license. When I got out of the army I was hired at WKOL in Phoenix as a broadcast engineer." He put down the sculpture and turned to Maggie. "And the rest, as they say, is history."

"But how did you make the transition from repairing microphones to talking into them?" Maggie wanted to know.

"Fate. Luck. Whatever. They needed someone for the graveyard slot and I volunteered to work without pay. It was an offer the general manager couldn't refuse." A shadow of a smile played on Mac's lips as he remembered. "I was such a cocky son of a gun in those days."

"Some things never change, do they?" Maggie drawled in her Magnolia voice.

Mac laughed. "Believe it or not, at the ripe old age of thirty-one I've mellowed. When I was in my twenties I was out to shock and enrage the listeners. That got me plenty of attention but I got sick and tired of it long before the audience did. Shock radio can be pretty exhausting. It's hard to keep topping yourself."

"Is that why you dropped out for two years?" Her eyes continued to follow him as he moved around the crowded parlor.

"That and other reasons." He went back to the nude bronze statue and studied it, tilting his head from side to side in exaggerated concentration. "You think Miss Jasper posed for this in her heyday? I'll make sure to ask her."

"Which would please her enormously." But Maggie wasn't going to be so easily distracted. "What other reasons, Mac? Why did you just give it all up at the height of your popularity?"

"Sorry, honey. I don't give interviews."

She felt the prick of his sharp retort and reined in her curiosity about him, feeling more than a little hurt. "Pardon me, but I didn't mean to be nosy," she said.

"And I didn't mean to be short with you, Maggie." He offered her his most engaging smile, which was hard to resist. "But I'm bored talking about myself." He returned to the sofa and sat beside her, and once again his clean, lemony scent and nearness filled her with something close to delight. "So enough about me. Why don't you tell me what a nice girl like you is doing in such an unsavory profession."

"I can think of a lot worse professions than being a disc jockey."

"I can think of a lot better ones, too." He stretched his long legs in front of him. "You must know by now that it's a cutthroat racket, Maggie. Job security is zero and except for the big markets like New York and L.A., the pay is nothing to write home about. Everybody wants to make it as a top-rock jock, but the higher you go, the stiffer the competition gets. And if you *do* make it to the top you have to kill yourself to stay there."

"Thanks for the pep talk," she remarked dryly. And then her heart tightened. "You want me to give it up, don't you, Mac? You decided this morning that I wouldn't work out on the show, and you want me to pack my bags and go back to Alabama."

"No, I don't." He looked genuinely surprised that she should think so. "I was simply talking straight about the business. If I wanted you out, I'd tell you so point-blank."

She believed him. He wasn't the sort of man to beat around the bush. Relief coursed through her, washing over her insecurities. He didn't want to get rid of her after all. At least not yet. "I don't think it's as bleak a business as you make it out to be," she said, gliding over her misinterpretation of his motives. "At least not in my experience."

He gave her a long, cool look. "Something tells me that you don't have a vast amount of experience, honey. And I don't mean just in radio."

She knew exactly what he meant and didn't reply. He was far too clever about guessing her past.

"How's that wimpy fiancé of yours, by the way?" he asked.

"Lamar is just fine, thank you," she replied stiffly. She gave him a sidelong glance. Sure enough, he was smirking.

"How'd he take the news that you were moving up north? Lying down, I bet."

Maggie looked at him directly, a frown marring her smooth forehead. "I don't know why you feel compelled to ridicule a man you've never even met."

"Neither do I," Mac said, more to himself than to her.

The shelf clock on Miss Jasper's crowded mantel began to chime. Neither of them spoke again until it stopped.

"Good Lord, it's already eight o'clock," Maggie said. "We've wasted an entire hour without accomplishing anything."

"Sure we did. We got to know each other a little better, didn't we?"

"Did we?"

They locked eyes, and Maggie leaned closer and closer to him, pulled in by the depths of his dark, fathomless gaze. How good he looked and smelled, she thought. How good it would feel to have his arms wrapped around her. She experienced an aching impulse to press against him, for only a moment.

"Would you care for a cup of coffee, my dears?" a chirpy voice rang out, as clear as the clock chime and even more timely. "I'm about to go into the kitchen to brew a pot."

Mac immediately rose to his feet and bowed to the sudden pixie apparition poised at the parlor threshold. "Miss Jasper, where have you been all evening? I missed you."

Miss Jasper smiled gaily, and despite all her wrinkles she looked youthful. "I didn't want to disturb you and Margaret while you worked, Madison. Besides, I have my own work to do."

"Miss Jasper is writing a book about her experiences in Zerbonia." Maggie stood, too. She didn't know what else to do. For some reason the old lady's unexpected appearance made her feel terribly awkward. She really didn't want to pinpoint the reason.

"Zerbonia? I've never heard of it," Mac admitted.

"You're not alone, dear boy. Very few people have," Miss Jasper said with kind understanding. Her sharp eyes immediately spied the shoe box beside the sofa and latched on to it. "But do have Margaret tell you about a certain Zerbonian mating ritual." She smiled impishly. "Now what about coffee?"

"That would be lovely," Maggie said, sensing that Miss Jasper wanted some company. "Let me help you, then we'll all have it together."

"I really don't want to interfere with your work," Miss Jasper stressed.

"Oh, we could use a break right now," Mac assured her, picking up Maggie's cue.

It was past nine by the time Miss Jasper excused herself and returned to her study down the hall. Maggie had downed two cups of coffee, which gave her an artificial energy boost. She'd had next to no sleep the night before, worrying about the show, but was determined to stay up for as long as necessary to make sure they were prepared for Tuesday's broadcast.

Determined as she was, she couldn't keep up with Mac's high-energy level. As the evening wore on, he became more and more creative, shooting off ideas like shotgun spray. Most of them had to do with the Magnolia character, and although Maggie appreciated his input, she began to grow suspicious.

"What are you trying to do? Make me the center of the show?" she finally asked him.

"No way, honey. But until you find your stride as Magnolia, I don't want Mad Dog to overshadow you."

"That's very generous of you." Too generous, she thought. She knew what hams jocks were. Once she got behind a mike, she was one herself.

"The truth is I find Magnolia Blossom a fascinating creature," Mac admitted.

And what about Maggie Bloomer? she found herself speculating. Don't you find her the least bit fascinating? She was tempted to ask him outright, but decided that it would sound too much like flirting. She would leave all the flirting to Magnolia—on the air.

They worked until midnight, roughly outlining enough segments and bits to carry them through their second show together. They would still have to wing a good portion, but Mac was confident that they could carry it off.

"It'll take a month or so for the show to develop and settle in," he said, standing and massaging the back of his neck. "After that, we'll be able to coast a little. But until then we're going to have to put in a lot of overtime together."

"I'd rather do that than flop on the air," Maggie told him. She was exhausted now, and sensed she looked it. It bothered her to have Mac staring at her when she looked less than her best. She got up and led the way to the front door.

"Better get some sleep," he advised softly, pausing in the shadows of the hall to stroke her weary shoulders. "We'll be on the air again in less than six hours."

Maggie groaned, partly to express her dismay, partly in pleasure as Mac kneaded her tense muscles.

"It'll get easier as the days go by," he assured her. And then, after giving her a reassuring pat on the back, he went out into the night.

He was an expert at quick exits, Maggie thought, immediately missing the touch of his strong fingers along her shoulders and spine. She went to bed with this thought heavy on her mind.

When her clock radio went off at four the next morning, Maggie awoke from a dream about Mac. The detail dimmed the moment she opened her eyes but the erotic nature of the dream had left her throbbing with pleasurable excitement. Alone in her bed, she blushed.

Chapter Six

Day two in the studio—6:03 a.m.

With two minutes to go before airtime, Mac stomped in like a grouchy grizzly.

"Good morning," Maggie called cheerfully from her desk. She'd come to work an hour early and was all set to go, headphones in place and folders containing live commercial copy, public service announcements and station promotions neatly arranged in front of her.

Mac growled back at her and settled down in front of the control panel.

"I would appreciate a civil greeting, please," Maggie said.

"You just got it, honey." After all his years as a morning disc jockey, Mac still loathed rising before dawn. But the critical early morning hours were the most vital for any radio station, snaring the biggest audience of the day, and Mad Dog MacNair had claimed them as his special territory long ago. If anyone had told him back in New York that he would be sharing this territory with a woman someday he would have howled.

Maggie decided that it wasn't her job to teach Mac proper manners. But maybe during the show her alter ego, Magnolia Blossom, could get in a few digs about his rudeness. Yes…that could be amusing. She jotted down a note on her pad.

When the six o'clock news report was over Mac opened his mike. "Awake and arise, you lazy bums out there!" he shouted. "It's six-o-five! Time to listen up to Mad Dog and Magnolia on station W…" Mac squeezed his nose. *"Pee Yew!"*

Maggie winced. She would have preferred a more genteel opening. Mac stuck a cassette in the cartridge machine and turned up the studio volume. "Born to be Wild" blasted through Maggie's headphones. She slipped them off.

"That song isn't on our computerized music sheet," she primly pointed out to Mac.

"Since when do computers have taste in music?"

"Since when do *you*? If you're going to open the show with a golden oldie, why not something pleasant like a Beach Boys song?"

Mac made a horrible face. "Take the bubble gum out of your ears, little girl, and listen to *real* rock and roll."

"I guess it's all just a matter of taste. And why must the volume be turned so high?"

"Because I like to feel the sound in my bones."

"Well, I don't." She put her headphones back on and made her own horrible face.

Mac adjusted a dial on the board. "Better?"

"Yes, thank you."

"Just remember I made a big concession for you, honey."

"You're all heart, Mac."

He put up a finger to caution her. "Don't call me Mac while we're on the air. I'm Mad Dog now and you're Magnolia."

"But we're not *on* the air now," she pointed out.

"Stay in character anyway," Mac said. "For the next four hours you aren't prissy Maggie Bloomer. You're provocative Magnolia Blossom. Okay?"

She nodded but didn't much care for his description of her off-the-air self. Refined, perhaps. Ladylike. But prissy? Certainly not!

"Let's start the show the same way we started this conversation," Mac suggested. "You complain about the song I chose in that husky drawl you put on and we'll take it from there."

"But what about the script we worked out last night?" Maggie protested. She'd risen at three just to prepare some lines for herself.

Mac gave her his first smile of the morning. "I guess it's time I told you the awful truth about me, honey. I've never stuck to a script in my life."

"I think I hate you, Madison MacNair."

"Mad Dog!" he reminded her once again. "Now play cool, Magnolia. We are *on*!"

She beat him to the trigger and opened her mike first. "I want you folks to know that Ah had nothing to do with the musical selection that just assaulted your ears," she cooed into it. "That varmint Mad Dog promised to play my favorite Beach Boys song right off this mornin', not some raucous tune from his preteen years. Grow up, Mad Dog! Born to be wild, my little toe. You were born with a tin ear, that's all."

"Oh, yeah?" Mac gave her a supportive wink. "Well, maybe if you took the bubble gum out of your own ears,

Magnolia, you could appreciate a higher form of rock music.''

"Honey chil', your problem is that you've got bubble gum for brains. Y'all call in if you agree with me that a rapscallion like Mad Dog MacNair doesn't have a smidgen of good taste.''

The buttons on the studio telephone panel lit up while Mac was reading the weather report, much to Maggie's surprise. Their invisible audience was responding and it gave her a heady feeling. How she loved the immediacy of radio!

Week two in the studio—6:03 a.m.

With two minutes to go before airtime, Mac stomped in like a grouchy grizzly.

"Good morning!" Maggie called cheerfully from her desk.

He stopped to glare at her. "Dammit, it's raining out. A cold, dismal rain. There is absolutely nothing good about this morning whatsoever.''

She gave him her brightest smile. "Sure there is. You're here.''

Her reply threw him for a loop and he smiled without intending to. "Don't try to sweet talk me, Magnolia. I know it's all an act.''

"Is it?" Maggie asked herself that question at the same time she asked him. No matter how bleak the predawn hours were, she always got up looking forward to that moment when Mac, sleepy eyed and grumpy, would make his appearance.

Mac took a swig of the unpalatable WPEU coffee but it didn't taste so bad going down when he was looking at Maggie. She was wearing a snug-fitting pink sweater with puffy short sleeves. Nice, he thought. Real nice. "I thought I'd open with 'Louie Louie' today," he said. "If that's all right with you."

Maggie had never heard of that particular song but didn't want to admit it. "Since when do you need my approval, Mac?"

"Come on, honey. Give me some input here. What moldy oldie would you like to hear? And if you say 'Good Vibrations' I swear I'll strangle that lovely neck of yours."

She touched her bare neck. Lovely? She smiled inside. "Actually, Mac, I think it's high time our show had its own theme song."

He nodded. "I've been thinking along those same lines myself. I have a few ideas."

"Let's talk about it later," Maggie said, pointing to the flashing red light above the clock. "But now Maggie Bloomer must leave her body to allow Magnolia Blossom to enter it." She covered her face with her hands and swayed in her chair, moaning and groaning like a possessed being.

Mac laughed. She was turning out to be a lot funnier than he'd initially supposed. If there was one thing he appreciated in a woman, it was a sense of humor. He also appreciated the way Maggie's full breasts moved under that sweater of hers as she swayed. Too bad their fans in radio land couldn't see her. He would do his best to help out their imaginations today.

He turned on his mike. "Awake and arise, you lazy bums out there!" he shouted into it. "Lousy day, isn't it? Well, for you, maybe. But not for me. I've got a big advantage over everyone out there. I've got Magnolia Blossom sitting right next to me and she's wearing this little fluffy pink sweater. Eat your hearts out, guys. She's one beautiful woman. And you're listening to *The Mad Dog and Magnolia Show* on station W..." Mac squeezed his nose. *"Pee-Yew!"*

Maggie didn't wince this time. She smiled as the color of her cheeks deepened to match her sweater.

Same day—10:15 a.m.

"This isn't an office, this is a broom closet," Mac said, pacing the short footage of it.

"Stan told us this was the best he could do," Maggie reminded him. She had to brush against Mac to get past the lumpy couch against the wall as she went to the desk wedged in the corner. All her nerve endings vibrated when their bodies contacted briefly. She sat down behind the desk, ignoring the quiver. "None of the other disc jockeys have office space."

"So what? None of them are as good as we are."

Maggie rolled her eyes. "Such modesty."

"Admit it, honey. We're great together!" Mac proclaimed. And then he immediately modified his statement. "On the air, I mean."

"I know that's all you meant, Mac. You didn't have to spell it out for me," she said irritably. "Don't forget that I'm the one who set the ground rules."

He looked at her carefully. "I won't forget if you don't."

Maggie forced a laugh. "You are the most vain creature alive, Madison. Just because we're stuck together for so many hours a day, do you think I'll actually fall in love with you?"

"Fall in lust with me, anyway." His tone was teasing. He leaned over the desk, resting his palms on the top of it. His grin was devilish. "I'm pretty hard to resist, aren't I?"

Maggie became lost in the depths of his warm brown eyes. Yes, she thought. He almost was irresistible.

Lola Medesa barged into the room, filling it with the scent of her perfume. "Am I interrupting anything?" She didn't wait for an answer. "Wow, this is a pretty small office, isn't it?"

"There's really only room for two in it," Maggie replied tartly.

Lola's smile was tight. "That's okay, Mags. You don't have to step out. You should hear my news, too. Our little luncheon with the New York media buyers last Saturday was quite a success. They were really impressed with Mac." Her jaw tensed, as if she were biting down on a bullet. "And you, too, Maggie."

"Great!" Mac said, wrapping his arm around Lola's shoulders. "Good work, lady."

Lady, my eye, Maggie thought. She was relieved when Mac removed his arm from Lola's shoulders and told herself to stop being so petty. "Yes, Lola, good work," she said. "This station is fortunate to have someone as sharp as you as its sales manager."

"Why, thanks, Mags." Lola gave her a genuine smile this time.

Week three at the coffee machine—5:30 a.m.

Maggie, who was measuring ground coffee into the filter, looked up, surprised. "Mac! What are you doing in so early?"

He ran a hand through his dark mass of hair, rumpling it even more. "I've been here all night in what is laughingly called the production studio. Talk about outdated equipment!" Shaking his head, he watched her pour water into the machine. "So that's why the java's been halfway decent lately. You've been making it fresh."

"I got sick of hearing you complain about Clyde Cobb's muddy leftovers. Do you like the pinch of chicory I've been adding?"

"Sure." He bent down and lightly kissed her cheek. "Thank you. I appreciate it."

"Oh, it's really nothing," she said. But his brief kiss delighted her more than she cared to admit to herself. "So what mischief have you been up to all night?" she asked.

"Come on." He took her arm and led her to the production room. "You can hear for yourself."

He rewound the tape he'd created, then played it for her. It was a multimedia mix down of the theme from *Gone with the Wind* and Springsteen's "My Hometown" with snips of their on-air conversations as a voice-over. Maggie listened intently, head tilted, hands to her face. And Mac watched her just as intently, his expression tense.

"Well?" he asked when it was over.

Her eyes were shining. "You're a full-fledged genius, Mac."

A grin of relief spread across his face. "I finally got you to admit it."

"I'm serious, Madison. It's a terrific lead-in to our show." Without thinking about it, she put her arms around him and hugged him tightly.

He hugged her back. "You're pretty terrific, too, honey," he murmured into her hair. And then he released her and busied himself rewinding the tape again.

A dark curl fell across his forehead as he bent over his task and Maggie felt the heart-pulling urge to embrace him once more. But because she had the time to think, she didn't allow herself the intimacy. How she longed to hear him murmur those words in her hair again, though.

Week four—6:02 a.m.

Mac stomped into the studio and smiled at Maggie. But this time she didn't look up from the notes she was studying.

"Hey, aren't you going to say good morning?" he asked gruffly.

"Why should I when all you do is growl back at me?"

"It's part of your job to put me in a good mood before we go on, that's why."

"Oh, is it?" She looked up at him but didn't smile. "Then who's going to put *me* in a good mood?"

"But you're always cheerful, honey. I count on it."

"It seems you count on me to do quite a lot around here."

"Uh-oh. Fame is going to your head, isn't it, Bloomers?" He slumped down in front of the control panel. "I guessed this would happen when those fan letters started coming." He sighed dramatically. "And this is the thanks I get for making you a star."

She pulled back her shoulders and raised her chin. "I think I had a little to do with the small success I'm enjoying."

Mac groaned. "Please don't turn into a prima donna on me, Maggie."

"I'd just like some words of appreciation from you now and then, that's all."

"I complimented your coffee, didn't I?"

"My coffee! If that's all you can think to compliment then it's a downright shame. I expect a little more consideration from you than that."

"I'm sorry. I was just being a wise guy."

Mac really was sorry for his dumb remark. Maggie was right. He didn't show his appreciation enough. She was organized, responsible, hardworking and talented. Damn tal-

ented. And because she was making this temporary gig for
him so much easier, Mac was feeling more and more guilty
about it. Where would that leave Maggie when he received
his "better offer" and quit WPEU? Better off, Mac assured himself. He'd given her a job when she'd needed one
and he could see her self-assurance growing with each passing day. She would do just fine on her own once they split
up the act.

Mac believed the important thing was to keep their relationship strictly platonic. But he constantly needed to remind himself of this. Lord, Maggie was tempting! But Mac
sensed that she would never enter a sexual relationship
lightly and he had no intention of persuading her to. When
the time came, he wanted to leave Rutland and Maggie behind with a clear conscience.

He smiled at her, a little sheepishly. "Don't be mad at me,
buddy. We've got us a show to do. And I really do count on
you to make it work. You know that."

Maggie sighed. "Yes, the show must go on," she said
dryly. *That's all he cares about, isn't it?*

But the moment their theme song surged through her
headphones, that's all Maggie cared about, too. Energy
flowed through her, even though she'd stayed up half the
night working on her daily report about Magnolia's crazy
relatives down in Alabama. Maggie sometimes wished that
her real family were as wild and crazy as her fictitious one.

Mac supplied the humorous sound effects as Maggie gave
the latest installment of the Blossom family saga, and then
he segued into one of the Top 40 songs listed on the music
sheet. He took off his headphones and hung them around
his neck so that he wouldn't have to listen to it. Checking the
program log, he told Maggie to read the library public service message after he played the station ID jingle.

He was very good at giving orders, Maggie thought. But he followed them, as she usually did. When they were on the air, Mad Dog MacNair was the boss. She accepted this because of his greater experience and supreme sense of timing. Maggie no longer doubted it. He really deserved to be called a superjock. She appreciated how much she was learning from him but it had begun to irk her that he didn't seem to appreciate *her* input.

She wasn't going to complain to him about it again, though. Mac had his irritating faults but he was generous about letting her share the spotlight. In fact, he usually gave her the best lines during their skits, usually let her have the last word when they ad-libbed and always went out of his way to make her look good on the air. Maggie was having the time of her life working with him and she was grateful for the opportunity.

Mac left the studio during the next news break and came back with coffee for both of them. He gently set Maggie's up on her desk. "You're not still ticked off at me, are you, honey?"

"No," she admitted grudgingly. "But I hope you value me for more than my coffee-making ability."

"Hey, where's your sense of humor? You know that was just a wisecrack." He chucked her chin lightly. "Do you have any plans for this afternoon?"

Her heart rose a little. "No, not really. What do you have in mind?"

"A new idea for a sketch. Let's work on it after lunch."

Of course. What else did she think he had on his mind? It was always on the show. "Sure," she said.

"That's my little trooper." He patted her head, which he knew infuriated her. There was a glint in his dark eyes, as there always was when he teased her. "For your reward, I'll take you out to lunch at the Greasy Grunt." That's what everyone who worked at WPEU called the nearby diner they patronized.

"Wow, thanks, Mac. You sure know how to treat a gal."

"Only the best for you, honey. I'll meet you there after I check out an apartment that just came up for rent."

"You've sure been taking your time about getting one."

"There isn't much time left to take when we spend most of it at WPEU," Mac replied. He thought it best not to add that he'd been having trouble finding a place that suited him yet didn't require signing a year's lease. It would only make Maggie uneasy to know that he wasn't planning on staying around that long.

"I couldn't stand living in an impersonal hotel room for any length of time," she said.

"It's not so bad. I've got all the necessities of life—hot shower, clean sheets and room service. I'm a man of simple needs, honey." He'd often longed to have Maggie in his lonely hotel room with him but thought it best not to mention that, either. "I really miss the great stereo system I still have in storage, though. I need a nice big apartment to set it up in."

"So you can blast your infernal rock music, I suppose." Maggie pretended a shiver. "Mad Dog MacNair moves in and there goes the neighborhood."

Mac smiled. "Believe it or not, when I'm off the air I manage to pass for a respectable citizen." He headed out the door. "See you at the Grunt later, Bloomers."

Maggie arrived at the diner at twelve-thirty. She walked down the booth-lined aisle to the big table in back where the WPEU personnel usually gathered for lunch. Stan was wolfing down an enormous salad. Night Owl Clyde, who never seemed to go home, was gnawing on a roast beef sandwich. Patti, the adorable eighteen-year-old reception-

st, daintily picked at her French fries as she sat next to Mac
and observed him with star-struck eyes. Maggie could eas-
ly understand her infatuation with him and was amused by
t. Lola Medesa was sitting on the other side of Mac and her
lagrant come-ons to him didn't amuse Maggie one bit. She
ook the vacant chair between Stan and Clyde.

"Don't order the pastrami today," Clyde cautioned her.
'It looks deadly."

"All meat is deadly," Stan said through a mouthful of
crunchy lettuce.

"Oh, Stan, stop being such a bore. Vegetarianism went
out with the sixties," Lola informed him in a superior tone.
'And please don't talk with food in your mouth."

He swallowed awkwardly. "Sorry, Lola."

Stan looked so crushed that Maggie squeezed his arm to
comfort him. "Ignore her," she whispered in his ear.

"I can't," he whispered back.

"Mac just informed us that he finally found an apartment," Lola said to Maggie across the table. "I told him he
should save his money and move in with me, instead."

"How sweet of you," Maggie replied. She did her best to
quell a spurt of jealousy. Mac and she had a working relationship and nothing more. Maggie wanted it to stay that
way, too. But she couldn't stop the erotic dreams she was
still having about him—more and more often as the weeks
went by. It had gotten to the point where she both dreaded
and greatly looked forward to falling asleep each night. She
turned to him now, hoping her smile didn't look obviously
artificial. "And are you going to accept Lola's generous
offer, Mac?"

He laughed, as if a little embarrassed. "It comes too late.
I already paid the first month's rent."

"Oh, darn my blasted luck," Lola said, ruffling Mac's
hair. "But here's an idea. We can swap sleep-overs, Mad

Dog. You spend the night at my place and then I'll spend the night at yours.''

"Oh, Lola, you really do have your vamp act down pat,'' Maggie said. Her smile was beginning to feel as tight as a Band-Aid plastered across her face.

"It's no act, Mags,'' Lola adamantly replied.

The table fell silent for a moment. Then Mac cleared his throat. "Did anybody besides Maggie and me catch the show this morning?''

"Everybody in Rutland listens to it,'' Patti piped up. "I'm a local celebrity for just knowing you two.'' She smiled at Mac and then had the grace to smile at Maggie, too. "All the guys want to know what you look like, Miss Bloomer. I tell them you're as beautiful as you sound.''

Maggie laughed disparagingly. "No need to go overboard, Patti.''

"But it's true,'' Mac said. "Our listeners can't possibly imagine you looking any better than you actually do, honey.''

His unexpected flattery warmed Maggie to the core but she tried to act cool. "Oh, Madison, you silver-tongued devil, you,'' she drawled. "Luckily my mamma taught me to pay no mind to such talk.''

But she couldn't stop herself from taking everything Mac said and did to heart. She couldn't stop herself even though the red light in her mind's eye flashed Danger whenever she looked at him. The last thing Maggie wanted was to fall in love with Madison MacNair. She considered herself far too sensible to ever allow that to happen. If only she could be as sensible in her dreams!

At first Mac didn't hear the knocking on his door. He had his stereo turned up high and was engrossed in the plangent notes of Tchaikovsky's "Pathétique.'' He kept his passion or classical music to himself, not because it didn't fit his ock-jock image, but because he was by nature an exceedngly private man. His father and he had shared the same aste in music—one of the few things they *had* shared while Mac was growing up. Mac had arranged for a symphony pianist to play his father's favorite Brahms concerto at his funeral three months ago. He and his father had reconciled only after Mac had learned that his father was dying. He was grateful that he'd been able to be with him during that painful last year of his life.

It always made Mac sad to think of his father, and all the years wasted apart not speaking. It was frightening how time could slip by, how a crack in a relationship could become a ravine too deep to dare cross. Contemplating this with a heavy heart, Mac finally heard the knocking on his door when it became progressively louder and more insistent.

His heart immediately lightened when he thought it could be Maggie. She was the one person he could appreciate seeing right now. His telephone hadn't been installed yet. Maybe she wanted to discuss the next day's show with him. He turned off the stereo and opened the door.

"Hi there, handsome. I hear there's a party going on here." Lola brushed against him and sashayed into his sparsely furnished living room.

Mac was tempted to tell her she had the wrong address and always would as far as he was concerned. "Sorry to disappoint you, Lola," he said. "But there's no party here."

"There is now." She raised a silver-wrapped bottle. "I brought champagne as a housewarming gift." She glanced around his new apartment. "Nice place you got here, Mac. Did you sign a long lease?"

"Actually I didn't sign any. I have a month-to-month arrangement with the landlord."

"That figures." Lola handed him the champagne. "I doubt you'll be hanging around Rutland any longer than necessary."

Mac gave her a cool look and made no comment.

"You'll be out of here as soon as you get a better offer, won't you?" Lola pressed. When he didn't respond she shrugged off his silence and continued. "Not that I blame you. I can't wait to leave this hick town and get back to corporate headquarters in New York."

"You do seem a little out of place in Vermont," Mac said with a faint smile, taking in her chic black velvet suit. "Poor Lola. All dressed up with nowhere to go."

"There's always Mac's place." Her bold eyes never leaving his, Lola slowly unbuttoned her jacket. "And I don't mind that the address is temporary. In fact, I prefer it that way." She threw the red silk-lined jacket on his couch; she was wearing a skimpy matching silk top beneath it. And beneath that, nothing at all, Mac noted.

"I'll go put the champagne on ice," he said.

"And what will we do with ourselves while it's chilling?" she breathed, stepping closer to him. "Something that will be worth celebrating later, I hope."

"I'll let you be the judge of that, Lola. And if you're disappointed, you can take back the champagne."

She threw back her sleek head and laughed. More like whinnied, Mac observed. "I certainly don't intend to be disappointed," she told him.

Subtle she wasn't, Mac thought, taking the bottle into the kitchen. He raised an eyebrow over the expensive French label—and groaned when he read the note she'd attached with a bright pink ribbon around its neck. "To a corker of a time together. We'll sip this in bed. Lola." Shaking his head, Mac dutifully placed the champagne in his empty refrigerator. He felt just about as empty of desire. It wasn't

Lola he wanted. It wasn't Lola he ached for from the moment he awoke until he saw her in the studio, then ached for even more when she became risqué Magnolia over the airwaves, her husky voice turning his spine into butter.

"Hey, Lola's getting lonely out here!"

Mac put his thoughts about Maggie on hold and reluctantly went back to Lola. She had arranged herself on the sofa, long legs tucked under, short skirt riding high up her firm thighs. No, Mac decided. He wasn't going to take her up on it. Even though she was so obviously willing to let him, he wasn't going to use Lola. Or any woman ever again. He found the situation more than a little ironic. Mad Dog MacNair hadn't gotten his wild reputation by turning down willing females. He'd eventually tired of such empty relationships, though. That was one of the reasons he'd married. And now that he was free again, he wasn't about to slip back into that meaningless life-style.

"What were you doing for so long in the kitchen?" Lola asked, pouting.

"Wrestling with my conscience." He thought that sounded a little too noble but he wanted to let her down gently. "I'm not looking to get involved with anyone right now, Lola. And you're way to classy a dame for a one-night stand."

Her eyes slithered over him. "If you pass the audition, it won't have to be a *one*-night performance, Mad Dog."

Mac laughed. Since Lola was so disinclined to be subtle he decided there was no need for him to be, either. "The truth is, Lola, I'm not interested in the part."

"Hmm." She considered his rejection for a moment. "Then I gather the rumors are true. Maggie's your leading lady on and off the air. That's how she got the job, and that's why you always make her look good on the show."

"Wrong, Lola. Maggie and I aren't having an affair. It's strictly business between us. I respect and admire her talent." He ignored Lola's sneer of disbelief and offered her his most gracious smile. "You know, you made my day by coming here." He had to work with her and he didn't want to alienate her completely. "You're damn attractive and I'm damn flattered."

"But you're also damn determined not to sleep with me, right? That sure doesn't sound like the Mad Dog MacNair I heard about. What did you do when you left the big time, Mac? Become a monk?"

He shrugged. "Maybe I finally grew up a little bit, Lola. There was a time when everything came too easy for me. Easy come, easy go. The trouble is that you can end up with nothing in the end that way."

"Yeah, tell me about it." Lola laughed bitterly. "Easy come, easy go, that's me all right. I've been around the block more than a few times, Mac, but I've never found a parking space. I'm beginning to wonder if I'll ever have a permanent relationship with a man."

"Do you want one?"

Her smiled faded. "You know that old song 'Whatever Lola Wants'?" Mac nodded. "Well, what if poor Lola doesn't *know* what she wants?"

Mac found himself liking her more. Maybe deep down Lola wasn't the tough-as-nails man-eater she made herself out to be.

"Can I stay around for a cup of coffee?" she asked him. "If I promise not to come on to you anymore tonight?"

"Sure. But all I have is instant and you'll have to drink it black."

Lola made a face. "Okay. That's how desperate I am for a little company tonight."

They ended up talking for over an hour, mostly about the station. They were both interested in making WPEU a commercial success. And they both intended on leaving it behind as soon as possible to move on to bigger and better things.

"What I can't understand is why a big corporation like yours would have any interest in a small station like PEU," Mac said, sitting across from Lola on an oversize ottoman.

"We've invested in a few dozen stations like PEU to test the waters," she told him. "Radio is big business. Over seven billion dollars a year." Her eyes glowed when she stated that figure. "What corporation wouldn't want a chunk of that action?"

Mac frowned. "But you can't mass-produce radio stations like you do computer parts, Lola. A good station has a unique spirit. It's got to somehow reflect the community it serves. That's what makes radio such an intimate medium."

Lola stifled a yawn. "My job is to worry about the bottom line, not some intangible *spirit*. The reason I've been sent here is that Stanmore Senior wants me to watch over Junior." She sighed into her coffee mug. "Keeping some overaged hippie from screwing up was never one of my career goals."

"Don't underestimate our funky station manager," Mac said. "Something tells me he's not as spaced-out as he pretends to be. And he has a real love for radio."

"Well, Stan *did* come up with the brilliant idea of having Mad Dog MacNair host the morning spot," Lola conceded.

"But my style would have been way too abrasive for this area if I didn't have someone to blunt my sharp edges."

"You mean your cute little second banana Maggie, of course."

"Come on, Lola. You know she's more than that on the show," Mac replied irritably. "The listeners appreciate her importance and so do the advertisers."

"And so, apparently, do you." Lola's snide smile returned. "But if you don't want to admit you're sleeping with her, that's fine with me, Mac."

He didn't bother to deny it again and he didn't protest when Lola said she would be on her way.

"Let me give you back the champagne," he said.

"No, no. Keep it iced. We may drink it together yet." She opened the door and paused on the threshold. "In bed, of course. That's the only place I drink champagne." And after supplying Mac with that tidbit of information, she closed the door behind her.

Mac was relieved to see her go and immediately turned on his stereo again. Tchaikovsky soon erased all traces of Lola from his mind. Another woman slowly crept into it, filling it completely—her fresh flower scent, her golden hair and eyes, her honeyed voice. He pictured her in a white strapless gown on a sultry southern evening, waiting for him beneath a blooming tree, bathed in moonlight and languidly fanning herself. "Ah, Magnolia." He sighed. In the deepest recesses of his heart Madison MacNair was a true romantic. But he would never admit that to anyone, even himself.

Maggie returned from a long afternoon walk in the woods behind Miss Jasper's house and came in through the back door. The soothing scent of melting chocolate hit her chilled nostrils when she entered the kitchen. Miss Jasper was at the stove, stirring it into a saucepan of warm milk.

"Oh, how delicious that smells." Maggie sighed as she shucked off her heavy knit sweater and sturdy shoes. "Is there enough for me?"

"Of course there is, Margaret," the old lady said. "I never bother to make hot chocolate for myself."

"How thoughtful of you, Miss Jasper. But how did you know I'd be arriving just now? I swear you really are clairvoyant."

"Stop giving me powers I don't possess, young lady. I happen to be making this beverage for a guest in the parlor. Not my *personal* guest, mind you, but one who called on you. A rather tall, handsome young man with the most beautiful eyes."

Maggie's heart picked up a few beats. "You must mean Madison."

Miss Jasper chuckled. "Now you're the one who is being clairvoyant."

"Just a lucky guess."

Miss Jasper clutched her own little hands to her breast. "Oh, those long eyelashes of his, Margaret! If I were half a century younger, I would surely swoon over Madison myself."

Maggie smiled and shook her head. "You are such a dear and foolish romantic, Miss Jasper."

"There is nothing foolish about being romantic, Margaret." She poured the hot chocolate into two thick old mugs and handed them to Maggie. "Now I must go back to my study and resume work on my memoirs."

When Maggie entered the parlor Mac was gazing out the long window, his hands behind his back. He was wearing an Irish knit sweater that accented his broad shoulders. He turned and smiled at her. "You look good, honey. Your face is all rosy."

"I've been out walking in the woods." She handed him a mug. "The trees are mostly bare now but the leaves were exploding with color all during October. How I adore New England! I can't wait to experience my first snowstorm."

Mac took a sip of the chocolate, observing her over the rim of the mug as she chattered enthusiastically. "You're beginning to sound like a confirmed Yankee," he said.

"Then I'd better watch myself next time I call Mamma. I still haven't broken the news to her that I won't be coming home for Thanksgiving. I think I'll write her a letter instead."

"Listen, honey, I've been thinking about that," Mac said. "Actually that's what I dropped by to discuss with you. If you want to go back to Tara for Thanksgiving, I'll let you take off a few days."

Rather than look grateful, Maggie studied him suspiciously. "But what about our show, Mac?"

He shrugged. "So I'll go solo for a couple days. No big deal."

"No big deal!" Maggie was crushed. "If that's your attitude then you obviously don't feel I contribute that much to it."

"Now hold on, Maggie. Don't act like I just insulted you. I figured you might be feeling a little homesick, that's all."

"Sure I feel twangs of it now and then," she admitted. "I miss my mother. And my sisters and darlin' nieces and nephews, too. Why, I even miss my staid brothers-in-law at times."

"Not to mention Lamar Bleaker," Mac added. "Which I notice you haven't. How come?" He grinned. "You don't have to answer that, honey. I suppose the memory of him pales in the bright light of my heady presence."

His teasing hit too close to the truth for Maggie to manage a quick comeback. She always felt an underlying tension when she was with Mac, and although it sharpened their repartee on the air, Maggie found their relationship exceedingly frustrating once they left the studio. It bothered her that she still couldn't figure Mac out after working with him so closely for almost two months.

He sipped from the mug and then licked the chocolate off his wide bottom lip. As Maggie observed him, the memory of the one searing kiss they'd shared came back to her full force. It was accompanied by regret that he'd never tried to kiss her again. Since she was the one who had enjoined him not to, this regret made Maggie feel rather foolish—and irrationally angry with both herself *and* him.

"You may not think it would make much difference if I'm absent from the show or not, Mac," she said, getting back to the subject under discussion. "But did it even occur to you that our audience might miss me?"

He impatiently flicked his hand through his hair. "I was just trying to be a little considerate for a change, Maggie. But if you don't want to go home for the holiday, that's fine with me."

She felt a pang of guilt because she really didn't mind missing out on yet another suffocating family dinner surrounded by well-meaning relatives who couldn't understand her choice of career, or her ambition to do more with her life than marry and settle down.

"All the other disc jockeys are doing their shows on Thanksgiving and I don't see why I should be the exception," she told Mac. "But you were kind to offer," she added, although she wished he hadn't.

They discussed the next day's show for a while, then Mac drained his cup of chocolate and left. Maggie often wondered how he spent his time when they were apart. Not that either of them had much spare time. Doing a live four-hour show six days a week wasn't easy. It still rankled her that Mac seemed to think he could easily do without her for a few days.

After their broadcast the following morning, they went back to their tiny office to work on new material for the show. But first Maggie settled down behind the battered metal desk to read and answer the week's accumulation of letters from listeners. Mac left that particular duty entirely up to her but she didn't mind. She enjoyed it. He claimed he wasn't interested in fan mail, but after Maggie read one particularly compelling request, she brought it to his attention as he lay on the lumpy sofa staring at the ceiling in what he called his "creative position."

"This is a letter from the director of the Jasper Nursing and Retirement Home," she said, handing it to him. "She says the residents listen to us every morning."

"So?" Mac gave the letter a cursory glance.

"So at least read it, Mac." He could be so exasperating at times, she thought. In fact, most of the time.

"Why don't you just summarize it for me, honey?" He tossed the letter back to her, then resumed staring at the ceiling. "But make it quick. We've got to come up with a new routine today with a Thanksgiving theme. What a drag holidays are. I'd just as soon ignore them all."

She wasn't surprised by his attitude. He was a loner, a maverick, a man who kept to himself for the most part, and getting enthusiastic about traditional holidays wouldn't be in keeping with this image she had of him. At the same time, she found him especially irritating at the moment. Perhaps because he was wearing his dreadful Hawaiian shirt, which Maggie took as a personal affront. Everything Mac did affected her enormously, even his smallest gesture or remark. And when they were apart Maggie constantly reviewed what he'd said and done. Madison MacNair had become a twenty-four hour obsession with her. He'd somehow managed to take possession of her mind if not her body.

"The gist of the letter is that it would mean the world to them if we celebrated Thanksgiving there," Maggie told him, taking in his strongly defined profile as he studied the cracks in the ceiling.

"Who?" he asked without blinking.

She knew that he was being infuriating on purpose and tried to rise above it. "Our listeners at the nursing home," she replied patiently, smoothing down the open collar of her creamy silk blouse. "I think it would be fun to have dinner with them."

"Fun?" Mac groaned. "Frankly, honey, having a bland turkey dinner with the geriatric set isn't my idea of a rollicking good time."

"Oh, Mac, I think it's the least we can do for such faithful fans."

"We do enough by entertaining them every morning."

"That's such an uncharitable attitude!"

Forgetting about the cracks in the ceiling, he sat up to look at her. "Listen, Maggie, those so-called fans out there will steal every minute of your time and every ounce of your energy if you let them. They'll take over your life."

"But this will only take a few hours of our time, Mac." She smiled sweetly, hoping her smile would encourage him to be more kindhearted and generous.

It didn't. "How much would we get paid for this gig?"

"Nothing, of course. You weren't paid to host that charity telethon in Phoenix, were you?"

"No, but that was different. First of all, I was doing a favor for a friend. Secondly, it was a worthwhile cause."

"Well, so is this," Maggie insisted.

"Perhaps. But let me explain something to you," he said patiently. "If we start making *gratis* personal appearances, there'll be no end to the requests. One good turn deserves another. And another and another. Hell, we're not social workers, Maggie. We're radio jocks."

"That doesn't excuse us from the human race, Mac. In fact, being in the public eye—"

"More like ear," Mac interrupted.

"Whatever." Wishing he could be serious for once, she continued. "Being local celebrities gives us a certain social responsibility. Whenever possible we should do our bit, if you'll pardon the pun, to help others."

His wide lips curled sardonically. "What do you think you are, honey? The Mother Theresa of the airwaves?"

She threw him a reproachful look. "Will you please stop being such a wise guy?"

"I will if you stop sounding so sanctimonious, Miss Goody Two Shoes. If you want to play the gracious star and go to this old folks' home to be admired and adored, then be honest enough to admit it."

Indignation heated Maggie's cheeks. "That's not the point at all, but how could I expect a reprobate like you to understand?" It hurt her to realize that she should never have expected anything from him.

"Come off it, Maggie. I see the way your face lights up when some local yokel asks you for an autograph."

"Why shouldn't I be flattered when people express how much they enjoy listening to me?" she asked defensively. Then she decided to take the offensive. "Don't tell me the big, bad Mad Dog MacNair is jealous of lil' ol' me for being popular here in Yankee land?" she asked, sliding into her Magnolia accent and batting her eyes, as if fanning the sparks of anger in them.

He laughed, as she guessed he would the moment the words left her mouth. "Why should I be jealous of your popularity, honey?" He rose from the couch and hovered over her. His tall, solid frame seemed to cast a shadow over

Maggie as she sat very still behind the desk, looking up at him. "After all, it's thanks to me that Magnolia Blossom exists in the first place. I invented her."

Maggie stood and stared him down. "You really are an egomaniac, aren't you? The next thing you'll be claiming is that you invented the radio, too."

"No, just *The Mad Dog and Magnolia Show*."

Deciding that the office was too small for her and Mac and his big, bulky ego, Maggie headed for the door.

"Where do you think you're going?" he asked. "We've got work to do on the Thanksgiving bit."

"Work on it yourself," she told him. "You can do the show yourself from now on, for that matter."

His dark eyes narrowed. "What are you going to do, Maggie? Go on strike just because I don't want to eat turkey at some old folks' home?"

"It's more than that." And she felt a lump of regret in her throat because he didn't understand how much more. "Don't you ever consider anybody but yourself?"

He studied her for a long moment. "What do you think?"

If only she knew. How she wished she understood him better. "I think you should come to that nursing home with me on Thanksgiving Day," she replied, trying hard to keep her voice light. If he agreed it would prove that he cared about her, or others, or *something* other than himself.

But he was shaking his dark, curly head even before she'd completed her sentence. "You're making this too much of an issue between us, Maggie." There was a warning ring to his voice.

She ignored it. "It's something I feel strongly about, Mac," she insisted. "You don't want me to go on strike, now do you?" He'd put that silly idea in her head and she made an effort to smile to show that she was joking. But it was such an effort it came out a grimace.

His brown eyes intensified, the softness in them receding without a trace. "Dammit, honey, don't give me an ultimatum."

Maggie returned his killer look without flinching. She wasn't about to be intimidated by him. Ever. She wasn't going to back down to him, either—it was way too late for that.

"I mean it, Mac. I won't do the show until you agree to go to the nursing home with me."

His smile was cold and bright and never reached his eyes. He leaned closer and closer to her and she watched him without moving or breathing or blinking, attentive as a cornered cat.

"Stalemate," he whispered in her ear, sending a shiver down her spine. And then he captured her in his arms.

Chapter Seven

Maggie leaned back and pressed against the solid boundary of Mac's arms, pushing her palms against his chest. At the same time she tilted her face upward, making her lips available to him and waited, breathless, for him to strike. But he made no move to kiss her this time. Instead he stared at her long and hard.

"So what are you going to do, honey?" he demanded softly. "I'll leave the next move entirely up to you."

How she wished Mac would stop challenging her. How she wanted him to simply acknowledge what was between them and take it from there. Acknowledge what, though? A mere sexual attraction? Unbridled passion? What? How could she possibly make the next move when she was so unsure of her own feelings, let alone where she stood with this mercurial man?

"You once warned me against daring you," she reminded him. "And now I'm warning you."

"Don't try to bluff me, Maggie." He pulled her closer. "That's such a risky game."

She could feel the strength of his long, hard thighs against hers and it made her knees a little weak. Her tone showed no sign of this weakness, though. "You'll realize I'm not bluffing when I don't show up in the studio Monday morning."

"I like it when you talk tough, honey. It's kind of cute." He smiled as he swayed against her sensually.

She knew he was playing with her—as he always had and probably always would. He'd refused to take her seriously from the very beginning. And that was one thing Maggie wanted from him with all her heart.

"That's it," she stated emphatically. "I'm officially on strike as of now. If you change your mind about visiting the nursing home with me on Thanksgiving Day, give me a call."

This time Maggie made a serious effort to break away from him, throwing her weight back as she pushed against his chest. She needn't have made such a show of force; he relented immediately. But only his physical hold on her. Mac's position on the point at issue remained inflexible.

"I won't change my mind," he assured her. "And if you're not at the station by airtime Monday morning, Maggie, you can kiss your Magnolia Blossom days here goodbye."

His words were a slap in the face, making her cheeks burn hot and bright. Her better sense pleaded with her to back off, retract her threat, somehow modify her stand. But her emotions were in high gear now, thrusting her forward, as if off a cliff. She swallowed hard and took the plunge. "Then I guess this is goodbye, Mac. Since you have so little regard for me—I mean, for my role in the show—I doubt you'll miss me around here."

"That's right. You won't be missed." He reached out and skimmed cool fingertips across her heated cheek. "Because you'll show up Monday, same as always, won't you, money?"

The underlying plea in his persuasive voice almost assuaged her. She needed more than that from him, though. Up until now she'd done everything his way. But Maggie realized the time had come for Mac to make some sort of concession to demonstrate he valued her, or at least her input.

"No," she said. "If you let me walk out now, I won't be coming back."

She went to the door and waited a moment, her hand on the knob. Mac made no move to stop her. She left, closing the door softly behind her, and walked briskly down the hall to the elevator. As always, it took forever for the creaky old car to rise to the summons—plenty of time for Mac to reconsider and stop her from leaving. He didn't. Maggie had no choice but to step into the car when it finally arrived. Her heart plunged all the way down to the street level.

"What are your plans for Thanksgiving, dear?" Miss Jasper asked Maggie the next day. It was a bright cool Sunday afternoon and Maggie was helping her clear dried leaves out of her chrysanthemum beds at the side of the house.

Maggie sighed and kept working, her fingers clumsy in the thick gardening gloves Miss Jasper had lent her. She was tired, but not from the light outdoor work. She hadn't slept well the night before. "I may be going home after all," she stated, then paused to swallow hard. "For good."

Miss Jasper remained, as usual, unruffled. "For good? Why is that?" she asked mildly.

Maggie related how she and Mac had reached an impasse over visiting the Jasper Nursing and Retirement Home. She stuck to the simple facts of the matter, her voice dispassionate. "So you can see why I can't back down now," she concluded. "Mac has forced the issue."

"Well, one of you has anyway."

"Certainly not me!" Maggie gave Miss Jasper a look of wide-eyed innocence.

She received a dubious one in return. "I'm sure your initial motives were pure," Miss Jasper said. "But it sounds to me as if you got sidetracked by ulterior ones. Why were you so determined to make Madison go along with your wishes?"

"Must you always play that particular devil's advocate, Miss Jasper?" Piqued, Maggie devoted her attention to plucking out tenacious leaves. But she found it impossible to ignore Miss Jasper's pointed question because it had pierced the heart of the matter. "The truth is I wanted Mac to show some regard for me by putting himself out a little," she admitted. "The more stubborn he got, the more important that became to me." She shook her head, considering her own words. "Maybe even more important than doing something nice for our fans at the nursing home," she acknowledged with a sigh. "I reckon my motives were downright selfish in the end."

"Not selfish, my dear. Only human." Miss Jasper gave Maggie a smile to reward her honesty. "But it all sounds like a tempest in a teapot to me. The nursing home residents will be delighted with a visit from you, with or without Madison. And if you show up for work tomorrow and act as if nothing has happened, I'm sure he'll have the good sense to act the same way."

Maggie shook her head stubbornly. "No. I can't do that. I won't return unless he begs me to."

"Oh, my." Miss Jasper shook a brown chrysanthemum bush hard to dislodge the fallen maple leaves that had caught in its branches. "Now if this were Zerbonia, the village mediator would step in, sprinkle orchid petals over your head and Madison's, and the ceremony would resolve your differences."

The image caused a small smile to soften Maggie's obstinate expression. "Too bad this isn't Zerbonia. Life sounds so simple and uncomplicated there."

"It's a beautiful place, indeed."

"Do you have any photographs of your time there, Miss Jasper? I'd love to see them."

"Alas, no. They were all lost on the boat coming back to the mainland."

The old lady looked so sad over this loss that Maggie decided to change the subject. "What are your plans for Thanksgiving?" she asked. "You must have lots of kin here in Jasper, considering your great-grandfather founded the town."

Miss Jasper stopped working and stood slowly, bones creaking. "All the ones I cared for are dead," she replied bluntly. "Except my brother, Oliver, who owns the mill. He and I had a parting of the ways, though, and I lost contact with his children during my many years in Zerbonia. It seems I've become a persnickety old maid with no one left to care about her."

"You sure got the persnickety part right, Florence."

The two women turned to see Ralph, Miss Jasper's chauffeur and handyman, quietly standing at the edge of the chrysanthemum beds, leaning on his rake. Since he was always around, his presence didn't surprise Maggie. Hearing him call Miss Jasper by her first name did.

"But you'll never be old in my eyes," he continued. "And being lonely is your own darn fault."

"It's my own business, too," Miss Jasper retorted sharply.

They locked eyes and Maggie was curious to see which one of them would stare the other down. They both looked away at the same time, though. Miss Jasper slipped off her gardening glove to adjust a wayward strand of gray hair, and Ralph turned his attention to the chrysanthemum beds.

"Nice job you're doing, ladies," he said. "Still, you should have left it to me." He gave Miss Jasper a sidelong glance. "You've got no need to do manual labor when there's an able-bodied man about who's more than willing to help out, Florrie." With that Ralph placed his baseball cap back on his bald head and walked back to the pile of leaves he was building at the far side of the lawn.

"Presumptuous old coot," Miss Jasper mumbled under her breath. "Thinks he knows everything."

It was apparent to Maggie that Ralph's remarks had flustered Miss Jasper and she became curious about him. Although Ralph spent a great deal of time tinkering around the house—inside and out—Maggie didn't know him well. He'd chauffeured her to the radio station in Rutland for a week or so but they'd never talked about anything except the weather during the ride back and forth. Then Maggie, not liking to impose or be dependent, had bought a used car that Ralph checked out for her. Now they had that to discuss along with the weather. But never anything more personal.

"Is Ralph married?" she asked Miss Jasper.

"Widower. And yes, he was one of my suitors when I was a girl if that's what you're trying to find out, Margaret."

What Maggie was really trying to find out was if Ralph was *Florrie*'s suitor at present. But Miss Jasper picked up her full basket of leaves and marched off with it before Maggie could think of a subtle way of asking her.

That evening Maggie leafed through a pile of old *National Geographic*s in the front parlor while Miss Jasper gave a talk

Say **Yes** to
romance

AND YOU'LL GET:

- **4 FREE BOOKS**
- **A FREE
BRACELET WATCH AND**
- **A FREE SURPRISE GIFT**

**NO RISK •
NO OBLIGATION TO BUY •
NO STRINGS • NO KIDDING**

EXCITING DETAILS INSIDE ⟹

Say YES to free gifts worth over $20.00

Say YES to a rendezvous with romance and you'll get 4 classic love stories—FREE! You'll get an attractive bracelet watch—FREE! And you'll get a delightful surprise—FREE! These gifts carry a value of over $20.00—but you can have them without spending even a penny!

MONEY-SAVING HOME DELIVERY

Say YES to Silhouette and you'll enjoy the convenience of previewing 6 brand-new Special Edition® books delivered right to your home every month before they appear in stores. Each book is yours for only $2.74*—a savings of 21¢ off the cover price, and there is no extra charge for postage and handling. If you're not completely satisfied, you can cancel at any time, for any reason, just by sending us a note or a shipping statement marked "cancel" or by returning any unopened shipment to us at our cost.

SPECIAL EXTRAS—FREE!

When you join the Silhouette Reader Service,™ you'll get our monthly newsletter, packed with news of your favorite authors and upcoming books—FREE! You'll also get additional free gifts from time to time as a token of our appreciation for being a home subscriber.

Say YES to a Silhouette love affair. Complete, detach and mail your Free Offer Card today!

* In the future, prices and terms may change, but you always have the opportunity to cancel your subscription. Sales taxes applicable in N.Y. and Iowa.

FILL OUT THIS POSTPAID CARD AND MAIL TODAY!

Sɪʟʜᴏᴜᴇᴛᴛᴇ Bᴏᴏᴋs®

FREE OFFER CARD

4 FREE BOOKS

FREE BRACELET WATCH

FREE SURPRISE BONUS

Place YES sticker here

FREE HOME DELIVERY

LOW MEMBERS-ONLY PRICES

FREE FACT-FILLED NEWSLETTER

Please send me 4 Silhouette Special Edition® novels, free, along with my free bracelet watch and free surprise gift. I wish to receive all the benefits of the Silhouette Reader Service™ as explained on the opposite page.

235 CIS R1X6
(U-S-SE-08/89

Name _____
(PLEASE PRINT)

Address _____ Apt. _____

City _____

State _____ Zip _____

DETACH AND MAIL CARD TODAY

BUSINESS REPLY CARD

First Class   Permit No. 717   Buffalo, NY

Postage will be paid by addressee

RUSH! FREE GIFTS DEPT.

Silhouette Reader Service™
901 Fuhrmann Blvd.
P.O. Box 1867
Buffalo, New York 14240-9952

NO POSTAGE
NECESSARY
IF MAILED
IN THE
UNITED STATES

at the Audubon Society of Vermont. She was disappointed
that she didn't come across an article about Zerbonia. She
was even more disappointed that the telephone in the hall
refused to ring. The lighting was poor in the parlor, a draft
came through the long windows, and Maggie would have
been more comfortable in her cozy quarters upstairs. But
she feared she wouldn't be able to hear the phone from her
room—and she didn't want to miss Mac's call.

The hours ticked by at an agonizing rate but she refused
to give up hope. Despite the display of bravado she'd put on
for Miss Jasper, she'd never really expected Mac to capitu-
late. But she had hoped a friendly call from him would
somehow release her from the corner she'd painted herself
into. Surely he owed her that much after all her hard work
on the show. Until yesterday she'd demanded nothing from
him. Nothing at all. *Please,* she begged silently. *Please call
me, Madison.* She sent that message to him with all the effort and force her mind was capable of projecting. But it
remained unanswered long past midnight, when Maggie finally released the last frail strands of hope she was clinging
to and went to bed.

She had no intention of getting out of it when dawn
broke. It was a matter of principle. More than that, it was a
matter of hurt feelings! Mac hadn't made the slightest effort to keep her from walking out on him—on the show,
that was. He'd treated her threat so cavalierly, as if it didn't
matter in the least to him if she went through with it or not.
So now she felt she had to.

She lay in bed, covers pulled to her chin, and listened to
the radio. Each time Clyde Cobb rang his cowbell and announced the time, Maggie tensed a little more. The dead-
line was nearing and Mac and she were still stalemated.
Maggie considered giving in. If she hurried she could still get
dressed and make it to the studio by six. But she remained

where she was, hands clenched beneath the covers. If only Mac had called her last night. If only he'd shown her the slightest concern or consideration. She blinked away hot tears of frustration when she heard a gentle knock on her door.

"Margaret? Are you awake?"

"Yes, Miss Jasper," she called back.

"May I come in?"

"Of course."

Miss Jasper, dressed in a bright green quilted robe, entered the room and stopped at the foot of Maggie's bed, shaking her head. "You're not ill, are you, my dear?"

Yes, sick at heart, Maggie thought. "No," she replied. "But I saw no reason to get up since I'm not going to the station today."

"I think you're making a mistake," Miss Jasper cautioned. "There's still time to rectify it, though."

"No. It's too late. It was up to Mac to set things right between us." Disappointment clouded her eyes, dimming their natural sparkle.

"Frankly, I'm surprised he hasn't, my dear. Madison doesn't seem the sort of young man who would let anything he cares about slip through his fingers."

"Then it's pretty obvious what he *doesn't* care about, isn't it?" Maggie's tone was grim.

Miss Jasper looked at her with great sympathy. "It's always dangerous to put a man's affections to the test, Margaret."

"This is a matter of principles, not affections," Maggie insisted.

"If I believed only principles were involved I would support your position completely and even serve you breakfast in bed," Miss Jasper told her. "But I know as well as you do what this is all about, my dear. You've fallen in love with Madison.''

Maggie turned her head aside and pressed her cheek to the pillow. "Have I? Or is it just—"

"A strong physical attraction?" the old lady asked with her usual candor. "Well, I wouldn't belittle *that*, my dear. If memory serves me correctly, that's the main reason the opposite sexes get involved in the first place. In Vermont as well as Zerbonia.''

"It's much more complicated than that."

"It strikes me that you have a way of making things complicated for yourself, Margaret. The simplest solution to your present predicament is to get up, get dressed and *go to work*.''

Maggie remained where she was, stiff as a board. "I can't do that, Miss Jasper. I've been taught to believe that once a stand is made, it must be upheld at all costs."

"Not at all costs, surely. Whoever taught you that?"

"My mother. She has very rigid standards of behavior."

"You're a long way from home now, Margaret. And you're certainly old enough to have your own standards," Miss Jasper pointed out gently. "So I won't attempt to influence you further." After giving Maggie a resigned smile, she left her alone.

Maggie continued to listen to Clyde Cobb and was unexpectedly reminded of the times when she was sick in bed as a child with the radio turned down low—her comforting bedside companion. She could almost hear background piano scales as her mother gave lessons in the living room. Between the lessons her mother would come in to check on Maggie and give her juice and toast and touch her hot forehead with her cool, soft hand. But Maggie also remembered how impatient her mother had been with her when she was ill, as if she'd gotten strep throat or the measles just to be even more trouble than she already was. Mrs. Bloomer always claimed that her youngest daughter was her most vexatious one. Try as she might, Maggie could never please her the way the other four always did.

Clyde's cowbell brought her sharply back to the present. "It's 6:00 a.m. and time for this Wild and Crazy Night Owl to go home to roost," he announced. "But don't touch your dial, folks. Mad Dog and Magnolia are coming up to lighten and brighten your morning right after the news."

Maggie bolted upright and turned up the volume. What was Mac going to *say* when he came on the air? Was he going to tell the audience that they'd heard the last of Magnolia Blossom? Or was he going to make up some excuse for her absence this morning? Maggie moaned and covered her head with her blanket, disgusted with herself for allowing pride and sheer mule-headed obstinacy to get in the way of what she really wanted. And what she wanted most at that moment was to be sitting in the studio across from Mac, feeling that surge of excitement she always felt right before they went on.

Mac was so angry he could barely see straight as he pulled cassettes out of the studio library stacks and lined them up on Maggie's vacant desk. His choices reflected his mood— Cheap Trick, Blondie, and Blood, Sweat and Tears. He would sure like to make one particular blondie sweat blood and tears for the cheap trick she'd played on him by not showing up this morning. But he was as cool and unflappable as ever when he went on the air. He made no mention of Maggie's absence to the audience. Instead he told them he was dedicating an hour of uninterrupted music to Princess Di, whom he would be interviewing later.

Half an hour later Maggie was still lying in bed, bemoaning her own stubbornness and half listening to the odd selection of songs Mac had selected—wondering what he was up to—when he burst into her bedroom. Marching across the room in long strides, he looked very tall and menacing from her vantage point on the bed. His sinewy masculinity filled the room and seemed to seep into her very bloodstream.

"Get up," he ordered succinctly.

She shrank back under the covers instead. As Mac towered over her bed, his anger was almost palpable. Already astounded by his sudden appearance, she wouldn't have been surprised if he started breathing fire, singeing the blanket she was clutching to her breast.

He yanked it away with one forceful tug. "Get up," he repeated. "You're coming back to the station with me."

"I'm doing no such thing." Maggie hurriedly pulled down her long flannel nightgown, which was twisted around her thighs. Not only had Mac revealed her smooth, bare legs, but also her woolly red ankle socks, which Maggie found even more embarrassing.

"What a sexy getup," he remarked dryly, wishing she hadn't covered up her golden legs quite so quickly. Her big toe had worked a hole through one sock and he found that somehow endearing. He reminded himself that he was damn angry with her.

"Well, it gets cold up north at night," she explained self-consciously.

"Only if you sleep alone, honey." His dark, knowing eyes glinted with humor as they swept over her. "I'm a little disappointed. I always imagined Magnolia Blossom wearing satin and lace to bed."

Disappointed, was he? Maggie tossed back her tangled mass of tawny hair and raised her chin to glare up at him.

"I didn't invite you into my bedroom, MacNair, and you have no right to be here."

"*You* have no right to be here at the moment, either, Maggie. You're supposed to be working. So haul your cute little butt out of bed and get dressed. I'll give you two minutes flat before I use force."

"That's how long I'll give you to get out of my room before I scream," she threatened back without budging.

"That won't do you any good. Miss Jasper promised me she wouldn't interfere. Now get moving. You're coming back with me."

"What's the matter? Can't the infamous Mad Dog handle a simple little morning show by himself anymore?"

Her taunt made no dent in his stern expression. "I'm not letting you get away with this stupid strike business, Maggie. Time is running out and so is my patience."

"Just admit how much you need me, Mac, and then maybe, just maybe, I'll reconsider my position." Her tone was still taunting but her heart cried out to hear him say those words.

"I'm going to reconsider your position for you, honey." With one quick movement he picked her up as if she weighed no more than a pillow and flung her over his shoulder.

She objected to his manhandling in the traditional manner, by beating her fists against his back and screeching her indignation. But the more she wriggled and writhed to free herself, the harder he gripped the backs of her thighs.

"Don't make me drop you, Maggie." He shifted her weight on his shoulder as one would a bulky sack of potatoes.

"Put me down this instant, you brute." She couldn't stop herself from saying that. It just sprang out of her mouth automatically, and then she started giggling over the absurdity of it all. "All right, Mac, you win. Put me down and I'll get dressed and go quietly." The blood was beginning to rush to her head. Enough was enough.

But Mac didn't seem to realize that the joke was over. "Sorry, Maggie. You had your chance to leave in dignity. Now you leave in your nightgown." He smoothed it down over her buttocks and legs with diligent care, taking his time about it, then carried her out of the room and down the stairs, ignoring her shouts of protest.

Miss Jasper was waiting at the foot of the stairs. "Oh, dear," she said.

"I don't mean to shock you," Mac apologized as he headed to the front door with Maggie. "But Margaret simply won't listen to reason."

"Oh, I'm not shocked, Madison. I've seen it all, believe me. But in Zerbonia it's the women who carry the men off over their shoulders." Miss Jasper bent down to look into Maggie's face. "You're all right, aren't you, my dear?"

"Call the police and tell them I've been kidnapped," Maggie instructed.

"Abducted," Miss Jasper corrected. "I don't believe Madison intends to ask for a ransom."

Mac snorted. "Who'd pay it?"

Maggie resumed pounding his back with her fists.

Miss Jasper hurried to the hall closet and took out Maggie's raincoat. "It's a bit nippy this morning," she remarked, draping it over Maggie's backside.

"And my purse, please," Maggie said.

Miss Jasper got that from the closet, too, and handed it to her. Mac carried Maggie to his car. The engine was running and the top was up. Miss Jasper waved a cheery goodbye from the porch.

They traveled down the winding country road in silence for a while, both a little out of breath from their heady exertion. It was the same road on which they'd met in early September when the leaves were still green. Most of the trees were bare now. After driving a few miles Mac pulled over to the shoulder and stopped. It was the same spot Maggie had stopped when she'd had her flat tire and she wondered if he realized this. What could be more romantic? She waited breathlessly for him to speak first.

"This is ridiculous," he said.

Those weren't exactly the seductive words she'd been hoping for. "If you mean your he-man tactic, I agree," she replied testily.

"What else could I do? The one cardinal rule in radio is that you always go on the air, no matter what. And you broke it, Maggie. I figured my choices were either to fire you or drag you back to work." He adjusted her raincoat around her shoulders. "And I didn't want to let you go."

Maggie shifted her weight in the leather bucket seat and leaned closer to him. She was smiling now. Obviously he needed her, whether he wanted to admit it or not—and he almost had.

She lifted her arms to wrap them around his neck and her raincoat slipped off her shoulders. From the moment he'd burst into her bedroom, she'd known that it would come to this. She had wanted some sign from him, some demonstration that he cared about her, and he'd dramatically given it to her. She kissed him softly at first, grazing his wide mouth with her full, supple one. Mac made no attempt to deepen the kiss, but he certainly made no attempt to pull away, either. His cool demeanor didn't fool Maggie. She'd picked up the quickening of his breath, so she pressed her mouth a little harder against his to test his reaction. He pressed back gently, still showing a great deal of restraint.

How delightful it would be to destroy his self-control, Maggie thought, and then set out to do exactly that. She ran her hand through his thick dark hair, as she'd been dying to do for weeks, slipping her fingers wantonly through the thick strands as she pressed kisses on the high planes of his face. She could almost feel the spark of desire ignite within him and smiled to herself. She recklessly slid her mouth across the rough expanse of his jaw and paused to nibble his earlobe.

"You'd better stop this, Maggie," he admonished thickly.

But she didn't want to stop. She covered his mouth with hers again to prevent further protest, assuming she was still in control of the situation. She had him exactly where she wanted him now and intended to show him no mercy.

The shift was so subtle, so sublime, that Maggie didn't realize right away that her control was slipping right into Mac's hands. But he began doing marvelous things to her with his fingertips, beginning with the lightest strokes up and down her back. Her spine tingled. She sighed. He slipped his tongue into her mouth and took over the kiss she had started.

He took over her entire body as he slid his hand over the curves of it through the layer of thin, flower-printed flannel. He cupped the indentation of her waist, the flat expanse of her belly and roundness of her breasts with a gliding lightness that tempered the intimacy of his caresses—making Maggie crave for more as a warm glow suffused her.

Mac could feel the heat of her pliant body through the soft material of her gown and he deepened his kiss, pushing her head back against the side window. The moan that escaped from her entered his body, filling him with an aching desire that was more poignant than any he'd ever experienced. He was lost then, as she invaded his senses, his heart, his mind. She was the woman he'd always wanted, the woman who had sprung from his yearning and imagination.

Tearing his mouth from hers to catch his breath and his sanity, Mac whispered hot in her ear. "Magnolia."

She laughed softly. "We're not on the air now. You can call me Maggie."

Her words broke the spell for him and he drew back as far as he could, to his side of the car, banging the stick shift with his knees in the process. "You sure picked a hell of a time and place to try to seduce me, honey," he joked gruffly.

She gave him her most innocent look but the flush of passion on her face belied it. "Is that what I was doing?"

"You tell me." His eyes were shining with intensity, the pupils dilated into great black disks. Maggie saw her own pent-up desire reflected in them and knew he wanted her as much as she wanted him. Her tongue felt thick when she spoke.

"Why shouldn't we . . . you know . . . make love?"

His smile was a little rueful. "Only acrobats could manage to make love in a car this small. Do you have special talents you didn't put on your résumé, honey?"

"I didn't mean *here*." She slapped his arm a little harder than she intended. "Can't you be serious for once?"

Wincing, Mac rubbed his arm. "No," he said. "That's not my style. That's why it wouldn't work between you and me, Maggie. If we started an affair, you'd expect me to take it as seriously as you did and I'd end up letting you down."

She turned away to gaze out the side window so he wouldn't see her face crumple with disappointment. "It seems you already have let me down, Mac. Or turned me down, anyway."

"Hey, don't get me wrong, honey." He placed a comforting hand on her shoulder. "You're as delectable as they come and more tempting to me than you probably realize.

But we have such a good act going together. Why let basic biological urges mess things up?"

She pushed his hand away. "How romantically you phrase things, MacNair."

"Come on, Maggie. Don't be mad." He tugged on the sleeve of her nightgown to get her to turn around, but she wouldn't. "I'm looking out for your best interests. A woman like you deserves a commitment from the man she gets involved with and that's something I can't give you."

She twisted her neck so that she could glare at him. "How do you know what sort of woman I am?"

"I know you don't sleep around for the hell of it."

She couldn't refute that and so she challenged him instead. "And I suppose you do?"

He shook his head slowly. "I stopped doing that years ago when I got married."

The high color in Maggie's face drained as if a plug had been pulled on her deepest expectations. "You're married, Mac?"

"Was. Past tense. I was lousy at it and I never repeat my mistakes."

The first part of his reply eased her mind. She took the second part as an unnecessary warning and wanted to set him straight. "I'm not interested in getting married myself."

Mac gave her a questioning glance. "What about that bozo you left down in Dixie, honey?"

Maggie ignored the denigration of Lamar's fine character—by now she was used to it from Mac. "That's over. We broke up." She was relieved to shake free of that little fib, then realized that a half-truth was almost as dishonest. "Actually Lamar and I broke up over a year ago. I don't know why I lied and told you I was engaged when we first met, Mac."

"Maybe you were trying to keep this Mad Dog at bay."
He bared his bright, white teeth in a smile.

"Maybe."

His expression turned serious. "That was smart, Maggie. And what you're suggesting now isn't. What made you have a change of heart anyway?"

Not only had there been a change in her poor heart, but it felt rather battered and bruised by his rejection. "Let's forget all about it, okay?" She'd never felt so dumb in her life. Or so greatly disappointed in not getting what she wanted.

Mac nodded, looking relieved, and started the car. He turned off the engine a second later. "Dammit, I *can't* forget it." His eyes latched on to hers. "I've wanted you since the first moment we met." His sigh was a deep shudder of surrender. "And God knows there's no way I can refuse you now, honey. Even if it goes against my better judgment."

He pulled her to him, a little roughly, and the fervor of his kiss made Maggie tremble. She could taste his hunger, feel the potency of his desire for her. It excited her beyond measure and frightened her, too. It flashed in her mind that she was sealing a bargain with the devil with this kiss, but that didn't make any sense. She was the one who had set out to tempt *him*!

"We'll go back to your place after the show," she said, her voice quivering a little when he released her. "Now we'd better hurry to the station. We're keeping our audience waiting."

Mac laughed deeply. With pleasure? Expectation? Or at her quivering boldness mixed with her innate practicality? Maggie wasn't sure. She could never be sure with him.

He started the car again and pulled onto the road so fast it sent her reeling back into the bucket seat. Feeling giddy, she started laughing, too. She had no intention of asking Mac to slow down. Hadn't she just thrown caution to the wind? Still, being the basically prudent soul she was, Maggie snapped on her seat belt.

Chapter Eight

Maggie smiled at Clyde Cobb's astonished expression when Mac carried her into the studio. He'd insisted on carrying her because she wasn't wearing shoes. She hadn't protested because she adored being pampered by Mac for a change.

"Thanks for covering for us, Clyde. We'll take over when this record ends," Mac said, offering no explanation for Maggie's tardiness or attire.

Clyde didn't act as if he expected any, either. He didn't so much as blink his heavy-lidded eyes as he promptly got up from behind the control board and stretched.

"I'm glad you two kids worked out whatever problem it was that you had," he said sleepily. After giving Maggie's nightgown and red socks a cursory glance, he left the studio shaking his head.

Mac settled down in front of the board and smiled at Maggie as she took her place across from him. It was his widest, most engaging smile—the one that always made her heart melt a little. "I would never want to do this show without you, partner," he told her softly.

Partner. How she liked the sound of that! They would soon become partners in a more intimate sense—in a *completely* intimate sense—and her nerve endings tingled with anticipation. "How are we going to explain going on an hour late?" she asked him, trying to keep her mind on the business at hand.

Mac shrugged. "Never explain yourself. That's one of the few rules I live by."

That sounded rather ominous to Maggie but her immediate concern was the flashing red light above the clock, warning them it was almost time to go on. "What's our lead-in going to be?" she asked Mac, hastily going through the copy on her desk.

"I promised them an interview with Princess Di when I came back on the air. How's your British accent, honey?"

Maggie rolled her eyes. "Honey chil', when it comes to puttin' on a British accent, I'm about as competent as a rubber-nosed woodpecker in a petrified forest," she replied in her husky Magnolia voice.

Mac glanced at the clock. "I don't have time to figure out what that means but it doesn't sound too promising."

"It isn't, believe me. The only accent in my repertoire is a down-home southern one."

"Okay, then *I'll* play the princess and you interview me."

"That's ridiculous, Mac! About what?"

"I don't know. What do women gab about when they get together? Ask me about clothes or something."

"Oh, Mac, you don't know a thing about clothes. This is the dumbest idea you've ever come up with."

"It will work, honey. Trust me. You set it up, and I'll jump right in."

Maggie gave him a nod of resignation and opened her mike. It was too late to come up with a better idea and she had no choice but to wing it. She told the listeners that she and Di had once been rivals for Prince Charles's affections and the princess had come to Rutland to bury the hatchet. She paused. Nothing funny so far, she thought, as flop sweat dampened her brow. She glared at Mac. "Tell me, Princess, how do y'all like Vermont?"

Mac glared back. Her pedestrian question gave him nothing to work with. Maybe this wasn't such a hot idea after all. "I say!" he screeched in a high-pitched voice. "I like it jolly well indeed!"

His reply was so corny, his accent so amateurish, the bit so absolutely dreadful and unfunny, that Maggie was stunned for a moment. And then she was overcome with a rush of laughter. Trying to stifle her giggles, she clutched her arms around her heaving chest and almost fell off her seat in silent mirth. Tears ran down her face from the effort.

Watching Maggie fall apart in amusement made Mac lose his own cool. Realizing that neither of them could contain their laughter a moment longer, he stuck a public service announcement into the cart machine to cover it up. He unplugged his headphones and rushed to her side. Taking her into his arms, he held her tightly as they rocked the room with an explosion of hilarity.

"Did I sound as bad as I think I did?" Mac howled.

"Probably worse!" Maggie shrieked, her ribs aching.

"What a colossal stink bomb of a bit!" His laughter subsided as he held Maggie close and breathed in her essence. "And it's all your fault, honey," he muttered into her hair.

Gasping for breath, she pulled away. "My fault? It was your idea, Mac."

He gently wiped the tears of glee from her cheek. "Of course it's your fault, honey. How can you expect me to think straight, let alone be funny, when the only thing on my mind is that we'll be making love in a few hours."

A little shiver ran through Maggie, from her crown to the tips of her toes. She wasn't laughing anymore when she looked up at him and gazed deeply into his eyes. Their lips met and as they floated together on the wave of their lingering kiss Maggie's heart was buoyant with optimism.

But then reality rudely intruded with a sharp rapping against the studio window, and Maggie, startled to her senses, jumped away from Mac. It startled her more to see the station manager's face pressed against the window, a goofy long-haired gargoyle mouthing frantic instructions she couldn't hear.

"Not a pretty sight, is he?" Mac muttered, turning away from the window to adjust his ardent expression.

"Dead air! Dead air!" Stan cried in alarm as he ran from the window and into the studio.

Swearing under his breath, Mac rushed to the control board and opened his mike. "Don't adjust your dials or hearing aids, folks. The silence you just had the pleasure of listening to was a test to see if you were paying attention. And you passed! Here's your reward." He grabbed another music tape and without bothering to check the song title, popped it in the cart machine.

Mac couldn't remember when he'd been so inept, so downright sloppy on the job. That's what happened when you mixed business with pleasure, he reminded himself. It was a mistake—a big MacNair-size mistake—to get physically involved with someone like Maggie Bloomer. Love and commitment were two things Mac didn't part with easily and he knew she would come to eventually expect both from him. He *did* pride himself on being a man of resolve, though. And he resolved to drive her straight back to Miss Jasper's after the show—for her good as well as the good of the show and his own peace of mind.

But a few hours later she was rummaging around his kitchen, trying to rustle up an early lunch for the two of them. So much for resolve, Mac thought sardonically as he leaned against the refrigerator watching her. But he wanted her, dammit. He had since the day he'd spotted her on the road, a vision of peach and gold femininity that would cause any red-blooded male to forget about his destination and come to a screeching halt.

"Don't you have even a can of soup hidden away somewhere?" she was asking, opening and closing cupboard doors.

"Nope. We could go to a restaurant if you're starving." It was a feeble suggestion, he knew.

And she immediately discounted it. "I can't very well prance into a restaurant wearing my nightgown, now can I?"

"I warned you that my cupboards were bare." And bare is the way Mac kept picturing her as she moved around. He could see the lush shape of her breasts through her gown when she reached up to browse through high shelves. He could see the rounded outline of her bottom when she bent to check under the counter. He'd had no idea such simple, domestic motions could be so erotic, but of course it depended on who was performing them.

"You've warned me about a lot of things, Madison," Maggie replied blithely, attempting to shove him aside so that she could open the refrigerator.

He moved quickly, but only to wedge her between the sleek, cool surface of the fridge and his warm hard body. "You should heed all my warnings," he told her in a low, dangerous tone.

She raised her chin and blew into his face, ruffling the dark wayward curls on his forehead. "Don't try to intimidate me, Madison. I'm not afraid of you anymore."

But he saw the way her pulse jumped at the base of her throat and he was sure he could hear her heartbeat, which sounded like a trapped rabbit's. "I can't forget how those big eyes of yours got bigger that first time we met and I took off my shirt," he said. "What were you thinking, Maggie? That I was going to ravish you?"

"I admit it crossed my mind." She kissed his neck. "Why shouldn't it have?" Her voice grew huskier. "A tall dark stranger ... you could have been capable of doing anything to me." She reached higher to kiss his cheek, his nose, his ear.

Her little kisses were driving Mac crazy. But he refused to let her take over the seduction. He still wasn't sure there should be one. "I'm even capable of ending this before it goes any further," he said, with more bravado than belief.

"My, oh, my, you do play hard to get, honey pie," she said in her Magnolia accent. "And to think I was worried all this time that you were a big ol' superstud."

Grabbing a handful of her golden hair and gently tugging, Mac tipped back her head to raise up her chin and luscious mouth. "Don't think you can get away with that kind of teasing off the air," he cautioned her, thrilled, as he always was, by the way she could thicken her honey voice. "Maybe it's high time Magnolia Blossom proved she wasn't all sexy talk and no action." He crushed her mouth with his and pressed insinuatingly against her so that she would know exactly what he meant.

So it was Magnolia who excited him, Maggie thought. Sharp pangs of jealousy shot through her and she stiffened. She realized how ridiculous it was to be jealous over a fantasy of her own making but she couldn't help it.

Mac immediately sensed her change of mood and reluctantly pulled away. "Aw, honey, don't run hot and cold," he murmured in exasperation. "What's the matter now?"

Her misgivings seemed too stupid to try to explain. Maggie wanted Mac to want her for herself alone, not the sultry creature she pretended to be on the show. But of course Magnolia was a part of her, a part she'd always been too conservative, too inhibited to release until recently. Why not live the fantasy if that's what Mac wanted? Straight-laced Maggie Bloomer, with her limited sexual experience, would probably bore him in bed. But a vamp like Magnolia Blossom? Why, she would absolutely dazzle him!

"Nothing's the matter, darlin'," she cooed, reaching up to run a finger along his strong prominent jaw. "This was all my idea, remember?" She slid her finger down his neck, slowly circled his Adam's apple, then dipped it under the collar of his denim shirt. "And I *do* believe it's an idea whose time has come."

"I doubt there's a man alive who could refuse you," he admitted.

She could feel the vibration of his deep voice through her sensitive fingertip. "No man south of the Mason-Dixon line ever has, anyway," she told him with false bravado.

Mac caught her finger, brought it up to his mouth and flicked his tongue against the tip of it, as if testing his taste for her. "Not this Yankee man, either," he said.

The gleam of desire in his eyes was exactly what she wanted to see. But the Maggie part of her, always vigilant, needed to clear up one thing right away. "The trouble is I didn't come up north prepared for..."

Mac's thick eyebrows meshed. "For what?"

"Intimacy." She gave him a level look. "I have no protection, Mac. I'm really sorry about that but—"

Her interrupted her with a low, understanding laugh. 'Oh, honey. The only time a woman has to apologize about hat is *after* the fact. Don't worry. I'll take care of it.'' He ook her hand. ''Let me show you my bedroom. That's what you came here to see, isn't it?''

She went back to being Magnolia. ''I hear tell the Chamber of Commerce is going to declare it a Rutland landmark.''

''Maybe after today they will.'' He tugged at her hand. ''Come on. Let's go make history.''

Like the rest of Mac's apartment, his bedroom was sparsely furnished—a double bed, a dresser, a portable television on top of it. A clock radio and a pile of paperbacks sat on the night table. The bed was neatly made but a few articles of clothing were strewed across the beige area rug. Other than that, the room was in order—and perfectly ordinary.

''I was expecting a water bed and mirrors on the ceiling,'' she said, only half joking.

Mac raised his thick eyebrows. ''And a video camera, perhaps? A trapeze? Maybe some velvet chains and whips if you really felt like getting kinky? Sorry, Blossom. I'm a simple man with simple tastes.''

''No need to apologize about *that*,'' she replied with relief, falling out of her brazen Magnolia character. She hoped Mac didn't notice the slip.

But apparently he did. He dropped her hand and studied her face carefully. ''You haven't been in many men's bedrooms, have you, Maggie?''

''Gentlemen do not ask southern ladies such delicate questions,'' she replied, giving him a sly little wink.

''Drop the act, honey. I'm talking to Margaret Bloomer now.''

She looked away. ''Just one,'' she answered truthfully.

"Lamar, right? And I bet you were already engaged."

"So?" She looked back at Mac defiantly. "I'm certainly not expecting a ring from *you*, Madison, if that's what you're driving at."

He had the grace to look a little chagrined. "I just want to get things straight between us because I like you, Maggie."

"How heartwarming."

He had to smile at her crestfallen expression. "You're also very beautiful and desirable but you don't need me to tell you that."

Yes, her heart cried. I do need that desperately!

"Making love could really complicate things between us," he said instead. "Think about how we got drunk on a few kisses this morning, lost our timing completely and botched up the show."

"God forbid I should complicate things for you and botch up the show, Madison!" Maggie walked over to the bed and flopped down on it, her ego deflated. Unaware of the classic drama of her pose, she rested her elbows on her knees and buried her face in her open hands. "I thought you wanted me as much as I want you," she murmured through them.

She felt the mattress depress as Mac sat down beside her. "I do," he whispered fervently. But that was all he would allow himself to say to her.

He delighted in looking at Maggie—the peachy glow of her complexion, the burnished gold wealth of her hair and the delectable body he'd spent many an idle moment undressing. He enjoyed the very smell of her, too—that special fragrance that was hers alone, so delicate yet pervasive. And of course he adored her voice. It could make the hairs at the back of his neck rise at times, the way certain movements in classical music could. But even though she thoroughly pleased all his senses, was he in love with Maggie? Mac simply didn't know. All he knew for sure was that he couldn't lead her on to believe that he was.

As he sat in deep silence beside her, Maggie thought how rare it was for them to be so quiet together. Silence was anathema in their business. She lowered her hands and took a deep breath, deciding that it was up to her to say what was on both their minds.

"Listen, Mac, I know what's bothering you."

Did she really? Mac wondered. Did she know that she was driving him crazy? He wanted her more than he'd ever wanted a woman, but at the same time his conscience kept making him draw back from her. Sex used to be so basic, so simple for him. But now it wasn't.

Maggie continued, her voice soft in his ear. "You think that once we make love I'm going to get all serious and committed and expect the same from you. You think I'll turn into some possessive, jealous shrew or something."

"Not that!" Mac said. "Well, not exactly," he added.

She gave him a comforting pat on the back. "But that's not going to happen," she assured him and at that moment she truly believed it herself. "You're an adventure to me, Madison MacNair, a wonderful, exciting adventure that began the day I arrived in Vermont when I met you on the road to Rutland."

Mac wasn't sure he liked being termed an "adventure." But he didn't mind being called wonderful and exciting one bit. He reached for Maggie's hand and played with her fingers. They were soft and pliant and delighted his sense of touch. "You sure didn't act as if you thought that highly of me at first, honey," he reminded her.

"I didn't know it myself at the time. I hadn't unpacked all the heavy baggage I'd lugged up from Birmingham yet. The emotional baggage, I mean. This is the first time I ever left home, you know. It's the first time I ever allowed my self to *be* myself, not trying to be a clone of my four perfec sisters.'' She opened her palm to him, like a flower unfold ing, and he ran his thumb back and forth over the padde planes of it in a soothing caress.

"And now you want to have your adventure up north, i that it, Maggie?'' That still nagged Mac a little, but h couldn't stop touching her. He pushed up her sleeve and stroked the exquisite smoothness of her forearm, imagin ing how silky her inner thigh would be to his touch.

Maggie could feel her very bones melting as he contin ued to stroke her. "I want *you*,'' she told him. Nothing lik stating the obvious, she thought. She released a tinkling tril of laughter, delighting in her own boldness.

It was that little laugh of hers that did it for Mac. It rang in his heart like a little silver bell and the sound of it drov away all his doubts and reservations. He would do his bes to give Maggie Bloomer the most wonderful adventure o her life, he decided. How could he possibly refuse her? She was the most beautiful, fascinating creature that had eve come into his.

"Oh, my precious one,'' he said in a hushed voice.

He pushed her down on the bed and sprinkled a showe of kisses over her face. When he trailed his kisses lower his mouth brushed against the flannel of her high-necked nightgown, tickling his lips. He impatiently untied the bow at the top of the lace-edged collar.

"That bow doesn't do anything,'' Maggie informed him "It's for decorative purposes only. And so are the button: beneath it.''

Mac was flummoxed. He'd coaxed many women out of many exotic outfits without missing a beat but he'd neve dealt with a flannel nightgown before. "Then what's the best way to get you out of this nightmare you're wearing, honey?''

"For that smart remark you'll have to figure it out all by yourself, Madison.''

"Don't start teasing me now,'' he pleaded, gliding his palms along the material that covered her. "I've already used up all my patience trying to keep my hands off you all morning during the show.''

"Patience is a virtue,'' she reminded him, then closed her eyes in pleasure as he fondled her breasts through the material. She heard his breath quicken as his circling thumbs made her nipples bud against the flannel.

"Oh, what a hidden delight you are,'' he said.

Maggie sighed. "Would you like me to strip for you?''

"I would love it.'' Mac pushed himself off the bed and pulled Maggie to her feet, too. "I'll even put on some music to accompany you.''

Maggie had immediate second thoughts about her impetuous suggestion. She was confident about her body to a point. But not *that* confident. "Why don't you take off your clothes first,'' she said.

Mac frowned. "That won't be very exciting.''

"It will be for me,'' Maggie told him. She perched on the edge of the bed and waited with polite attention, staring up at him with her big, golden eyes.

Mac needed no further encouragement. "I'll give you whatever you want today, honey,'' he said.

His shirt came off first. No surprises there for Maggie; he'd showed off his muscular chest to her within the first few minutes of their acquaintance and she'd retained a photographic image of it that often flashed through her mind at unexpected moments.

Mac kicked off his worn leather moccasins next. As Maggie demurely admired his well-shaped feet he unbuckled his belt, unzipped his jeans and shucked them off in easy, uninhibited motions. She raised her eyes and swallowed hard. All he was wearing now was a pair of extremely brief black cotton briefs. The olive tones of his skin looked magnificent against the black material. He *was* magnificent, she concluded.

"Tah-dum!" Mac sang out, flinging wide his long arms.

Maggie applauded the slimness of his waist and hips and the power of his sinewy thighs.

"No need to clap just yet," Mac told her. "The best is yet to come."

Maggie clutched her hands together. "You mean when your black briefs come off?" She sucked in her breath.

He laughed. "I mean show time is over for me and it's your turn, honey."

"My turn?" Maggie didn't move a muscle.

"Wasn't that the deal? I take off my clothes for you and then you give me the pleasure?"

Maggie knew that she could never be so physically sure of herself as Mac was of his athletic body. "No way, Madison," she said. "You're too tough an act to follow."

Mac wasn't going to let her get away with it so easily. "Are you kidding, love? I'm just a big ugly brute. It's your luscious form that all these people have come to see unveiled." He pointed to the imaginary audience at the foot of the bed. "They're waiting, Magnolia Blossom. And so am I. The spotlight is on you and it's time to perform."

Maggie felt the reins of inhibition tightening around her and she refused to go along with the game. "I'm not an exhibitionist like you," she informed Mac primly.

He smiled, baring his teeth. "Sure you are, honey. Deep down in a secret place every beautiful woman is. Don't tell me you've never posed naked in front of a full-length mirror before."

"That's different!" Maggie blurted out before realizing she was admitting that she had.

Mac's laugh was warm and encouraging. "So pretend I'm that mirror," he said. A wicked gleam flickered in his dark eyes. "I promise you I'll be more fun to pose in front of."

Maggie's lips tugged up into an insuppressible smile. His suggestion did have a certain appeal.

"Please," he whispered.

She found herself on her feet, spurred into action by that simple, soft word. "You cajoling demon," she said.

Mac smiled, taking it as a compliment. "I'd like to bring out the devil in *you*, Maggie Bloomer. I'll go put on some music."

Maggie watched him pad to the stereo in the living room, a sleek male animal in his absolute prime. The powerful expanse of his back was breathtaking. The sight of his taut buttocks moving under the clinging cotton of his briefs caused a quiver of pleasure deep within her.

Music flooded through the speakers in the bedroom a moment later, and the pure glorious notes astonished Maggie. She had expected some tacky bump-and-grind tune. Or, even worse, some raunchy rock.

"Isn't that Mozart?" she asked when Mac returned.

He nodded. "Only the best for you, love."

"Well, I'm certainly not going to do a striptease to Mozart! That would be almost sacrilegious."

"Nonsense. Old Wolfgang would have flipped his powdered wig in delight to see a beauty like you take off her clothes during one of his concertos."

Maggie looked dubious. "Somehow I can't help imagining that I'll be performing in front of an entire symphonic orchestra."

"Forget about them. Just concentrate on the conductor." Mac began waving an invisible baton. His movements were elaborate to the extreme, an energetic parody of an earnest maestro.

Maggie couldn't help but laugh at his antics. And she couldn't take her eyes off his lean, muscular body as he stretched and bent and swayed with exaggerated flair. Pretty soon she was swaying along with him, improvising on ballet steps she'd learned as a girl in dance class. She delicately picked up the hem of her long flannel gown to show off her woolly red socks to advantage, did an arabesque or two with aplomb, and went right into a few *jetés* that may have lacked finesse but certainly not energy. Then she gave up all attempts at ballet steps and simply twirled around the room on a swell of strings and trumpets until she was dizzy and giddy. Mac caught her up in his arms to stop her. She was grateful for that because she was quite out of breath.

"Calm down now," he whispered in her ear. "This is my favorite part of the concerto. I want you to slowly undress to this movement."

It was a haunting movement, a poignant dialogue between the piano and solo wind instruments. "Oh, Madison, I can't," Maggie confessed, pressing her flushed cheek against the smooth, cool flesh of his chest. "I really am too shy for that sort of thing."

She could feel the rumble of his deep laugh vibrate through her. "Never mind, Miss Bloomer. I'll help you," he said, stroking her brow.

She gazed up at him, a little dazed by her frantic exertions. "Will you?"

"It will be my pleasure," he assured her. Holding her hand, he bowed over it, and grazed his lips across her knuckles.

This sudden formality on his part should have been ludicrous, considering his attire, but Maggie was deeply touched. Her heart expanded with a sweet, overpowering love for him as he went down on bended knee and slowly removed her socks. It almost burst when he kissed one high arch and then the other.

"Ballerina feet," he remarked, looking up at her with a piercing gentleness that filled his large brown eyes.

She was sure then that he knew all her secret fantasies and longings and she wanted to cry out her love for him. But she was afraid to speak the words, afraid that this moment and all future ones would be ruined by such a confession. Instead she bent down to take his face in her hands and buried her lips in the wild curls of his hair. Then she stood quietly before him and waited, as the beautiful music filled her soul.

He lifted her nightgown with excruciating slowness, inch by inch, rising to his height as he uncovered her breasts. "Perfection. Lift up your arms, Maggie."

It was a motion of complete surrender on her part and when he pulled the nightgown over her head and tossed it aside, she breathed out a sigh of relief. "There!" she said, as if she had done it herself.

"Pirouette for me, princess."

She did.

He nodded his approval. "Even better than I imagined."

"It would look better performed in a tutu."

"No. It would look even better without these." He slid a finger under the lacy band of her panties and snapped the elastic. But he made no move to remove them for her.

Maggie knew that the next move was up to her in this erotic love dance. The trouble was, she didn't know the steps as well as Mac did. Was she expected to take the lead? She felt a throbbing pulse of excitement, yet she was also surprisingly calm. Perhaps that was because of the sublime music.

"I've never made love to Mozart before," she said.

"And you never will, unless they allow that sort of fun and games in the Great Beyond," he replied.

She was a little hurt that he could make a joke at a time like this. But he'd already warned her that he could never be serious. She'd been wise not to blurt out that she loved him a few moments ago. Yet he'd seemed so very serious then. So intense. Would he always be this changeable, this unpredictable? She wasn't going to think about that now.

"Well, if I can't have Wolfgang I'll settle for Mad Dog," she said, straining to keep the mood light.

He chuckled. "That sounds just fine to me, love." He picked her up in one swift, easy movement and carried her to his bed. He placed her down gently, then stood above her to take in the lush length of her, his eyes slow and languid as they moved up and down her body. "Oh, you are a delight, Magnolia Blossom," he said thickly. "You would have inspired Mozart to even greater genius, I'm sure." At that moment the record ended and Mac made no move to change it. "We'll make our own music now."

He lay down beside her and took her into his arms. At first they kissed and touched lightly, delicately, as if they were both made of the most fragile crystal. Then Mac's caresses became bolder as he explored her sumptuous curves. He continually muttered his approval along the way.

"I knew you would be this beautiful the first moment I saw you. My lovely Dixie lady, all peaches and cream."

He caressed her breasts until the tender tips became hard, aching buds, and she moaned.

"Luscious fruit," he said, dipping his head to taste them. He circled her nipples with his tongue until she was floating in a heated whirlpool of passion.

"You're making me all swimmy headed," she said in a thick, honeyed drawl.

He laughed at her southern expression. "Swimmy headed? Honey, I want to drown you in love." He stroked her smooth stomach and thighs. "Silky cream," he whispered, sliding his mouth across the expanse of her abdomen, making her muscles quiver. "How delicious you feel and taste and smell, my perfect blossom."

She shivered as the hot breath of his whisper tickled her sensitive flesh. She moaned again as he slid his hand down to explore her more intimately. "Do you like this, love?"

"Yes." She sighed. She threw back her head and closed her eyes, melting under his knowing touch.

"I love pleasing you." He covered her body with the long expanse of his, propping up on his elbows so that his full weight wasn't on her. "I want to give you pleasure in a million ways."

"A million?" Her eyes flew open and she looked directly into his. "My, my, I surely hope that's not just bragging, Madison."

He laughed again and nuzzled his face against her neck. "Oh, honey, you're not going to make me live up to my hyperbole, are you?"

She slid out from under him and pushed him down on his back. "Either that or die trying, Yankee man."

"Gladly!" he assured her, grabbing her slender waist and pulling her on top of him. "Let's take forever, Maggie. Let's make our first time together last for as long as we can bear it."

She didn't protest. That was exactly what she wanted. She rolled off him and began exploring his perfectly proportioned body with the same fascination and attention to detail that he had given hers, finding his secret pleasure points along the rolling, muscular expanse of him.

"Crazy." He sighed. "You're surely making me crazy, love."

Maggie continued to caress him, loving the feel of his firm flesh beneath her palms. "Oh, Madison, you were crazy to begin with."

"But you're driving me over the edge for sure."

"Then take me with you," she suggested softly.

"Honey, I'd like to take you with me to the end of time."

His dark eyes glittered with bright sparks of desire and Maggie was sure she would never in her life want a man as much as she wanted this one. She trusted him completely at that moment and he didn't betray her trust. He didn't forget his promise to protect her, either.

He cushioned her buttocks with a pillow before he entered her, then took her on a long, languorous journey into the realm of mutual pleasure. It was a territory Mac knew well, and he slowly guided her to secret places that she never knew existed. He would wait until she caught her breath and then take her farther still, until she was so lost that she was sure she could never return. But what did that matter? She let him take her deeper, deeper. Higher, higher. And she clung to him at the top of the highest peak they reached together and felt a release so great she cried out with joy.

They held each other tightly until they slowly returned to the real world again. The first thing Maggie saw when she opened her eyes was exactly what she wanted to see—Mac.

He smiled gently and brushed a lock of hair from her flushed face. "It was damn good, wasn't it?"

She stretched her damp, limp body against his. "It was lovely." She slid her tongue along his shoulder and tasted salt. Delicious. "You're a man of your word, Madison. I lost count after I reached one million."

He chuckled softly. "And I'm still alive to hear you tell me you did."

They cuddled awhile and then Maggie spoke again. "Shall we go for a trillion, Madison?"

She could feel the energy flow through him at the very suggestion. "Can you count that high, honey?"

"Try me."

"With pleasure." He kissed her softly. "You're a woman of amazing talent and energy, Maggie Bloomer."

"Only because I have a man with exceptional talent himself as my partner. And perfect timing, too."

He roared at the compliment. "You give me such a kick, honey."

The light in the room changed as morning drifted into late afternoon but time stood still for them. They made love again and again. It seemed they would never get enough of each other. The last thought Maggie had before falling into a deep, satiated sleep was that now she and Mac were as committed as two people could be.

She awoke some time later with laughter on her lips. Mac was sitting at the edge of the bed, tickling her ear. His thick dark hair was slicked back, wet from a shower, and he was fully dressed.

She gazed up at him expectantly, hoping for some kind of declaration from him that would formalize their love.

"Time to get up, honey," he announced cheerfully. "I sent out for pizza. We can work on tomorrow's show while we eat." With that he gave her a friendly pat on the rear through the blanket, stood and headed for the living room. He stopped in the doorway and turned back to her. "I left fresh towels for you in the bathroom." And that was all he said.

Chapter Nine

You're a big girl now," Maggie muttered aloud in the shower as the hot, soothing water sprayed over her. "You went into this with your eyes wide open." She closed them and let the water hit her hard in the face. "Only a fool would think that a man like Mad Dog MacNair would feel the need to make a commitment to a woman just because he enjoyed making love with her." She shut off the water with a hard twist of her wrist. "Fool!"

Mac had left her an oversize bath towel and she dried her body and the few tears she'd shed before noticing that the towel had a huge nude picture of *him* printed on it. Was this man a complete, raving egomaniac? Stunned, she held it out at arm's length to examine more closely. And then she began laughing despite her discomfort. It was Mac's face all right, mugging a wink and a leer, but the torso it was superimposed on was that of some incredibly overdeveloped body builder with bulging muscles of terrifying dimensions. The measurement Maggie was most curious about, though, was coyly hidden under the call letters of the New York station where Mac had been top disc jockey. The towel had been one of their promotional gimmicks.

She wrapped it around her like a toga and went looking for Mac in the living room. He was lolling on the couch, in his usual insouciant manner, and smiled at her when she entered the room.

"You look good in that," he said.

"And you look much better than the body pictured on it," she replied with heartfelt honesty.

"Aw, shucks, ma'am. All the ladies tell me that."

Maggie didn't find that the least bit humorous. "Would you kindly lend me something to wear," she requested stiffly. "I really don't want to wear my nightgown all day."

"You haven't worn it *all* day," Mac reminded her. But when she stared at him without smiling he eased himself off the couch. "Would you like me to drive over to Miss Jasper's and get you some clothes?" he offered. "Just for today, I mean," he hurriedly added.

"Oh, is that what you meant?" Maggie sighed dramatically. "I was hoping you were offering to pack up my suitcase and have me move in with you." Did his face pale from her suggestion or was it her imagination? "Just joking, honey chil', just joking," she said in her Magnolia voice. "So stop looking like you've been eating a green persimmon."

He laughed. With sheer relief, she was sure. "What do they taste like anyway?"

"Sour. Real sour." She tossed back her wet hair, flicking droplets.

"Then I'm sorry I looked that way. I didn't mean to." He crossed the room to her and dipped his head to lick the beads of water off the slope of her shoulder. "You certainly don't taste like a persimmon, honey. You taste like dewdrops.''

"That's just regular old tap water, Mac." She wasn't going to let flattery get him anywhere now. She wanted a little more than that from him. Sincerity, for starters.

He nuzzled her ear. "And you smell like a refreshing summer rain."

"That's just the soap I found in your shower stall." She stepped away from him. "I'm getting cold, Mac."

"You sure are, Maggie."

She ignored the implication. "Well, that's what standing around in a wet towel will do to a body. Surely you have something in your wardrobe that will fit me."

"Choose anything you want." He spread his arms wide in a munificent gesture. "Even my Hawaiian shirt."

"You're all heart, Mac," she said sarcastically.

He narrowed his eyes. "You're angry with me now, aren't you? Why? Seems to me that we parted real good buddies back in the bedroom."

Buddies? Well, of course she still wanted to be friends with him, Maggie reminded herself. She had to make herself stop hoping for more.

A knock on the door distracted his attention from her. "That must be the pizza delivery. Go get dressed while I handle this, honey. Then we'll talk about what's bothering you."

Maggie went back to the bedroom and closed the door behind her. How could she possibly tell Mac what was bothering her? It would be so difficult to put the chaos of emotions clashing in her heart into words. She didn't regret for a moment having made love with him. What she hadn't allowed herself to consider, though, was how she would feel after sharing such intimacy with him. He was a part of her now. Not only her body, but her heart and mind had bonded to him.

She let the damp towel slip to the carpet and stared down at the winking, grinning face imprinted on it. It was the face of a man who had no intention of ever taking anything seriously. And the worst part was she'd known that from the very beginning. She could hardly blame him for leading her on. No, she had only herself to blame.

When she opened his closet the sight of his clothes caused a warm flow of love to sweep away all other emotions. She buried her face in his tweed jacket, remembering that he'd worn it on the first day they'd done the show together. How furious she'd been with him then. Since the moment they'd met he'd driven her crazy. "Oh, Madison," she whispered, her lips brushing against the wool material.

She straightened, threw back her shoulders and began examining his clothes, hanger by hanger. She told herself that she wasn't really snooping, only looking for something she could wear. But she gave each article her close examination, even filing away the name of the dry cleaner he used. Every detail that in any way touched his life was important to her. She was familiar with some of the clothes—the brightly colored and boldly striped sport shirts, the pleated corduroy slacks he wore when he wasn't in his jeans, the leather bomber jacket that accented his broad shoulders and narrow waist and made him look especially dangerous.

She'd never had the opportunity to see him in the burgundy robe with navy piping, though. She brushed her hand down the front of it. Cashmere. No doubt it had cost a fortune. It wasn't the sort of garment men usually went out and bought for themselves and she couldn't help speculating that some woman had given it to Mac as a gift. For Christmas maybe? His birthday? Their anniversary? Stop this stupid train of thought! she chastised herself. She raked the hanger across the iron pole.

What she revealed behind the robe was another surprise—a black tuxedo and a stiffly starched white pleated shirt. It was difficult for Maggie to picture Mac in such civilized, proper attire. She wondered if he'd worn the tuxedo on the charity telethon he'd hosted in Phoenix. Maybe he made it a practice of devoting his time and talent to good causes.

Then why had he refused to go to the nursing home with her? Maggie shook her head. Mac was no saint and she shouldn't try to make him out to be one. He was a wonderful lover, though. He'd shown her the gentle, generous side of his nature along with his hot-blooded passion. It was an exhilarating combination and her head was still spinning from it. Perhaps that was why she was standing in his closet communing with his clothes like some silly, love-besotted woman. Well, part of that couldn't be helped. She *was* a woman in love. What she couldn't allow herself to be was silly or besotted. She knew, both intellectually and with every fiber of her female instinct, that being the least bit maudlin would drive Mac away.

And so Maggie forced herself to concentrate on the age-old question of what to wear. She was determined to look terrific when she made her entrance back into the living room. But that was going to be a tough act to pull off. The flannel nightgown was most definitely out. She was truly sorry Mac had caught her wearing such dowdy attire in the first place. A smile tugged at her lips as she recalled the way he'd flung her over his shoulder and carried her away. One thing they had in common was a penchant for the dramatic.

She selected one of his shirts in a bright red-yellow-and-black plaid, and the cotton fabric felt as soft as a kiss against her naked body. The shirttails hit a few inches above her knees.

She found his hairbrush on the dresser and noted the quality of the teak wood and natural bristles. That was something else they had in common, she thought. They both appreciated quality in small objects used daily. Telling herself to stop grasping at straws, she pulled the brush through her wet hair. Mac and she had absolutely nothing in common but their work...and their sense of humor...and their sense of intimate pleasure. She put down the brush and pressed her hand to her breast. Wasn't that enough? Wasn't that more than so many couples had? She closed her eyes and made a simple little wish. *Make this work out between us.* She left the bedroom with a hopeful smile, but it faded the moment she entered the living room. Mac was leaning against the frame of his open front door, cozily chatting with Lola Medesa.

Maggie's first impulse was to retreat to the bedroom. She was sure there was no way Lola could have seen her. But then it struck her that there was no reason to hide. After all, she and Mac were both unmarried, consenting adults. And she was aware that most of the personnel at the radio station either assumed they were having an affair or wondered why they weren't. She could think of no good reason to keep her presence in Mac's apartment a secret, and many reasons to let Lola know about it. She started to cross the living room, her bare feet making no sound.

"Really, Mac," Maggie overheard Lola say in that breathy yet demanding voice she found so irritating. "I don't see why we have to continue this conversation while I'm out here standing in the *hall*. Are you going to invite me in or not?"

"Now's a bad time for me, Lola." Mac arranged his body in a more secure blocking position. "Later, okay?"

"Later not okay with Lola," she simpered. "Now good. Later bad. Come on, Macky, let Lola in."

Macky? Maggie stopped in her tracks. Later? Did Mac plan to usher her out and replace her with Lola for his evening enjoyment?

Mac patted Lola on the back. "You've got real bad timing, honey."

The endearment roared in Maggie's ears. She'd assumed that she was the only woman Mac called honey. Dumb assumption. Real dumb, Maggie. She had trouble deciding who she hated most at that moment—Mac or Lola, or herself for being so naive, so stupid.

"Hey, I get the picture," Lola said. "You don't have to paint it in a thousand words." She leaned against his shoulder, which was barring her entrance. "That doesn't sound right," she mumbled. She fished in her handbag and clumsily pulled out her car keys.

Mac sighed. "I think you had better come in after all, Lola." He reached for her keys but she drew back.

"Too late, pal. You lost your chance. When Lola gets turned down, she doesn't stick around." She giggled. "Hey, I just made a rhyme. I'm a poet and don't know it." She giggled again.

Mac grabbed her by the waist and hauled her into the living room. Maggie stared at him, horrified. How could he humiliate her like this by inviting in another woman? How could he be so unbearably cruel? For a brief instant she wanted to die, she wanted to melt into nothingness and dissolve from the face of the earth. And then, as Mac deposited Lola on the couch, Maggie realized that she was drunk.

"Well, looky who's here!" Lola cried, giving Maggie a fluttery wave of her fingers. "Seems we both had the same idea but you beat me to it." She hiccuped.

"I'll go make coffee," Maggie said coolly and with a majestic toss of her head she marched toward the kitchen.

"Nice shirt you're wearing," Lola shouted, addressing Maggie's stiff, retreating back. "But frankly, I much prefer Mac in it—" a pause "—no, out of it."

Maggie pushed the swinging door shut to muffle another spurt of Lola's intolerable giggles. She found a jar of instant coffee in the cupboard and her hand shook as she spooned the granules into a mug for Lola, wishing they were dusted with arsenic. She remembered one of her mother's many dictums. *A lady must always be a gracious hostess when unexpected guests drop in.* She wondered how her dear mother, the self-declared arbiter of southern gentility, would handle this situation. *A true lady would never allow herself to be in such an unseemly situation in the first place,* she heard her mother distinctly reply. *But you, Margaret Amelia Bloomer, unlike your sisters, have always been a disappointment to me.*

Maggie took the kettle from the stove and gripped the handle tightly. "Oh, Mamma, get off my case, will you?" she muttered. She turned on the faucet but the rushing water didn't drown out the sound of her mother's next words in her mind. *You must leave immediately, child. The longer you stay, the more you are compromising yourself.*

"Compromising myself! Hah!" Maggie smacked the full kettle on the burner. "Oh, Mother dear, if you only knew how far I've compromised myself today."

Mac pushed through the swinging door at that moment and Maggie glared at him with fire in her eyes.

"I'm sorry about this, honey," he said softly.

"Don't call me that anymore." She turned away and began searching for matches to light the gas. She couldn't bear to look at him. It hurt too much. "I heard you call Lola honey, too. Are we interchangeable to you?"

"Of course not. That's an absurd thing to say."

"You called her *honey*!" Maggie repeated like a broken record, but she couldn't help herself. It kept echoing in her ears.

Mac shrugged. "Did I? I don't even remember. It didn't mean anything."

The shrug infuriated Maggie. She wanted to shake him, until he understood how she felt. Instead she gave him a disdainful smile. "And I suppose what we shared didn't mean anything to you, either."

"Of course it did, hon—" Mac caught himself. "Maggie. You know it did."

"All I know for sure is that there's another woman, a giggling horror of a woman, sprawled out on your couch right now." Maggie found a box of matches on the hood of the stove and struck one with a trembling hand. "Or did you escort her to your bedroom while I was in here making coffee for her like a chump?"

"That's a cheap shot, Maggie." Mac ran his hand through his hair impatiently. "I'm not interested in Lola and I would have sent her on her merry way if she was in any condition to drive. But you saw for yourself that she isn't. I couldn't very well let her get behind the wheel and be a menace to herself and others, now could I?"

"What a Good Samaritan you are, Mac." The smile that was frozen on Maggie's lips was becoming painful. "Maybe they'll erect a statue of you on the town green. Mad Dog MacNair, the patron saint of drunken women in need!" She forced out a laugh. "How utterly ennobling."

Mac leaned closer to her and blew out the match before it burned her fingertips. "You're coming very close to sounding like a jealous female, Maggie. It's not attractive."

"Oh, I'm not attractive to you now?" She could barely squeeze the words out of her tightening throat.

"That's not what I said. And it's certainly not what I meant." He reached out to take her into his arms.

She backed away from him, hitting her spine hard against the counter, but she was numb to the pain. "Yes, you did," she insisted shrilly. "What *do* you find attractive, Mac? A nymphomaniac like Lola Medesa?"

"Shh. Keep your voice down," he cautioned. "She'll hear you."

"You think I care if she does?"

"Honey, please show a little sympathy for her," Mac said softly. "When Lola sobers up she's going to feel terribly embarrassed about this. Think how *you* would feel."

"Me?" Maggie's eyes widened with indignation. "I would never, ever behave in such a coarse, crude, vulgar, crass—"

"Okay, okay, I get your point. You're above the rest of us lowly humans who sometimes make fools of ourselves."

"Of course I'm not," she said, realizing that she was making quite a fool of herself at the moment by acting outraged. She looked into Mac's compassionate eyes and calmed down. "You were right to ask Lola in. I'm sorry I lost my temper and said those nasty things."

When he moved near her again, Maggie didn't back away. He kissed her forehead, the tip of her nose and her chin. "I'm sorry, too, that Lola ruined our wonderful time together. I wanted to strangle her when I opened the door." He looked a little abashed. "Egotist that I am, I actually thought it was the pizza boy again, coming back to ask me for my autograph."

"Lola came to ask you for a lot more than that, didn't she, Mac?" Maggie said this as casually and as lightly as she could, but she held her breath and gripped her hands so tightly that her knuckles turned white as she waited for his response.

He gave her the one she was hoping for. "Lola and I have never slept together, Maggie. I was as surprised as you were to see her."

"But you told her to come back later."

She saw the flicker of irritation in his face. "Did I? I don't remember everything I said to her as clearly as you seem to, but I'm sure I was just trying to be polite."

Maggie arched her eyebrows. "I never realized that you were such a gentleman, Madison."

"You didn't?" There was hurt in his voice. "That's too bad, Maggie, because I've done my best to be one with you."

She quickly looked away from him. She was making a horrible botch of the present situation but she didn't know how to handle it well. She was in love with this man and all she wanted was for him to take her in his arms and tell her that he loved her, too. "Please," she said. "Please let's not argue anymore."

He *did* take her into his arms then and stroked her back to comfort her. "We have nothing to argue about," he assured her. "Listen, here's the plan. We'll give Lola some coffee, maybe get her to eat some pizza. And as soon as she's more herself I'll drive her home and hurry back here to you, honey. We'll pick up where we left off as if nothing happened. Okay?"

Maggie didn't know if it would be okay. She wasn't even sure where Mac thought they had left off or how he felt about what had happened in between. Maybe, when they were alone again, he would tell her everything she needed so desperately to hear from him. She took a deep breath and put on a brave smile.

"That's as good a plan as any," she said. "Go keep Lola company while I get her coffee ready."

"Make it real strong," he said. "The sooner she's out of here, the better." He gave Maggie a quick kiss and went back to the living room.

When Maggie came out with the steaming mug of coffee she immediately saw that Lola wasn't going anywhere soon. She was zonked out on the couch and Mac was throwing a blanket over her.

"Forget the coffee. She's out like a light," he said grimly.

Maggie's own face had a grim set to it as she carefully set down the mug on the end table. "She probably wouldn't have drunk it anyway. I couldn't find any cream in your refrigerator and Lola never drinks her coffee black."

Mac shrugged his insufferable shrug. "Well, that's hardly important now. We might as well just let her sleep it off. She may be out for the whole night."

As still as a statue, Maggie stood staring at Mac. She'd had quite a shock when she looked in his refrigerator for cream and found nothing in it but a bottle of champagne with a note attached. "To a corker of a time together. We'll sip this in bed. Lola."

"How many times has Lola spent the night here, Mac?" she asked in a voice just above a whisper.

"What?" His eyes narrowed. "I thought we already settled that between us."

"What's between us is not only settled, it's ended." Maggie had brought her purse from the kitchen and now looked around the living room for her raincoat. She spotted it draped over a chair and barely had the energy to put it on. She was heartsick.

"What are you doing, Maggie?" Mac asked, eyes still narrowed as he carefully watched her.

"I'm going home, of course. Would you mind calling me a taxi? I'll wait downstairs for it."

"I certainly would mind. I'll take you home if you want to leave."

"If I want!" She glanced at Lola, sleeping as soundly as a baby, and with great self-control lowered her voice again. "You can't expect me to stay here with Lola and you. Does *she* dance to Mozart for you, too, Madison?" A little sob escaped from Maggie's throat. She managed to swallow down the next one as she hurried to the front door. She couldn't break down in front of him. She had to at least try to leave with a shred of her tattered dignity.

When she yanked open the door Mac was by her side in a flash to slam it shut again. They both looked in Lola's direction but the sharp sound hadn't disturbed her. She smiled in her sleep. There was no smile on Mac's face, though, when he grabbed Maggie by her shoulders and swerved her around to face him.

"What the hell has gotten into you?" he demanded in a harsh whisper. "You seemed fine just a few minutes ago when I left you in the kitchen. But now you're talking crazy."

"I was crazy to believe you in the first place," she said, meeting his angry glare without blinking. "I found the champagne in the refrigerator, Mac. I read Lola's note."

Mac swore under his breath. "We'll talk in the car," he said. Keeping a tight hold on Maggie's arm, he pulled her across the room to get his keys on the coffee table. He considered a moment, then took Lola's keys, too. "Just in case she wakes up and decides to take off while we're gone," he told Maggie. And then he did something that made Maggie's heart wince. He gently tucked the blanket around Lola's shoulders.

They didn't talk at all for the first few minutes of the ride to Miss Jasper's. Maggie stared out into the hazy autumn twilight and found it difficult to believe that it was only this morning that Mac had burst into her bedroom. Only this morning that her life had turned upside down, inside out. If loving Mac was going to cause this kind of upheaval in her heart, then Maggie wanted no part of it.

But he *was* part of her and there was nothing she could do about it. If only they could go back to the way they were before they'd made love! The moment Maggie wished that, she took it back. She didn't want to go back to that limbo of yearning. She'd wanted this man more than she'd ever wanted a man before and for once in her life she had acted upon her deepest impulses, her most fervent desires. She'd never been more completely herself as when she and Mac were making love. How could anything so right turn out so wrong?

She glanced at his strong, stern profile as he drove, his eyes never straying from the road ahead, and she remembered how he'd cautioned her against beginning an affair with him. But hadn't it begun long ago, before culminating in such ardent intimacy? She'd been falling in love with him day by day, hour by hour, minute by minute during their symbiotic partnership on the air. She'd learned to trust him completely during the weeks they'd performed live, without a parachute, and he'd never made her look bad or let her down. Then why couldn't she trust him *now*?

Because she was becoming exactly what she'd assured Mac she would never be, that's why, Maggie told herself. She was acting possessive and jealous. She was breaking the subtly agreed upon pact they'd made before they'd become intimate. *You're an adventure to me, Madison MacNair, a wonderful, exciting adventure!* Didn't the very definition of adventure involve risk? And he'd certainly never asked her to wager her heart.

Mac cleared his throat sharply and the sound cut through her introspection. "Listen, Maggie, I don't like explaining myself to anybody but—"

"No explanations are needed," she hurriedly interrupted.

"Obviously they are, or you wouldn't be so upset now." His voice was cool and his eyes remained on the road.

"I *was* upset. But now I'm not. I'm sure the humor of the situation will hit me at any moment." Maggie began talking faster as her mind raced. "Maybe we can develop a radio bit out of it. A takeoff on one of those stupid TV sitcoms where the guy's got one date hidden in the closet and another really dumb one in the kitchen and then maybe there's a knock on the door and—"

"Maggie, stop it!" Mac's deep voice thundered through the small car.

"Not funny?" she asked in a very small one.

"You don't hear me laughing, do you?"

"I hear you shouting."

Mac took a deep breath. "I won't shout anymore, I promise. Now can we simply discuss this like the two sensible, civilized adults that we are?"

Maggie didn't see anything simple about it. Or sensible. Or even civilized for that matter. Women in love didn't use words like that. Men who *weren't* apparently did.

"There's nothing to discuss, Mac," she said, trying her best to sound untroubled. "We made love and it was fun."

"It was *fun*?" Mac glanced at her then looked back at the road. "Is that all it was to you?"

"No." It was impossible to lie to him. "It meant a great deal to me."

"And me, too, honey," Mac insisted.

Maggie waited, hoping he would say more, but he didn't. They fell back into silence. By the time Mac pulled into Miss Jasper's driveway Maggie was beginning to feel that they'd become more like strangers than lovers.

"Well, good night," she said, starting to get out.

Mac placed his hand on her shoulder. "Wait, Maggie. We have to settle things between us."

She turned back to look at him but had difficulty reading his expression in the descending darkness. "Settle what?" she asked as her heart tightened.

"This impasse."

"That sounds awfully bleak," Maggie said.

"Only if we can't get over it."

"And is Lola the big obstacle, Mac?"

"If you build her up high enough to make her one she is, honey. I've never gone to bed with her and never intend to. But I want to remain friends with Lola. I think she could use a few. And if you don't like that, Maggie, then that's too bad. Jealousy shouldn't play a part in our relationship. Am I making myself clear?"

"Loud and clear." She raised her chin. "You and I both remain free agents, as always."

Seemingly satisfied with her reply, he caressed her face. "Look at you," he said with soft concern. "Wet hair. No shoes. You'll be lucky if you don't catch a cold. We don't want Magnolia Blossom to sound like a foghorn over the air, do we?"

"All you care about is the show."

"That's not true, Maggie." The exasperation in his voice softened to tenderness. "I care about you, honey. I think you're wonderful. I'd do almost anything for you and to prove it I'm going to make a huge concession."

Her heart picked up a few beats. "You are? What?"

"I'm going to go to that old folks' home with you on Thanksgiving Day."

"Oh." If that was Mac's idea of a huge concession Maggie feared they would never reach a complete understanding.

"You don't sound terribly thrilled, honey. Wasn't that what all this strike business of yours was about?"

"Yes. Of course." She forced some enthusiasm into her reply. "And I am pleased, Mac."

"Maybe we can come up with a special skit for them," he suggested. "One they can participate in. We'll even record it and play parts of it on the show the next day. They'd get a kick out of that, I bet. What do you think?"

Maggie looked at him and smiled. How could she not? He really was doing his best to please her. "It's a great idea," she said.

"We'll talk about it more tomorrow." He gave her a quick kiss. "Now get inside where it's warm, honey."

But Maggie lingered on the porch and watched him drive away. She tried not to dwell on the fact that Lola was no doubt still sleeping on his couch. She had to trust Mac now because it would do no good if she didn't. And she wanted to trust him with all her heart.

Chapter Ten

Mac found Lola awake and watching TV when he returned to his apartment. She had washed her face and coated it with a new paint job, he observed, but she still looked wan and haggard.

"You have every right to be mad as hell with me, Mac," she immediately told him. "Not only did I crash your little party with Maggie, but I ate all your pizza while you were gone." She groaned. "An entire pizza! This is sure my day for excesses. I'm really, really sorry."

"Forget it. I'm glad you got some food in your stomach. Maybe it'll soak up the alcohol."

Lola groaned again and got up to shut off the TV. Her gait was steady and when she turned to face Mac her eyes were bloodshot but focused. He was relieved to see that she'd sobered up.

"Now you think I'm a horrible lush and an absolute jerk, don't you, Mac?"

He shook his head. "It happens. There was a time in my life when I did a lot of things to excess." He took her car keys out of his pocket and tossed them on the table. "You were a real jerk to drive in that condition, though, Lola. And you'd still better take a taxi home."

"I will. I didn't realize I'd had that much. I guess that's what can happen when you drink alone. I don't make a habit of it, Mac. But today's my birthday and I was feeling pretty low that I had no one to celebrate with me. Not that there's anything to celebrate." She attempted a smile. "The big three-o. I'm over the hill, Mac."

"Nonsense, kiddo." He gave her a hearty pat on the back. "Your best years are yet to come."

"Come off it, Mac. You sound like our flower child of a station manager now. You know what Stan did this afternoon? He paraded into my office in a clown suit, carrying a bunch of balloons and proceeded to sing 'Happy Birthday' to me at the top of his lungs."

Mac laughed. "Stan's a sweet, thoughtful guy."

"Thoughtful? Hah! He should have thought twice before barging into my office like that. I was meeting with two important media buyers from New York, trying to convince them to place money on PEU. And in walks the station manager making a complete jackass of himself."

"Men in love sometimes do that, Lola. Stan's got a big crush on you."

"Lucky Lola!" She rolled her weary eyes. "The last thing I need in my life is an over-the-hill hippie in a clown suit." She smiled despite her scornful tone. "He did look kind of cute, though. And you're right. He is sweet."

"You could do a lot worse than Stan, Lola."

"I have. Believe me." Her shoulders sagged. "And I'm not going to do better with you, am I, Mac? You should have leveled with me about Maggie the last time I came calling.''

He ran his hand through his hair. "I haven't leveled with *myself* about her yet.''

"What's that supposed to mean?''

"Oh, hell, I don't know, Lola.'' He sank on to the ottoman. "All I know for sure is that Maggie has become very special to me and I'm not quite sure how to proceed from here.''

Lola raised her sleek, plucked eyebrows and cupped her hand to her ear. "Hark! Do I hear wedding bells in the distance?''

"No way! At least I'm deaf to them. I'm not good marriage material. Ask my ex-wife, Sheila. I made her miserable for two years.''

Lola settled down on the couch again and gave him a knowing look. "You cheated on her, right?''

"Yep. But not the way you're thinking. I played around plenty before I got married but once I made the commitment I stuck to it. There was one love I could never get out my system, though.'' Mac sighed. "Radio.''

"Yeah, you superjocks don't have a great reputation for keeping the home fires burning.''

"That's because we're never home. It's an all-consuming profession. More demanding than any mistress. Sheila never saw me. I left by four each morning. I never came back till late.''

"Little wifey felt ignored, did she?''

"She had every right to, Lola. She *was* ignored. My New York show soaked up all my creative juices and left me drained. When I wasn't doing the show, I was constantly thinking about it. Sheila got fed up and threatened to divorce me.''

"And you said bye-bye wifey and went back to the station."

"Wrong, Lola. That's why I quit."

"Mad Dog MacNair walked away from the most successful radio show in New York to save his marriage? You're joking!"

He smiled grimly. "The joke was on me. It turned out that Sheila and I were better off seeing as little of each other as possible. We'd never had much in common and there wasn't much of a marriage left to save. But I thought I owed it to her to give it a try."

"Poor Mac."

"Save the sympathy, Lola. Quitting was the best thing I could have done. Turning thirty hit me hard, too." He smiled as Lola grimaced. "It made me realize I had no life at all beyond that radio show. My ego, my heart, my soul were all wrapped up in it, which meant that I was *nothing* without it. Maybe I quit to save myself as much as my marriage. I needed some time off."

"But you're not going to waste your talent here in the boonies forever, I hope." Lola looked horrified at the very idea. "You want to go back to the big time, don't you?"

"Sure." Mac stood and stretched his long frame. "The phone hasn't exactly been ringing off the hook with offers, though."

"It will," Lola assured him. "Your name was mud in the business when you walked out and lost your station millions in ad revenues. But greed heals wounds much faster than time, Mac, and the big metro guys know you can still bring in the bucks. Trust Lola on this—they'll be calling you soon enough."

"I suppose." That had been Mac's original conviction but right now he couldn't drum up any enthusiasm.

"I might speed things up by putting out the word that you're chomping at the bit for an offer," Lola suggested.

"Thanks but no, Lola. I want to cool it out here for a while longer."

"But *why*?" She stared at Mac, dumbfounded for a moment, and then gave him a shrewder look. "Oh, I get it. Maggie. You've acquired a taste for that little southern fried chicken and you want to play around with her for a while."

Mac's eyes flashed with anger. "Hey, I'm not playing with her, Lola. And I'm getting fed up with your snide remarks about her, too."

"Okay, okay." Lola got up from the couch and slung the strap of her handbag over her shoulder. "It seems I've worn out my welcome around here."

"Yeah, it seems you have."

"*Mea culpa* again, Mac. I didn't know you were so touchy about that particular subject."

His anger subsided a bit. "Neither did I, Lola."

"Are we still friends?"

"Sure. As much as we've ever been, anyway." Mac picked up the phone and called a cab to take her home.

Maggie tossed aside the book she was reading in bed, unable to concentrate, and looked at the old-fashioned clock on her night table. She held it to her ear to make sure it was ticking. It seems more like midnight than eight, she thought. The hours since she'd parted from Mac had crawled by at a snail's pace. She heard a car pull into the driveway and got up to look out the window. She was disappointed to see that it was Miss Jasper's limousine rather than Mac's car. Not that she expected him to come back that evening. But she would have been overjoyed if he had.

She went back to bed and picked up her book. She read a few pages without anything sinking in, then vaguely heard

the telephone ring in the front hall. She was about to rac
downstairs to answer it but it stopped after the second ring
Miss Jasper must have picked up.

A few minutes later Miss Jasper tapped on her door and
stepped in. "Good evening, Margaret," she said. "I wasn'
sure you'd come home yet and here you are all tucked i
bed. I was attending a church meeting. We're planning a bi
Christmas bazaar and I was wondering if you could possi
bly publicize it on your show."

"Of course we will," Maggie assured her.

"Then I gather that you and Madison worked ou
your ... little disagreement this morning."

Maggie appreciated how tactful Miss Jasper was being b
not mentioning the indecorous way she'd left the house wit
Mac. "Yes. I'm no longer on strike and Mac has volun
teered to come to the nursing home with me on Thanksgiv
ing."

"That's lovely, dear." The elderly lady smiled sweetly.

"But what bothers me now is that you'll be spending th
holiday alone, Miss Jasper. Why don't you join us for din
ner at the nursing home?"

Miss Jasper considered a moment. "All right. I will. I
will be nice to go someplace where I'm not the oldest per
son present for a change."

Maggie clapped her hands together. "Great! Mac and
are planning a little entertainment after dinner. Why don'
you give a talk on Zerbonia, too? I'm sure everyone woul
enjoy hearing about your adventures there."

"Oh, my, no." Miss Jasper's parchment cheeks turne
pink. "I could never talk in front of an audience."

"Sure you can. You just gave a talk about bald eagles a
your Audubon meeting, didn't you?"

"But that was different, dear. That was reality." The pink
in her cheeks deepened. "I mean, that was in front of a

group who had an avid interest in the subject. Nobody wants to hear about Zerbonia.''

''Of course they do! It's a fascinating subject.''

''I said no, Margaret. And that's final.'' There was irritation in her voice.

''I'm sorry. I didn't mean to be pushy.''

''Nonsense. You weren't. And I didn't mean to be curt, dear,'' Miss Jasper said, sounding like her genial old self again. ''Oh! I almost forgot why I came up to your room in the first place. Your mother just called and she wants you to call her back immediately.''

Maggie was in no mood to talk with her mother but she got up, put on her robe and went directly downstairs to call her.

''Maggie Amelia, your letter has broken my little ol' heart,'' her mother said right off. ''Ah am devastated that you prefer to spend Thanksgiving with strangers up north than with your very own kin.''

''Mamma, I have no choice in the matter. I have to *work* that day.''

''You don't have to do any such thing, child.'' As always, Maggie cringed at being called one. ''You can pack up your bags today and come home where you belong.''

''And do what when I get there? Go on welfare?''

''No Bloomer has ever been on welfare. What a thing to say!''

Maggie began to hunch over, caught herself and stood straight again. ''Try to understand that my job is important to me, Mamma.''

''Your job in ra-di-o?'' Mrs. Bloomer twanged out the offensive word. ''How a daughter of mine could grow up to be a disc jockey is beyond me. What kind of profession is that for a lady? Your sisters were all perfectly happy tutoring children from the finest families in Birmingham before they got married and started raising their own fine families.''

Maggie closed her eyes. "I am not my sisters, Mamma," she said.

"Oh, that tone of yours, Maggie Amelia. Your sisters neveh, eveh use that impatient tone with me."

Maggie sighed. "How is everybody doing?" she asked to change the subject.

It worked like a charm as it always did. Mrs. Bloomer enjoyed nothing more than telling her youngest daughter how well her sisters were doing, how successful their husbands were and how brilliant and good their children were. Since Maggie enjoyed hearing good news about her family, the conversation went well for a while. Then Mrs. Bloomer dropped a bomb into it.

"Lamar is back," she said.

"From France?"

"Well, where else, child? Where else has he been doing research on the French Revolution for the last year?"

"I give up. The Mongolian People's Republic, maybe?"

"Is that intended to be one of your jokes, Maggie Am?"

"Forget it, Mamma. How is Lamar?"

"As handsome and charming as ever, darlin'. Fine southern gentlemen like Lamar Bleaker never change. They remain perfect until the day they die," Mrs. Bloomer said with a sad little sigh. "As your dearly departed father did."

Maggie had no memory of her father, who died when she was a baby, but she always felt a little pull at her heartstrings when her mother brought him up.

"Anyway, Lamar dropped by the other day to ask about you," Mrs. Bloomer continued in a cheerier voice. "He was *crushed* when I told him that you were way up in Vermont, of all places. Oh, Maggie Am, you should have seen that handsome face of his fall at the news. He so wanted to see you again.''

"He was just being polite, Mamma.''

"What a fool thing to say. Polite as Lamar is, that had nothing to do with it. He still cares for you, darlin'. He's never recovered from the time you two parted ways.''

"Need I keep reminding you, Mother, that it was *he* who broke off our engagement?''

"Hush!'' Mrs. Bloomer enjoined. "That's best left forgotten. And I'm sure you made him do it, Maggie Am. You have a way of upsetting all those near and dear to you.''

"Do I?'' Maggie's shoulders hunched again. "I don't mean to, Mamma.''

"Well, that's just the way you are, Maggie Am. You've got a streak of I-don't-know-what in you and I often fear you will never end up content like your sisters. But if there's one man who can make you happy, then his name is Lamar Bleaker.''

"No, Mamma. His name is Mad Dog MacNair.''

"What?'' The energy Mrs. Bloomer put into that simple question almost made the phone sizzle in Maggie's hand.

"Forget it, Mamma. That just popped out.''

"Mad Dog MacNair!'' her mother cried. "The name alone makes me sick with despair. He's that awful man you're working with now, isn't he? That New York radio personality. Oh, my darlin' child, come home immediately, before it's too late. Lamar will marry you in the end. I just know he will. You'll have a proper wedding same as your sisters did. You'll get married in the same church, we'll invite the same fine guests, you'll wear a lovely white gown and—''

Click. The sound was sharp in Maggie's ears as she pressed down the button. She replaced the receiver very carefully, as if it could potentially explode, and went to the parlor to confess her transgression to Miss Jasper.

"For the first time in my life I just hung up on my mother," she said.

"That's why telephones were invented," the old lady told her, putting aside her needlework. "To have the pleasure of hanging up on people." She took in Maggie's disturbed expression. "But maybe not mothers. You can physically hang up on them but never mentally. I speak from experience."

"My mother drives me crazy," Maggie said.

"Mine did, too."

"So you took off for Zerbonia and I took off for Vermont." Maggie attempted a smile. "You were smarter, Miss Jasper. I bet there aren't any telephones in Zerbonia."

Miss Jasper looked away and made no reply.

"Well, I don't mean to bore you with my problems," Maggie said. "I'm probably keeping you from your work on your memoirs."

"No, Margaret. You're not keeping me from anything at all. If you need someone to listen to you now, I'm here for you."

Maggie sat down on the settee and thought how odd it was for her to feel so comfortable talking with a woman almost three times her age.

"I'm in love with Madison," she blurted out to the elderly pixie. "Completely and absolutely. I can't remember life before him or imagine it without him. I've got it bad, Miss Jasper. Real bad."

"How nice," the older woman replied mildly.

"Nice! It's agony. Pure agony. He's given me no reason to believe there's a future for us."

"Then you must simply enjoy the present, my dear. Let the future take care of itself."

"But that goes against everything I've been brought up to believe," Maggie protested. "Mamma worried about the future dreadfully and who could blame her? She had to raise five daughters on her own. She wanted us to plan our lives carefully and not take any chances whatsoever. But for some reason I've never been able to fit into a safe secure mold as easily as my sisters did, try as I might."

"Then stop trying," Miss Jasper suggested blithely.

Maggie's laugh was hollow. "If only it were that simple! You see, there's a part of me that really *is* very conservative, Miss Jasper. I'm hardly a rebel. The most daring thing I've ever done is leave home to take this job in Rutland. And if I didn't have such a passion for radio, I would never have done it."

"Yet you risked losing that very job today."

"I know." Maggie shifted uncomfortably. "I realize now that my feelings for Mac caused me to act in a totally irrational manner. And that's what frightens me so! He stirs up all these crazy emotions in me. Emotions I didn't even know I had!"

"Well, of course they were always there, my dear. You just needed the right man to tap them."

"The *wrong* man, you mean. Maybe Mad Dog and Magnolia complement each other perfectly on the air, but Madison and Maggie have never been on the same wavelength."

"Never?"

The memory of their afternoon of love flashed hot in Maggie's mind and she bent her head to examine the buttons on her raincoat to hide her blush. "Well, almost never," she mumbled. "He makes me behave so impetuously, Miss Jasper."

The old lady shook her head. "I don't think Madison would ever make you do anything you don't want to do, Margaret."

"You're right," Maggie softly agreed. "He never has. I have to take full blame for my own lack of discretion."

Miss Jasper chuckled. "Blame, dear? Don't be so hard on yourself. It's no crime to fall in love."

"But why with *him*?" Maggie cried. "I knew he was dangerous from the very beginning. There's no security in loving a man like Mad Dog MacNair!"

"What do you want? A safe little lap dog of a man?"

"No, it doesn't seem that I do." Maggie's voice was wistful. "But the prudent part of me can't help from wanting one who is willing to make some kind of commitment."

"Give it time," Miss Jasper advised. "Everything works out for the best in the end, if you'll pardon the bromide. I've lived long enough to recognize the truth of it."

Maggie gave her an appreciative smile. "You're so wise. And it comforts me to know that you speak from experience. You dared love a man who was all wrong for you and even though there was no happy ending, you went on to do great things in your life. I admire you very much, Miss Jasper."

"Oh, Maggie, please stop. You're embarrassing me."

"But I *do* admire you and I want you to know it," Maggie insisted. "It's an honor to know you. You've become a mentor to me. I came here so set in my ways of thinking but you've made me recognize how limiting that was. You've never put limits on your life, Miss Jasper. You've—"

"Stop!" the older lady commanded. She covered her eyes with her hands. "I'm a complete fraud and I can't have you believing in me anymore, Margaret. I have led the most severely limited existence possible."

Maggie jumped up from the settee and went to Miss Jasper's side. "What are you talking about? I don't understand."

Miss Jasper lowered her hands to look Maggie directly in the eye. "Please understand this, my dear. I meant no harm. Whatever advice I've ever given you has come straight from my heart. But all the stories I've told you about myself are complete fabrications."

Maggie moved to the mantel and took up the photograph of Slade Berrymore. She turned back to Miss Jasper but before she could ask about him the old lady supplied the answer.

"There has never been a man in a white suit for me, Margaret. I don't even know the name of the one in that picture," she said. "I cut it out of a magazine and framed it years ago because the image appealed to me. I made up the name Slade Berrymore for your benefit, dear. It has a rather nice ring to it, doesn't it?"

Maggie nodded. That's all she could do. Miss Jasper's confession had left her speechless.

"Ralph Klugg was the only man who paid me any attention in my youth," Miss Jasper continued. "How flattered I was! Ralph was popular with the girls in town but it was me, plain little Florrie Jasper, who caught his eye. My mother convinced me to discourage his attentions, though. He was the son of a mill worker and my family owned the Jasper mill."

Maggie replaced the picture. "And you never took off for Zerbonia to make a life of your own."

"No, Margaret." Miss Jasper shook her head wearily. "I've never been to Zerbonia because there's no such place."

"You're joking now, aren't you?"

The old lady directed her bright blue eyes at Maggie. "No, my dear. I'm not joking with you or myself anymore. Zerbonia only exists in my mind. I invented it to catch your interest, as I invented Slade Berrymore. I've spent my entire life here in Jasper, contributing my small share to the community and observing my feathered friends.''

Maggie was now beyond surprise and entering the realm of amazement. Ever since she'd crossed the Vermont state border she'd felt much like Alice going through the looking glass. "But why did you make up such outlandish stories, Miss Jasper?"

"Because I'm a lonely old lady in need of companionship and I thought they would make me more interesting to you." Miss Jasper kept her head high as she confessed this. "And I sensed that you needed to hear them. You initially impressed me as being far too stolid and unimaginative for one so young. But that was before you allowed the Magnolia side of your nature to blossom."

"Madison claims *he* invented Magnolia."

"Perhaps he's just inspired her. Are you angry with me, Margaret? You have every right to be."

"No, I have nothing to be angry about." Maggie sat down beside Miss Jasper and took her hand. "Even though the stories were fiction you have never told me anything false, Miss Jasper. And I still value your advice."

"You know what I regret most now, Margaret."

She squeezed the old lady's hand. "What?"

"That I never had a granddaughter like you."

Maggie blinked away a tear. "You can adopt me," she suggested lightly.

Miss Jasper wiped her own eyes and beamed. "Very well. I shall! You are now my honorary granddaughter, Margaret."

"Oh, we should have some kind of formal ceremony, don't you think?" Maggie gave her a conspiratorial look. "Tell me, Miss Jasper, how would they do it in Zerbonia?"

The old lady didn't miss a beat. "Well, the Zerbonians believe in simplicity at all times." She stood and motioned

Maggie to do the same. "First, the shaking of the hands."
They did. "The kissing of the cheeks." They did. "And then
you would be commanded to start calling me Florrie from
this day forward."

Maggie laughed. "Thank you for the privilege, Florrie.
I'm so glad we had this talk."

"And I'm so relieved that I finally told you the truth."
She hesitated a moment. "About Thanksgiving, Margaret—"

"You're not going to change your mind, I hope!"

"Only the frame of it, dear. I was wondering if Ralph
could join us. He asked me for a date over sixty years ago
but my mother made me refuse. Maybe it's high time I asked
him for one."

"I'll say it is, Florrie!" Maggie hugged her. "It's going to
be the best Thanksgiving ever."

Maggie slept in Mac's shirt that night and her dreams
were sweet and tender. But when she awoke they quickly
faded, overshadowed by doubts. How would he look at her
in the morning light? Would there be love in his dark, ex-
pressive eyes? At least affection? Or would there be nothing but total disregard?

She tried convincing herself that she was foolish to worry.
Mac may not have told her he loved her the day before but
he had behaved in a loving, caring way. He had given her the
sweetest, most gentle kiss in parting before he had driven
back to...Lola.

Maggie sidetracked that train of thought immediately. If
she truly loved Mac then she would have to trust him. That
was all there was to it. She dressed with care—her prettiest
dress, which was a pale blue jersey, gold earrings that made
her eyes sparkle all the more, gracefully designed ecru shoes
that had cost far too much and were worth every penny. She

had selected her underthings with even more care. Her slip, bra and bikini pants were of ivory silk, her pale panty hose were sheer to the waist, and as she'd put on these delicate garments she had entertained herself by imagining Mac taking them off. After anointing all her pulse points with expensive perfume, Maggie hurried off to work and the man who awaited her there—Madison MacNair, her grand adventure.

Chapter Eleven

The elegant shoes were somewhere in the living room. The blue dress was draped over the ottoman. The slip was a silk puddle at the threshold of the bedroom door and the panty hose a cloud at the foot of the bed. The bra and bikini pants were nestled near a pair of men's briefs—bright red today—decorating the beige area rug. Maggie and Mac were in bed. She was still wearing her gold earrings and perfume.

"What time is it?" Maggie asked sleepily.

"Who cares?"

"Mac! We've in bed for hours. We have to work on tomorrow's show before I leave."

"Today's went pretty well, don't you think?" He nuzzled against her and kissed her neck.

She should be immune to his kisses after receiving so many, Maggie thought, but the touch of his lips made her shiver with delight. "Pretty well." She sighed. "But that bit between Magnolia and the dentist needs tuning up."

Mac laughed, his breath warm on her neck. "Cleaning up, you mean. Magnolia was pretty wild with her double entendres today, honey. She made oral hygiene sound like an advanced form of lovemaking."

"Maybe she *did* get a little carried away. But that's because Mad Dog kept goading her on with that leer of his." She rolled over to face Mac and his eyes glittered with appreciation at the sight of her swaying breasts. Maggie smiled. "Like you're leering now."

"It's better when I don't have to use my imagination. I couldn't stop picturing you with your clothes off all morning."

"Is that why Mad Dog asked Magnolia to undress in order to examine her teeth?" She stroked his handsome face and his beard scratched against her fingertips. It was a delightful sensation. "We're going to get a lot of irate letters from dentists about that, Mac."

"Nah. Dentists have a sense of humor, too."

"Do they?" Maggie looked doubtful. But there was something bothering her a lot more than getting angry letters from dentists. "We have to be careful when we're on the air, Mac. I think we're starting to let our personal relationship slip into the act."

"Don't worry about it, Maggie. The act is going just great."

"But I do worry about it," she insisted. "We mustn't bring our personal lives into the show. We have to keep ourselves separate from our radio personalities. What we do off the air is strictly our own business and I don't want our audience privy to it."

"Well, neither do I!" He moved away from her a little, irritated. "You're not the only one with a sense of privacy and propriety, Lady Bloomer."

"I just wanted to remind you that we have to be careful," Maggie said. "So don't pout now."

"I do *not* pout. Real men don't pout."

"Aww, then what's that wittle bottom wip of yours sticking out for, sweetikins?" Maggie could not believe her own ears. Was she actually talking baby talk to him? It was amazing what love could reduce you to do. She tickled his lip with the tip of her finger.

"Stop that, Maggie."

"Why?"

"It's very irritating to have your lip tweaked, that's why."

"I'm not tweaking your lip, I'm tickling it." She reached for his ear and pulled. He yelped. She laughed. "Now *that* is a tweak. Did you feel the difference? Or shall I do it again?"

"Be careful, Maggie. You're flirting with danger here."

But she was enjoying the game. "And this is a pinch," she said, her fingers like pincers all over his chest. He was so lean and muscular, though, that she couldn't get a good grip of excess flesh.

"Pinching is very immature behavior, Maggie. Very immature."

She could tell that he was doing his best not to smile. "And then there's the nip," she said, dipping her head to nibble his shoulder and neck.

"Ouch!" he cried when she bit a little too hard.

"Sorry." She licked the injured spot. "But you know what I think you're going to find the most excruciating torture of all, Madison?" She lowered her voice to its most husky timbre.

"What? A man can only take so much, honey."

"But you're a *real* man, Madison. Real men are tough."
She slowly slid her hand down his chest, stopped along the
way to circle his navel, then inched farther down. His
stomach muscles tightened with a sharp intake of breath.

"You're roaming into a highly sensitive area, honey. One
I value highly, too. You're not going to tweak or pinch or
nip anymore, are you?"

"No, my darling man. I will demonstrate the slow, gentle
squeeeeze."

He moaned. "Oh, I like that."

"I kinda figured you would."

"You want me to show you how much?"

She laughed. "I can already see how much, love."

"But do you want to *feel* how much, honey?"

"Hmm. Let me consider that offer a moment."

"Sorry. Time's up." With a quick movement he pushed
her onto her back. As eager as he was, he took the time to
protect her, and then slowly entered her. "Oh, Maggie, I can
never get enough of you," he murmured in her ear. "Never,
ever, ever."

"Good," she whispered, pressing her palms against his
back as his strokes and thrusts gave her exquisite pleasure.
"That's good, Madison. That's real good." And she was
lost in voluptuous bliss once again.

They sent out for Chinese food that night and no unexpected guests interrupted them as they worked on the next
day's show. Maggie had made a point of not mentioning
Lola to Mac. She intended never to bring up the subject
again because she didn't want anything to ruin their time
together. She wanted to enjoy every moment of it for as long
as possible. Forever, she hoped, but forbade herself to express this hope to Mac. She would be the kind of woman he
seemed to want—a spontaneous, amusing, a sexy free spirit.

Not that it was a difficult act to pull off. Maggie had always longed to be all those things.

They sat cross-legged in front of the coffee table in the living room because Mac had never gotten around to buying a kitchen table. Maggie had a notepad on her lap instead of a napkin, and it was spotted with grains of pork fried rice. She'd never quite gotten the hang of using chopsticks.

"Please pass the General Tso's Chicken," she requested.

Mac handed over the white cardboard container. "This dish dates back to the Ching dynasty," he informed her.

Maggie made a face. "I thought it tasted a little moldy."

"Jot that down. Maybe we can use it."

She sighed. He was always thinking about the show. Not that she minded. So was she. "It's not funny enough," she said. She perused the take-out menu. "But there's got to be a good joke in here somewhere. Neptune Blessing? Triple Delight? Oh, here's a great one. Seven Stars and a Moon."

"Eat, Maggie. Your food's getting cold. All you think about is the show, for Pete's sake."

"My thoughts exactly."

"You were thinking about some other guy named Pete? How could you, honey? I'm hurt to the core."

"Bad joke. Bad joke." Maggie formed a cross with her chopsticks and held them up, as if to ward off further ones.

"That won't protect you from Count Macula, honey." Mac pushed away the chopsticks and leaned over the table to kiss her neck. "Oh, you smell delicious. Spicy garlic sauce always turns me on."

"*Everything* turns you on, Madison."

"Everything about you does, love." His eyes glittered as he looked at her. He smiled contentedly. "That was some Triple Delight we had this afternoon, wasn't it?"

"I give it Seven Stars and a Moon," she replied, smiling back.

"You don't have to go home tonight. Spend it with me, Maggie."

"I can't. I didn't bring a change of clothes for tomorrow or anything." She pushed herself up from the floor, determined not to let him become a habit she could never break. She needed some time away from him or she would be lost completely.

When she glanced down at him she saw glum disappointment in his face. How he always liked to get his own way, she thought. But she wasn't going to let him change the rules on her now—not on a whim.

"Are you going to start pouting again, Madison?"

"If it gets you back to bed with me I will."

"Oh, no you don't. I'm leaving right now. I'm exhausted. And I don't need to tell you, of all people, how early I have to get up tomorrow." She turned away from him and began searching the room for her shoes.

Maggie continued to be exhausted for the next few weeks. There never seemed to be enough hours in the day anymore, never enough time with Mac. But she still refused his invitations to spend the night. It became a point of pride with her. If he had asked her to move in with him it would have been a different matter, but he'd made it clear from the beginning that he didn't want a live-in companion. Maggie doubted that she would have accepted that offer, anyway. Inherent in such an arrangement was the eventuality of moving out and Maggie was sure that she would not be able to bear that when the time came.

So for six, at the most eight hours out of the twenty-four each day, Maggie and Mac separated. And each morning, when Maggie awoke alone, her heart immediately pounded with the anticipation of seeing Mac at the studio again. She would leap out of bed ready to seize the day. As exhausting as loving Mac was, it was also exhilarating.

Their show had never been better. When they weren't making love they were working on their skits. And the extra time they put in paid off. Fan letters poured in. They developed an ever-increasing audience of faithful listeners.

When they did a remote at a newly opened shopping mall outside Rutland, Maggie was amazed at the crowd they drew. Families came with cameras and asked her to pose with their children on her lap, which she gladly did until her dress was a mass of wrinkles. Mac somehow always managed to stay in the background when fans approached for autographs and pictures and at first Maggie thought he was being aloof and supercilious. But a woman in love doesn't miss much in regard to her man and Maggie understood soon enough why he hung back. He was shy. Mad Dog MacNair, a total extrovert on radio, was innately shy!

"Come on," she said, taking him by the arm when their broadcast was over. "Let's go mingle with the people for a while."

"No, we'd better get back to the studio," he mumbled. "I've got some production work to do."

"That can wait," she told him, keeping a tight hold on his arm. "Some of our fans have come quite a distance to meet us. We can spare a little time for them." She tugged him into the crowd.

And once he was warmed up by the glowing smiles and enthusiasm of his admirers he was wonderful, as Maggie knew he would be. He chatted and joked with everybody, gave women the most outlandish compliments, and actually patted a baby's head.

"You can hold little Jake if you'd like," the mother offered.

Mac backed away. "No, that's okay."

"Hold Jake," the father ordered, reaching for his camera. "And you, Magnolia Blossom, get into the picture, too."

Mac took the baby into his arms awkwardly but gently, as if the child could crack like an egg with the slightest jolt. "Cute kid," he remarked stiffly.

"Smile," the father ordered.

Mac and Maggie complied. Jake howled.

After the camera clicked, Mac quickly handed the crying baby back to his mother. "He doesn't seem to like me."

"Oh, he likes you all right," the mother assured him. "He's just hungry, that's all. You'll get used to crying babies soon enough, Mad Dog, when you and Magnolia get hitched and start having them."

Maggie quickly spoke up. "Mr. MacNair and I have a professional relationship, ma'am." Well, that was true enough, she told herself, not wanting to come right out and lie about it. "What you hear on the air is all an act."

"So when do you two plan to tie the knot?" Jake's father asked as if she hadn't spoken at all. He gave Mac's arm a playful punch.

"Never," Mac said between clenched teeth. "Didn't you just hear Ms. Bloomer? Our relationship is strictly professional. You got that straight, buddy?"

"Well, yeah, sure." The man's chummy smile faded.

"Thank y'all for coming to see us," Maggie hurriedly interjected, putting on her Magnolia accent. "We're real pleased to get this chance to meet with our listeners in person. And that little ol' Jake of yours, why, he's just as cute as a button. Looks the spittin' image of you, sir." She winked at the baby's father.

He smiled again, appeased. "You're as nice as you sound, Magnolia. I wake up to your lovely voice every morning."

"Time to go now," his wife said, pulling him away.

"Time to go now," Mac repeated, guiding Maggie away from the crowd and toward the WPEU van. She refused to look at him during the drive back to the studio.

"Okay, what's the problem?" he asked when they were alone in their shoe-box office. They hadn't spent much time in it lately.

"The problem is that you were unnecessarily rude to that man." She took a seat behind the desk and started going through their pile of mail.

"You mean that guy who kept insinuating that we were more than a radio couple?" Maggie gave him a curt nod without looking up from her task. "Well, excuse me for trying to be your knight in shining armor, lady!" Mac said in his most injured tone. "You're the one who made a big deal about keeping our love life personal. I was just trying to protect our privacy."

"You didn't have to be so adamant about it." Maggie pushed aside the mail. "You jumped down his throat as if he were accusing us of heinous crimes when all he was suggesting was that we might eventually get married." As soon as the words were out of her mouth it occurred to Maggie that Mac *did* consider marriage a heinous crime.

He began pacing the small quarters like a caged animal. "You know, Maggie, I sometimes wonder if I can do anything right to please you."

"What's that supposed to mean?" Surely he knew by now how much he pleased her. She'd never hidden that from him. She couldn't have even if she'd wanted to.

"For instance, I keep asking you to spend the night with me and you always refuse, as if I'm insulting you or something," he said. "I don't ask just any woman to spend the night with me, you know."

"I should hope not!" Maggie sputtered.

Mac held up his hands. "Wait a minute. Let me rephrase that. What I meant to say is that you're the first woman that I've ever wanted to spend as much time with as possible, love."

"What about your ex-wife?"

"Sheila?"

"Oh, is that her name? Since you've never discussed her with me, I wouldn't know." Now Maggie's tone was injured.

"Why the hell would I want to discuss my ex-wife with my lover?"

Maggie could feel the burn of tears behind her eyes. Was that all she was to him? His lover? "Pardon me for forgetting my place, Madison."

"Your place?" Mac stopped his impatient pacing. "Your place is with *me*, okay?"

It certainly wasn't okay with Maggie. She could still hear Mac's booming reply when the man asked if they were going to get married. *Never!* She bit her bottom lip and remained silent.

"You want to hear about Sheila? Okay, I'll tell you about Sheila," Mac said, resuming his restricting gait between one wall of the room and the other. "I was passed out on a plane one night about four years ago, flying back from a big rock concert I'd emceed on the west coast. I used to do a lot of gigs like that on weekends when I wasn't doing my show. The money was great and the action was better."

Maggie leaned back in her chair, not sure she really wanted to hear this. But she didn't interrupt. She had to know everything there was to know about Mac because he was in her blood, a part of her now.

"Anyway, I wake up," he continued. "I look out the window and see only darkness, a void. I realize that I don't know where I am. I mean, I realize I'm in a *plane*, I'm not that far gone. But I can't remember if I'm coming or going. I have no idea what my destination is!'' He gave a shudder, remembering. "Let me tell you, I was scared mindless. I was a big, hotshot deejay making tons of money but I was still going nowhere way too fast. Understand?''

"I want to,'' Maggie said in a small, soft voice.

Mac didn't acknowledge that he had heard her. He was engrossed in his own memories. "So I almost panic. I don't remember ever feeling so scared since my mother died when I was a kid. I break out in a sweat, I look around for the nearest exit.'' He gave a short, harsh laugh. "Like I'm going to throw myself out of the plane or something, right? I close my eyes and pray, trying to keep a hold on my sanity. I promise myself I'll change my crazy life-style if I can only survive this blasted plane ride. And when I open my eyes again I see Sheila hovering over me. She's a stewardess on that flight. She gets me some warm milk to calm me down and we chat awhile. She gives me her number. Two weeks later we marry.'' Mac took a deep breath. "But it didn't work out, Maggie. She wasn't the answer to my prayers, after all. And I certainly wasn't the answer to hers. She made it clear that the breakup was all my fault.''

"Do you think it really was?'' Maggie asked gently.

Mac nodded. "I realize now that I got married for all the wrong reasons. I expected Sheila to be my salvation and it isn't fair to expect anyone to be that. I never really shared my life with her. She was my wife but not my partner. So I failed her in the end. I was a lousy husband.''

Maggie couldn't sympathize with a woman she didn't know. But she could with the man she had come to know as having a loving and generous nature. "Sheila certainly managed to make you feel plenty guilty about it, didn't she?''

Mac gave Maggie a rueful grin. "Yeah. That she did. But I'm an easy target." He circled the area of his heart with his forefinger. "Just aim right there, honey, and you can get me every time."

Maggie had no intention of doing any such thing. Ever. Mac's admission had made him far too vulnerable. She sheathed all the weapons with which she was armed. "I think you're a good man, Mac," she said simply. "In fact, I know you are."

"Then you know more than I do, Maggie."

She couldn't bear the pain in his voice. "Well, of course I do," she said, lightening hers. "Haven't I always told you that, MacNair?"

"From the very beginning, Bloomers." His smile relaxed as they fell into their easy banter. "You think you're the greatest thing since sliced bread, don't you?"

"Honey chil', I think I'm the cat's meow."

"Mad dogs have a way of hushing uppity southern cats, don't forget."

"But I do forget. How?"

He crossed the small room, lifted her from her chair and showed her with a long, lingering kiss. Maggie was almost sure that everything would be all right between them. But just in case, she sent up a silent little prayer.

They spent a perfect Thanksgiving Day together. They went directly to the Jasper Nursing and Retirement Home after the show and met Ralph Klugg and Miss Jasper there. Ralph was wearing a blue suit and a spiffy red bow tie—and had apparently left his baseball cap at home for once. Miss Jasper was all gussied up herself. She'd paid a visit to the local beauty shop the day before and her hair was a shimmering silver arrangement of waves. She was dressed in rose instead of green for a change—a classic suit of nubby wool—and her cheeks were rosy, too. She looked lovely.

The residents greeted their guests warmly and even Mac said the dinner was delicious. It had been catered by The Bear and Elk Inn, the finest restaurant in the area. After a glass of wine or two, a few elderly men did their best to be funnier and more outrageous than Mad Dog. And they succeeded, causing some of the more refined ladies to blush. Miss Jasper, though, giggled like a schoolgirl throughout the meal and Maggie caught her squeezing Ralph's hand more than once.

After coffee and dessert were served everyone participated in the skit that Mac and Maggie had created, reading from scripts they handed out. It was a silly piece about the first Thanksgiving dinner, but there were Pilgrim and Indian parts for everyone. The tape recorder mike was passed back and forth around the long table.

Mac planned to edit the tape in the production studio later, deleting stuttering mistakes but keeping the most hilarious bloopers and ad-libs. Background music and sound effects would be added and then they would play it on the show next morning. Mac smiled at Maggie, who was at the other end of the table. She'd never seen him look so happy and relaxed and a warm, sweet love for him flooded her heart.

They celebrated their own private Thanksgiving later that day in bed. They had reached a perfect harmony in pleasing each other but Mac never failed to surprise Maggie with new suggestions. She often delighted him with her own creativity, too. Their mutual trust allowed them to reach unexplored vistas of sensuality. Sometimes their lovemaking was playful and at times so serious and intense that it left them gazing at each other in stunned wonderment.

They were gazing at each other that way now, satiated and speechless. But not speechless for long, Maggie knew. One of the many delights of their relationship for her was that they enjoyed talking together so much. They found each other constantly amusing. Serious conversation, though, was usually avoided. Maggie recognized this as the major fault in their relationship but tried not to press Mac to reveal his deepest feelings too often. She had seen how uncomfortable and withdrawn that usually made him.

"This is the best holiday I ever had," he told her, breaking the silence. His voice was drowsy with love. "I never liked them much as a kid."

"Tell me why." She stroked his hair, hoping to coax him into talking about himself. She couldn't help herself.

"Well, for one thing school was out, which meant my father was around. I told you he was a principal, didn't I?"

Maggie nodded. She had filed away every detail about Mac that he had eked out to her.

"He would always take vacation time as the opportunity to lecture me about my failings. And tutor me. He was a born educator, my old man. But he didn't know much about raising a son."

"Oh, you didn't turn out so bad, Madison." She caressed his cheek.

"Sez who?"

"Sez me. Now go on."

"About holidays?" She nodded. "Well, without a woman in the house they were dreary events," Mac continued. "I was twelve when my mother died. Too young to understand that my father was mourning the loss, too. He became distant. I became rebellious. We ended up hating each other's guts."

"Hush, Madison." Maggie pressed her hand to his lips for an instant. "I'm sure you didn't really."

"Yes, really," he insisted. "After I left home we didn't speak for almost fifteen years. I occasionally sent him a nose-thumbing postcard while I was hitchhiking across the country. He wrote me a few letters I never answered while I was in the army. And then, when I became a success on radio, I'd send him news clippings about myself to show him I wasn't the failure he always predicted I'd be. He'd send them back to me in care of the station, all torn up. No note. No nothing." Mac laughed. "He was a doozy, my old man."

"Was? Is he dead, Madison?"

The muscles around his eyes were tense. "I buried him last July. Get this, Maggie." His smile was tense, too. "He took his last breath on the Fourth of July, managing to ruin yet another holiday for me."

"Oh, darling," she said, cupping her cool hand beneath his strong jaw. "Don't try to sound so callous and selfish. You're not like that."

"Don't be so sure, Maggie."

"But I am," she insisted. "I'm smart enough to see through an act. So drop yours, Madison MacNair, the way I dropped mine when you asked me to."

"Sometimes I'm not sure what part of me *is* an act, Mag."

"Me, too," she said. "But real people are a lot more complicated than radio personalities." She gave him a soft pat on the cheek. "Now go on with your story."

"But I just got to the end of it."

"You mean you never saw your father again before he died?"

"Thank God I did. My aunt wrote to tell me he was dying of cancer. That old goat never would have let me know himself." Mac shook his head. "He would have gone on to his greater reward leaving me holding the guilt bag."

"So you went to visit him after you got the letter?"

"Visit him? Hell, Maggie, I moved back into the house with him! I was Dad's nurse and companion for over a year." He shook his head and smiled sadly. "We were the quintessential odd couple. Dad was a terrible patient. And I was no Florence Nightingale, believe me. We usually managed to find something to argue about. Dumb things. For instance, he always wore this ratty bathrobe, so I get him a fancy one to cheer him up and—"

"A burgundy robe with navy piping?" Maggie interrupted.

Mac looked at her, startled. "How on earth did you know that?"

"I saw it hanging in your closet and wondered about it. It looked as if it had never been worn."

"It never was. Dad accused me of being a spendthrift and refused to wear it. I don't know why I've kept it. But I bought it especially for him and haven't had the heart to get rid of it." He laughed softly, as if over his own sentimentality.

"You were with your father when he most needed you, Madison. Take pride and comfort in that." She kissed his forehead. "You were a good son to him in the end."

"Don't make me sound so noble, honey. I may have made his last year on earth more comfortable but we never really resolved our differences. That only happens in the movies. Dad and I never had one of those heartwarming scenes between father and son where they look eye to teary eye and understand each other at last. Sorry to disappoint you, honey, but real life ain't that way."

"You haven't disappointed me, Madison," she said quietly.

"But I will, Maggie."

His tone was so foreboding that Maggie shivered. She didn't dare ask him why. Instead she rose from the bed and slipped on one of his soft bright shirts. "I still have that shirt I borrowed from you that first time we were together," she told him.

He sat up and leaned against the headboard, his upper torso as spectacular as a centaur's in Maggie's eyes. "I was wondering when you were going to fess up to that, Bloomers. But I've been way too polite to mention it, of course."

"Hah! You polite?" She picked up his brush and ran it through her tawny hair. "You probably forgot all about it."

"I haven't forgotten one detail of our first time together, honey. Or any other time we're together. Every moment with you is etched in my heart."

She turned to look at him. His face was serious. His confession spurred her to make one of her own. "I sleep in that shirt of yours almost every night, Madison."

She had expected him to look pleased but he frowned. "A lot of sense that makes when you could be sleeping in the arms of the man who owns it instead. What's with you, Maggie? Why the hang-up about spending the night here? Do you think that going back to your own little bed keeps you respectable or something?"

She raised her chin. "That has nothing to do with it. I'm not a hypocrite, Mac. And I don't feel our relationship is unrespectable."

"Then stay tonight, honey." He patted the space she'd just vacated, still warm, and his smile was coaxing. "Come back to bed and cuddle. I'll even make you breakfast in the morning."

"How? Out of thin air?" she asked archly, skirting the issue. "Don't you ever go grocery shopping? There's never any food in this place. You don't even have enough furniture. You haven't hung one picture on the wall or added any personal touches whatsoever.''

Mac watched Maggie brush her hair vigorously. The electricity snapped and crackled with each stroke. He watched her carefully but remained silent.

"You live like a nomad, Mac," Maggie continued. "What do you plan to do? Fold up your tent and sneak off in the night when the mood strikes you, leaving no traces behind?"

"I can go out to the corner deli and pick up some breakfast," Mac said in lieu of an answer. It was his turn to skirt the issue Maggie had brought into their discussion. She had hit close to the truth and it made him very uncomfortable. "I'll serve it to you in bed."

"Oh, hang breakfast! That's not the point and you know it, Madison.''

"The point is that you won't stay tonight."

"And what about tomorrow night?"

"We'll play it by ear."

"Just the answer I expected from you." Maggie threw down his hairbrush. "Everything is so temporary with you, Mac. Don't you ever think about the future?"

"You mean *our* future?"

"No, the future of radio in the age of electronics," she replied dryly. "Of course I mean our future!"

Mac heaved a sigh. The time had come, he decided, to have it out with her. A part of him was relieved it had. Maybe that's why he'd pressed her to stay. "It's not that I haven't thought about asking you to move in with me, honey. Sometimes I miss you so much during the night that I ache. Maybe we should give it a try for a week or two and if it doesn't work out—"

"You can bounce me out on my bottom, right?"

"Now, honey, you know I respect that adorable bottom of yours way too much to do that."

Not a smile out of her, Mac observed. Not even an inkling of one. He had known this was going to go badly. But now that they'd opened the subject, they would have to pursue it to the bitter end.

"Here's a news flash, MacNair," Maggie said, jabbing her forefinger in his direction. "I wouldn't move in with you if you got on your knees and begged me."

"Even if I promised you could hang frilly curtains on all the windows and get a fluffy bathroom mat and matching seat cover?"

"You're not being humorous now, Mac. You're being tedious." She flicked back the bed covers, looking for her new lacy teddy.

Mac caught her arm and pulled her onto the bed. "Listen, Maggie, if you moved in with me it would be on a temporary basis only because living here is temporary for me, too."

She tensed. "How temporary?"

"You know how it is with us radio jocks. A better offer comes along and—" He snapped his fingers. "We're off."

"You'd do that, Mac? You'd leave PEU just like that?" *You would leave me?* "I thought you were so happy with the way the show was going." *I thought you were so happy with me!*

"I *am* happy with the show," he said, rubbing her back. "But let's face it, honey. Rutland is hardly the big time. When New York calls, you gotta answer."

"Yeah, a man's gotta do what he's gotta do." She made no effort to hide the bitterness in her voice. "So when did you get this big offer, Mad Dog? Is your carpetbag already packed?"

"I haven't gotten one yet, Maggie. I have no immediate plans to leave. I just thought it was time that I leveled with you about it and we—"

"No *immediate* plans!" She leaped off the bed and stared down at him, her face flushed with rage. "Oh, that's a relief, MacNair. Maybe we can fit in a few more good times in the sack before you take off for the Big Apple."

It pained him to hear her talk like that. It pained him even more to know why she felt compelled to. "Please hear me out, Maggie."

He reached up to take hold of her arm again but she jumped out of reach, crossed the room and slammed the bathroom door behind her. Mac lay in bed for a while, listening to the rush of the shower, then got up, got dressed and went to make coffee for them. That's the only thing he could think to do at the moment.

When Maggie joined him in the kitchen she was dressed and poised. Her hair was wet but Mac was relieved to see that her eyes were dry.

"I wish I could remember to bring a shower cap when I visit you," she said.

That sounded optimistic. Mac gave her a hopeful smile. "I'll buy one for you. First thing tomorrow."

"Wow." Her voice was flat. "Sure that's not too big a commitment, Mac? You know what they say. Once you give a woman a shower cap, she's going to expect a toothbrush next."

He ignored that and pointed to the stove. "Look, honey. I went out and got myself a real, honest to goodness coffeepot. I know you can't stand the instant stuff."

Maggie watched the perking bubbles for a moment, as if fascinated. "I am moved by such thoughtfulness, Mac. I am genuinely moved."

She didn't sound very genuine *or* moved. Beneath the cool veneer of her voice Mac heard deep hurt. And that made him hurt, too. He rebelled against the pain. "Maggie, I cautioned you from the very beginning about getting involved with me."

She rolled her eyes to show her disdain for his timely reminder. "Too bad you neglected to tell me about your plans to leave here as soon as possible." She had grown so attached to the community. She'd foolishly assumed that he had, too. "Go soak your head in your brand-new coffeepot, MacNair." Maggie pushed hard on the swinging door and went out.

Mac stopped the door before it swung back in his face and followed her out. "Oh, that was a great exit line, Bloomers. Who writes your material? Some kid in fifth grade?"

"Yeah, the same one who called me Bloomers." She looked around the room for her shoes until Mac stopped her frantic search by taking her into his arms.

He pressed her head against his chest and stroked her hair. "I'm crazy about you, honey, and I hope we stay together for a long, long time. But you're always going to consider it an impermanent situation without a wedding band, aren't you?"

"Yes," she admitted. "I see no future for us without a commitment and although I try not to think about it, it frightens me."

"Marriages can be impermanent, too," he reminded her. "Mine sure was."

She stepped away from him. "What happens when you get that offer from a big market station?"

"We can decide that when the time comes, honey."

She sniffed. "Boy, I'm really glad we discussed this, Madison. I feel *so* much better now that I know the ending to our story."

"There doesn't have to be an ending, Maggie. That's wha' I'm trying to tell you. We'll work things out day by day."

"So we're right back to where we started," she saic grimly.

"It's not such a bad place to be, is it, Maggie? We have ? wonderful time together."

"I'm not having such a wonderful time right now." Hov she regretted they'd ever had this conversation! "I think I'l' go home."

"Please, Maggie. Don't leave in a huff."

"No, I'll leave in my car. Good night, Madison."

She walked out very calmly, drove away, and when she was halfway back to Jasper she finally realized that, thanks to Mac, she was barefoot once again.

Chapter Twelve

When Maggie returned to Miss Jasper's house she was surprised to find Ralph still there, sitting beside Miss Jasper on the parlor sofa, his red bow tie askew.

"We have a bit of news, Margaret," Miss Jasper announced.

"Oh?" Maggie mentally pushed aside her own problems for the moment. "What have you and Mr. Klugg been cooking up together?"

"We're going on a cruise," Ralph said.

"To Zerbonia," Miss Jasper added.

Maggie couldn't prevent the rise of her eyebrows. "How nice," she said.

"Where the heck is that?" Ralph asked. "It isn't listed on the itinerary. Florrie and I are boarding a boat headed for the Caribbean tomorrow, Maggie. We'll stop at many islands along the way. Maybe Zerbonia, too, for all I know."

"Tomorrow?" Maggie was more than a little surprised. "This is rather sudden, isn't it?"

"It certainly is for me," Miss Jasper said, eyes bright. "I've been trying to get rid of Ralph all evening in order to pack. But I can't!"

Ralph chuckled. "I'm stuck on her like glue."

Miss Jasper gently pushed away his hand before it settled on her knee. "We'll be away for two weeks, dear," she told Maggie. "You won't be afraid to be alone, I hope. Please feel free to invite someone to stay with you if you have qualms."

"I'll be fine alone. But I still can't understand how you managed to arrange this trip so quickly."

"It's been arranged for months," Ralph said.

"He won a magazine contest," Miss Jasper explained. "One of those silly promotions for a romantic holiday for two. Why Ralph entered it is beyond me."

"Because I'm a born optimist is why, Florrie. Don't you know that by now?"

"All I know, Ralph, is that you were going to let that trip slip right through your fingers."

"Well, I didn't want to go all by myself. What fun would that have been?" He turned his happy face to Maggie. "I offered the trip to my sons and their wives but none of them could get away. I was about to tear up the tickets when Florrie called. Needless to say, I refused all other Thanksgivings and accepted hers." Before she could prevent him, Ralph managed to fondle Miss Jasper's knee. "And now she's accepted mine!"

Miss Jasper didn't attempt to push Ralph's hand away this time. "Waste not, want not is what I always say," she did indeed say. "A free vacation cannot be ignored."

Ralph grinned. "And neither can I be ignored anymore, right, Florrie?"

Miss Jasper blushed but didn't reply. "Are you sure you'll be all right alone here, Margaret?"

"Of course I will," Maggie assured her. "Y'all have a wonderful time." After chatting with them awhile she excused herself and headed for the stairs.

"Did you notice that Margaret was barefoot?" she overheard Ralph ask Miss Jasper.

"Oh, that's nothing new. Margaret has her little quirks, as we all do."

"Tell me some of yours, Florrie. Whisper them in my ear."

"Ralph, you silly old coot!"

Maggie climbed the stairs to the sound of Miss Jasper's giggles.

There was a gift-wrapped box on Maggie's desk the next morning. She picked it up and shook it.

"Why do people always do that?" Mac asked grumpily, shuffling into the studio with his cup of black coffee. "What if there's something breakable inside? What if there's a *bomb* inside?"

Maggie set down the box gingerly.

"Oh, go ahead and open it, honey. It's not a bomb. At least I hope not."

She gave him a suspicious look. "A dead cat on the line," she said in her Magnolia accent.

"Huh?"

"That's a southern expression for something fishy."

"There's nothing fishy about it," he said in that injured tone she knew so well. "I went out and bought you a present last night, that's all. Hurry up. Open it before we go on."

She tore off the bright paper, remembering the last gift he'd given her—her own shoe! She looked inside. A shower cap. And ten toothbrushes in various colors and styles. She stared at Mac, not smiling.

"I didn't know if you liked hard bristles or soft or what, so I got you every style the drugstore carried," he explained.

"You expect me to be touched by this, don't you, Madison?"

His dark eyes pleaded with her. "Yeah, I was hoping and praying you would be, honey."

Maggie shook her head. "The sad thing is I *am*. Despite my better judgment Madison MacNair, I am touched by this small, no doubt meaningless gesture on your part. I guess that makes me a born pushover."

"It's not meaningless, honey!"

She sighed with resignation and gave the smile he was waiting for. "Oh, Mac. What am I going to do with you?"

He smiled back in relief. "I'll show you when we go back to my place this afternoon." His smile wavered. "You *are* coming back, aren't you, Maggie?"

She glanced down at the program log without replying and began circling commercial spots. She'd decided to let him stew for a while.

"Aren't you, Maggie?" he asked with uncharacteristic doubt in his voice.

"Hush please, Mac. I have two minutes to get organized before airtime and desperately need them."

"And I desperately need an answer, honey! Are you still ticked off with me?"

"Ticktock, ticktock," she said. "Time is a wastin', Mac. Are you all set to go on with that tape from the nursing home?"

"Of course I am. I worked on it all night."

Mac settled down in front of the board and silently sulked for a few minutes. But when he turned on his mike and shouted into it, his voice was as self-assured as ever. "Awake and rise, you lazy bums out there! It's six-o-five! Time to listen up to Mad Dog and Magnolia!"

The first three hours of the show went well. But during the nine o'clock news break a good-looking man in a navy blazer tapped on the control-room window. Maggie glanced up and gasped, her eyes wide with astonishment. And then a bright smile eased across her face as she waved to him enthusiastically.

"Who the hell is that?" Mac demanded.

"I can't believe it!" Maggie replied.

"Who is he, dammit?"

Maggie took off her headphones. "Lamar Bleaker," she informed him as she hurried out. "Cover for me while I go talk to him, Madison."

"Hey, wait a minute. You've got a job to do here, Maggie. You better be back here by the end of the news or..." Mac let his threat trail off; she hadn't stuck around to hear it.

He gazed through the studio window with narrowed eyes and watched her run into Lamar's arms and give him a hearty hug. Then Lamar picked her up and twirled her around. Then they stepped back to look at each other with glowing eyes. Then they hugged again. Then Lamar twirled her around again.

"If he keeps doing that he's going to make her throw up," Mac muttered. But he was the one who felt like throwing up at the moment. He felt as if he'd just been kicked in the stomach. Hard. Real hard.

Maggie was back in front of her mike, a little breathless, a second before the news segment ended. Even so, Mac glared at her. She smiled back. Lamar stayed at the window, his eyes never leaving Maggie as she performed.

"What's that bozo doing here?" Mac asked during a commercial break.

"He's come to see me, of course."

"Well, I didn't think he came to see me! I mean what does he *want*, Maggie?"

"I don't rightly know." She turned to Lamar and waved. He waved back.

"Stop making goo-goo eyes at him and try to remember you're a professional," Mac told her. But a moment later he was the one who stumbled his way through a public service announcement. He felt as if his mouth were stuffed with cotton, a recurring nightmare he'd had when he started in the business. Except this wasn't a nightmare. Lamar Bleaker was a reality.

When Maggie introduced Mac to Lamar after the show he was actually civil and suggested they all go to the diner across the street for coffee. At first Lamar hesitated. It was obvious to Mac that all he wanted was to be alone with Maggie after traveling all the way from Birmingham to see her. Mac insisted, grabbing Lamar's arm in a buddylike fashion. If Lamar refused again, he was going to yank it off. Luckily Lamar didn't.

"So, Bleaker, what brings you to Rutland," Mac asked when they'd settled in the booth. He'd made sure, with none too subtle maneuvering, that Maggie was sitting with *him*.

"I've come to see Maggie, of course," Lamar replied.

What did these two do, rehearse their answers? Mac wondered. "Yeah, but why?"

"Oh, call it an impulse." Lamar laughed.

The laugh of a wimp, Mac decided. "Why, Lamar, you mad impetuous fool, you," he said.

"Maybe I acted a bit too impetuously. I assumed I wouldn't have any trouble finding a place to stay but all the inns and motels in the area are filled because of the holiday.''

"Try some other area," Mac suggested. "Like Cleveland.''

Maggie pinched his leg under the table. "Lamar, don't be silly. You're going to stay with me, of course. There's plenty of room at Miss Jasper's house. I'm all alone there now and I'd appreciate the company, sugar.''

Sugar! Mac scowled at Maggie. "What do you mean you're alone? Where's the old lady?''

"Miss Jasper and Ralph took off on a cruise ship today.''

"Well, isn't that convenient," Mac said. "Now you and La, here, have the whole place to yourselves." Animosity emanated from Mac's glinting eyes like radar when he looked at Lamar. "It's okay if I call you La for short, isn't it?''

"Actually no one ever has before, but I don't mind.''

"Well, *I* mind, dammit!" Mac hit the table with his leg when he stood, making the coffee cups rattle in protest. "You've got no business here, mister. So catch the next plane back to Birmingham.''

Lamar dabbed at the spilled coffee with his paper napkin. "I don't intend to do any such thing, MacNair," he replied calmly. "I plan to stay for as long as Maggie will have me.''

"She doesn't want to have any part of you, Bleaker. You're out of the picture now. *Get* the picture?" He banged his fist on the table, spilling more coffee. "You tell him, Maggie.''

She started dabbing up coffee with her napkin, too. "I don't intend to do any such thing," she replied as calmly as Lamar. "And please keep your voice down, Madison.

You're not on the air now and I'd prefer you didn't make this conversation a public broadcast.''

"Are you coming back to my apartment with me or not?" he roared.

The way she looked at him left no doubt about her answer. Mac stomped his way out of the restaurant and diners held on to their coffee cups as he passed.

"Gee, he didn't stop to pay the check," Maggie said to Lamar. "Didn't he say this was going to be his treat?"

Lamar's face remained serious. "You're in love with him, aren't you?"

"Yes." She gave out a weak laugh. "Poor me."

"Poor me," Lamar said.

When Maggie and Lamar returned from dinner at the Bear and Elk Inn that evening she suggested having brandy in the parlor.

"Shall I light a fire?" Lamar asked as he walked into the room. "I meant in the fireplace of course, darlin'. You've made it quite evident to me that I don't stand a chance of lighting one in you anymore."

She laughed and poured them drinks from the decanter on the library table.

"Not that I ever could," Lamar added.

She stopped, midpour. "Oh, sugar, what a thing to say. I was madly in love with you at one time."

He busied himself putting logs on the andirons, keeping his back to her. "But you never felt real passion for me, did you, Maggie Am?"

"I was awfully young and inexperienced," she hedged.

"You're not so very much older now."

"Lamar, why did you come to see me?" They'd talked about family and friends for most of the evening, avoiding that very question.

He slowly turned to her. "To ask you again to marry me."

Maggie put down the decanter and walked over to him. "You're serious, aren't you? But when you left for France you made it clear that it was over between us."

"You hurt me, Maggie, by refusing to come with me."

"I don't think there's much of a demand for American disc jockeys who speak atrocious French in Paris. I couldn't give up my career. It wasn't fair of you to expect that of me."

"I know. That wasn't the real problem, anyway. I always felt that you had accepted my proposal to please your mother."

"No!" Maggie protested although she wasn't quite sure. "I wanted to marry you because you're one of the finest, most responsible, most honorable men I've ever known, Lamar. I feel so safe when I'm with you. So comfortable."

"But you don't feel passion."

She shook her head sadly. "No," she admitted. "But you already guessed that. So why do you want me back?"

"Because we're so good together in so many other ways, Maggie. We think alike. We have the same background and values. My research work is completed and I'm ready to settle down and teach. I've been offered a full professorship at the University of Birmingham."

"That's wonderful, Lamar. Congratulations."

"It would be even more wonderful if I had someone to share my life with. Someone like you, darlin'. You'd be with your family again. We could start one of our own. We could have a good, solid life together."

She reached up and touched his cheek. "Oh, Lamar, you honor me."

He bowed his head. "That's a gracious no thank-you, isn't it?"

"I'm so sorry, Lamar. But I can't."

"Because of Mad Dog MacNair." Lamar leaned against the mantelpiece and his elbow knocked over the picture of Slade Berrymore. "Oh, Maggie, listen to me as a *friend*. I try not to judge people on first impressions but it's so abundantly obvious to me that MacNair is all wrong for you. I can't for the life of me understand what you could see in that boor beyond his looks. And I know you're not the sort of woman who gets carried away by a man's physical appearance."

"Don't be so sure." She smiled at Lamar's shocked expression. "I'll tell you what I see in Mac. I see myself! Or at least a part of myself that I've always kept buried. I know you won't believe this, Lamar, but I really do have a passionate nature."

"I never claimed you didn't, darlin'. I only expressed regret that I couldn't bring it out in you. Maybe I just wasn't lowbred enough."

"That's really hitting below the belt."

"Well, isn't that where it's all centered between you and him?"

"I can't believe my ears, Lamar Bleaker! I've never heard you be so uncouth." But Maggie wasn't really angry with him. She actually smiled. "Sometimes it's centered there," she admitted. "Mac and I have a very physical relationship. But we have more than that, too. We have the same passion for our work, we make each other laugh, we energize each other. I feel *complete* when I'm with him."

"You're not thinking clearly, darlin'," Lamar said in a patronizing tone edged with irritation. He sounded exactly like her mother at that moment. "Somehow that hellhound has managed to bedevil you. Get away from him as soon as possible, Maggie Amelia. Come back home with me."

She laughed at such an absurd suggestion. "I don't want to get away from Mac! I want to spend every minute of every day with him for as long as it lasts."

Lamar immediately picked up on that. "For as long as it lasts?"

"Nothing in life is permanent," she said uncomfortably.

"What *I* offered you is permanent!"

"Oh, Lamar, you poor dear. You're stuck in an emotional rut." Maggie hugged him, then took his kindly, familiar face in her hands and spoke gently. "You don't really want me, sugar. You've just gotten into the habit of thinking you do. I'm the convenient, comfortable girl next door. What you need is a woman who'll bring out the devil in *you*."

He smiled at such a notion. "I'm very fond of you, Maggie. I always will be. But I reckon I'm going to have to give you up, aren't I?"

"You did once before and made the right choice for both of us," she reminded him.

He brushed her lips with his and stepped away. "I won't light a fire, after all. It seems our discussion is over and there's no sense in keeping you up. You must have to get up very early for work."

She had never appreciated his courteous manner more. "Four o'clock to be exact," she said. "Did you like what you heard of the show today?"

"It was pretty amusing," he said. "I never knew you had such a sense of humor."

"Neither did I!"

"But I'll tell you one thing, Maggie. Your mother wouldn't like it one teeny bit. She'd like Mad Dog MacNair even less. And she's going to be downright disappointed that I'm not bringing her baby home where she belongs."

"I belong here now, Lamar."

"I sincerely hope that man doesn't end up breaking your heart, little girl."

"I'm not a little girl anymore, Lamar. And it's worth the risk."

He held up his hands as if in surrender. "Good night then. I know my way to the guest room. I'll be leaving before you're through work tomorrow morning so I guess this is goodbye for a while."

"You know I'm very fond of you, too, Lamar," she said.

His smile was resigned. "Maybe you're right, Maggie Am. Maybe we both deserve more than lukewarm fondness, comfortable as it is." He kissed her cheek, then turned and went up the stairs.

Maggie didn't know what to expect from Mac when she entered the studio the next morning. And he surprised her once again by giving her a breezy greeting and then studying his notes for the day's show, cheerfully whistling as he did so and ignoring her completely.

Maggie certainly wasn't going to bring up Lamar's name if he didn't. She could play little mind games as well as he could. Checking over her own notes, she began whistling, too.

She watched him carefully when the show began, as she always did. His constantly changing expressions and eyes gave her the cues she needed to do her job well. And he always looked for feedback and encouragement in her face, too. But not today. Today he wouldn't so much as glance her way. Maggie noted how hollow eyed and drawn he looked. Poor boy probably didn't get much sleep last night, she thought with satisfaction.

She immediately reined in such a thought. Surely she was above such shoddy, spiteful games! She had always been forthright with Mac and she wasn't going to change now.

She waited for the first commercial break, a recorded spot, to set things right with him.

"I'd like to talk to you about Lamar," she said, taking the direct approach because it was fastest and the commercial was short.

"Lamar?" Mac gave her a disinterested look. "Lamar who?" He put up his hand. "Wait. Don't tell me, Maggie. Let me guess. Lamar Bleaker, right? The bozo you asked to come all the way up here to make me jealous."

"I did no such thing, Mac!" She took a deep breath and put her flaring temper on simmer. "Only *you* would think of something so childish," she said in a quieter tone.

"Maggie, Maggie, Maggie." Mac shook his curly head. "To stoop so low. You've really disappointed me, honey."

"Oh, stop being ridiculous if you possibly can."

He ignored her tart request. "Maybe, just maybe I'd have cause to worry if Bruce Springsteen had moved in with you. But a total wimp like Lamar Bleaker?" His laugh was a perfect imitation of unconcern. "Sorry, honey. It ain't gonna play."

Since Maggie had heard through the laugh she continued to keep her temper on the back burner. "Mac, you'll be happy to know that Lamar—"

"Stifle it, honey. We're back on in two seconds and I don't want to hear one damn thing more about your precious La." He shuffled through his notes. "Where's the crummy bread-and-rolls copy, dammit? It's the next live spot coming up."

Maggie, ever organized, handed him a sheet, which he snatched from her hand without thanking her. He read the commercial for a local bakery in an angry tone, as if fresh rye bread and flaky croissants were somehow the cause of all human misery. Then he slammed number ten on the music list into the cart machine and punched it up.

"How I hate this song," he muttered, slipping off his headphones and hanging them around his neck. "It's such a lousy rendition of a Buddy Holly classic."

"I don't think the folks at the Have A Good Day Bakery are going to appreciate your rendition of their commercial, either, Mac."

"Then let them eat cake."

She had to smile. "You really are jealous, aren't you? I know I shouldn't let that please me so much but I can't help it."

"Well I'm not pleased one damn bit, Maggie. I want Bleaker out of that house and on a plane back to Birmingham today. You hear me?"

"Ah do believe you forgot to add the *or else*, Mr. Macho Man," she drawled out in her Magnolia voice.

"Yeah, I did. Thanks for reminding me. Now listen up, my little blossom. He goes today *or else* I go."

That did it. Her temper passed the simmering stage and went into a rolling boil. "You can go to hell in a hand basket for all I care, MacNair. You have no right to tell me what to do. Absolutely none." The flashing red light above the clock caught Maggie's eyes. She pointed to it.

Mac hurriedly selected another prerecorded commercial, rammed it into the cart machine and pressed the start button. "This is going to be our most boring show yet," he predicted grimly. "But it's hard to be funny when the woman in your life, the one you've come to trust and respect, is trying to manipulate you into marrying her."

"What?" Maggie screamed, over the tire commercial coming through her headphones. She yanked them off.

"You heard me right, honey," he said. "I know what you're up to with your Bleaker stratagem. But you didn't have to use him to get to me. You didn't have to resort to playing those kinds of games."

"Oh, Mac, that swollen ego of yours has given you brain damage."

"Of course you're going to deny it. You're embarrassed. And you have every right to be embarrassed, honey. I'm willing to forgive and forget, though." He paused. "But I still want him out of the house by this afternoon," he reiterated. "And that's my last warning, lady."

The heat of rage consumed Maggie, scorching her composure and judgment. Coolness of mind was no longer possible. Reasonableness had been fried to a crisp. The last thing she was going to tell Mac now was that Lamar had already left. "It's your turn to listen to me, Madison," she said. "Margaret Amelia Bloomer will not be intimidated by anybody. Especially by the likes of you. I will see whomever I choose whenever I choose. That's the deal we made. That's the deal we keep."

"That wasn't the deal!" he protested vehemently. "We're still obliged to remain faithful to each other. It doesn't matter if we're married or not."

"You know, you're the one who always brings up marriage, not me."

"But you're the one who's always thinking about it. I can read your eyes, Maggie."

"Oh, really? Well, try reading my lips for a change. I wouldn't marry you now if my life depended on it, Madison MacNair."

"Oh, my God," he said.

She followed his horrified gaze. The flashing red light was no longer flashing. It was a steadfast beacon indicating that they were now on the air. Maggie quickly looked down at her mike, hoping for some miracle she knew she didn't deserve. All hopes were dashed when she saw it was switched on and so was Mac's. She covered her face with her hands and ran out of the studio.

Chapter Thirteen

Maggie rushed to the ladies' room to compose herself. But she found no refuge there because Lola followed her in.

"It's a lucky thing I came to work early today," Lola said. "Looks like you could use a friend right now."

Maggie swiped at her eyes, brushing away tears. "You?"

"Hey, I'm available."

Maggie had no inclination to accept the offer. "Were you listening to the show in your office?"

"I sure was, just like thousands of others."

"Thanks for reminding me, Lola. How much did they hear?"

"You came on during the part when you were saying you couldn't be intimidated. I didn't know your middle name was Amelia, Maggie. That's my favorite aunt's name."

Maggie groaned. "So they know I wasn't playing the

Magnolia part at the time. What else did I say? I can't remember now."

"You told Mac that he was the one who was always bringing up marriage, not you, and that you wouldn't marry him if he was the last man on earth—or words to that effect."

"I have never been so mortified in my life."

"Really?" Lola looked surprised. "It's no big deal, Mags. So what if everybody in Vermont and the neighboring three states knows you're sleeping with Mac? You're probably the envy of New England right now."

"Are you trying to comfort me, Lola? Or make me even more miserable?

Lola sighed. "I guess we don't see things the same way, Maggie. All I know is that this is going to be great for the ratings."

"My personal life has just been made public and you talk about ratings!" Maggie turned away and took a deep breath to steady herself. "Please go away, Lola. I need some time alone now."

"Don't take too much time, Mags. You've still got the rest of the show to do."

"You've got to be kidding! I can't go *on* again. I'm going home and burying my head under the covers for the rest of my life."

"No, you're not." Lola gave her a long, steady look. "What you're going to do is wash your face and go back to the studio, Maggie"

"Hah! Let Mac handle this mess. It's all his fault in the first place."

"It's both your faults. You were both unprofessional. But that's in the past now. At the present moment this station has got air to fill, sweetie. If you don't go back on you'll be letting down your audience. You don't want to do that."

"You're right," Maggie said, amazed that she was. "I never thought I'd be saying this to you but...thanks, Lola."

They made a quick gesture that came close to a hug but wasn't quite one. "We better watch it, Maggie," Lola said on her way out of the ladies' room. "Or we may end up actually liking each other someday."

When Maggie joined Mac in the studio she was cloaked in composure. But it was gossamer thin. Any wrong word or signal from Mac could easily tear it to shreds.

Mac immediately sensed this and quelled his first impulse to take her into his arms.

"I'm glad you came back, Maggie," he said softly. He knew for sure that their relationship had been ruptured. But mortally? He couldn't even face that possibility now. He could barely face Maggie. He blamed himself entirely for what had occurred. He was the one in charge of the board. He had let Maggie down and he hated himself for it.

"We'll continue as if nothing has happened," she told him.

And Mac hoped with all his heart that she wasn't only referring to the show.

They proceeded with their planned broadcast, falling right back into their Mad Dog and Magnolia characters. Mac ignored the constantly winking yellow buttons on the studio phone. The last thing he was going to do was take a call from a listener. By ten o'clock he was more exhausted than he'd ever been in his life. He threw off his headphones, stood slowly and offered his hand to Maggie.

"We got through it, partner. You're a real pro."

"Same goes for you," she replied.

Her hand was like ice when she shook his.

"We have to talk now," he said.

"No. We already did that with thousands of eavesdroppers."

"Is that what bothers you? That everybody overheard our argument?"

The tiny muscles beneath her eyes pulsed with tension. "I'll recover from that humiliation," she told him. She grabbed her purse and jacket and headed for the door. "Oh, by the way, Mac. Lamar left this morning. I told him I was in love with you and I meant it at the time. But I'm not so sure anymore."

Mac didn't try to stop her when she walked out of the control room. He didn't know how.

He went back to their office and sat behind the desk. Maggie's desk. He picked up a pen and twirled it through his fingers. Maggie's pen. He threw it aside. He examined the top of the desk, the papers and paraphernalia so neatly arranged. With one long swing of his arm Mac wiped everything off it. He regretted his action immediately. It was his day for regrettable actions.

"Oh, wow," Stan Stanmore said, coming in without knocking. "Looks like a tornado hit this place. Did you and Maggie continue your fight in here when you got off the air?"

Mac ignored Stan, hoping he would go away, and gathered strewn papers from the floor. Stan stood where he was.

"The switchboard is lit up like a Christmas tree," he said. "That's what's happening to our switchboard right now. Patti is going bananas. I told her to keep tabs. Want to know the vote count so far?"

"What vote? What the hell are you babbling about, Stanmore?" Mac threw the papers he'd picked up back on the desk and scowled at the station manager, his thick eyebrows almost melding.

"Hey, man, don't look at me that way," Stan said. "I'm not the one who was *babbling* private stuff on the air without realizing it." He grinned. "You and Maggie put on quite a show today."

Mac's dark look became even more fierce. "If you're getting the slightest enjoyment out of what happened, I'll wring your scrawny neck, Stan. I swear I will."

Stan immediately put on a straight face. "The lucky thing is that neither of you swore on the air, man. FCC regulations and all that."

Mac slumped down in the chair behind Maggie's desk again and buried his head in his hands. "I don't even remember what we said," he mumbled through them.

"Oh, I can fill you in," Stan offered eagerly. "I heard it all. You told Maggie that you were both obligated to be faithful to each other."

Mac looked up. "I said that over the air?"

"Yeah. It was pretty touching. And then she told you that she would rather rot in hell than marry you, or something like that."

Mac moaned.

"More bad news, Mad Dog," Stan informed him in a cheery voice. "Patti's count on the calls so far is Maggie, ninety-nine. And you have ten, half of which were obvious nut cases according to our frantic receptionist."

"A count on *what*, dammit?"

"On who won the argument, of course. But the general consensus is that you two should bury the hatchet and get married."

Mac balked. "I don't need a general consensus to tell me what to do." He stood and shoved his hands into the pockets of his corduroy slacks. His fingertips grazed against a round object in one of them—a little gift he'd intended to give Maggie after he'd had it out with her about Bleaker. His heart sank. She would never take it from him now. He'd allowed jealousy to get the better of him after cautioning Maggie not to let it enter into their relationship. He felt like a complete jerk. "Do you know where Maggie is now, Stan? I've got to talk to her."

"She left the building a few minutes ago." Stan looked at Mac with pity. "Maybe you should let her cool down, Mad Dog. I mean, when a woman says she'd rather rot in—"

"She didn't say that!" Mac shouted. "She said she wouldn't marry me if her life depended on it."

"Hey, same difference, man."

Mac moaned again. Maybe Stan was right about waiting awhile before talking to Maggie. He left the office and headed down the hall. Fat Man Spratt, stuffing himself with doughnuts by the coffee machine during his show's news break, stopped him. *"Mmhfry frerr,"* he said.

"What?"

Fat Man swallowed his mouthful. "Marry her," he repeated. "If she'll have you, that is."

Mac nudged him aside. He proceeded past the receptionist desk and Patti waved at him frantically. He waved her away as he passed. "I don't want any messages."

"But there's one from a Mr. Copla who claims he will come to Rutland and hold me personally accountable if you don't get it!" Patti called.

Mac stopped dead in his tracks. Frank Copla was the general manager of one of New York's top-rated stations. He turned back and took the pink message slip Patti so desperately wanted to hand him.

By late afternoon Mac was sitting across from Copla in the Oak Bar at the Plaza Hotel in New York sipping India Pale Ale. Copla hadn't wasted time getting to the point. He wanted Mac to take over the morning show at his station.

"It's a tempting offer," Mac told him. "But I've got a partner now. Hire her to work with me and it's a deal."

Copla shook his head. "Forget it. We've already got a male-female duo in our afternoon drive-time slot. Too much of a good thing is a bad thing, Mad Dog. Leave that partner of yours behind. We want you solo."

"But she and I are so *good* together. Have you ever heard our show?"

"Nah." Copla waved away the very idea. "I never listen to the backwater stations. But I remember you..." He pointed a pudgy finger at Mac. "When you were the best jock in New York. It's time you came back, MacNair. I've already made you my top offer, but I can throw in a limousine to and from work every day to sweeten it."

Mac leaned forward. "I want to keep working with my partner, Frank. If you listened to our show you would understand why. It's the two of us or nothing."

"Okay, okay," Copla said. "You can have the limousine full time, Mad Dog. At your beck and call, twenty-four hours a day. How's that?"

Mac pulled back. "You're not hearing me, Copla."

The general manager's eyes got hard. "And you're not hearing *me*, Mad Dog. You're in. The broad is out. That's final. Take it or leave it."

And Mac said the words he had never expected to say while he'd been sitting it out in Rutland waiting for this very opportunity. "Then I'll have to leave it."

"Are you crazy?" Copla looked a little mad himself at that moment, eyes bulging out. "If you're so hung up on this woman, move her back to New York with you. Hell, for the money I'm offering you can move the entire population of Vermont back here with you!"

Mac smiled, always appreciative of hyperbole. "I can't work without Maggie as my partner anymore," he said. "Sorry, Copla." He finished off his glass of ale. "Thanks for the drink and thanks for the offer."

"You really are crazy, aren't you, Mad Dog?"

"Yeah, crazy in love," he replied before leaving the bar. He drove straight back to Vermont.

Maggie was lying under a blanket on the sofa in Miss Jasper's parlor, immersed in her misery, when the doorbell rang. She made no move to answer it. There was no one on the face of the earth that she cared to see at the moment, even Mac. Especially Mac! But the ringing was insistent and incessant. She flung off the blanket and shuffled to the door in her thick red socks. The flannel nightgown she was wearing gave her extra protection against the chill. But unlike Mac's shirt, it did nothing to warm her heart.

"Go away!" she shouted through the thick door.

"I won't! I'm going to camp out here until you let me in."

"Lola?" Maggie pressed her ear to the door. "Is that you?"

"No. It's Snow White and the Seven Dwarfs."

Deciding that the quickest way to get rid of Lola was to hear her out, Maggie let her in.

"You're the last person I expected to see tonight," she said.

Lola gave her a quick once-over as she sashayed into the parlor. "You've been lying around crying and feeling sorry for yourself all evening, haven't you?"

Maggie snatched up the blanket on the sofa and folded it. "Why are you here, Lola?"

"For Mac's sake."

"He asked you to come talk to me?" Maggie forced a laugh. "Since when does Mad Dog MacNair need anyone to do his talking for him?"

"He doesn't. Mac has no idea I'm here. The way I figure, he's still driving back from New York."

"He was in New York today?" So that's why he hadn't called. Not that she would have spoken to him, Maggie reminded herself.

"He went in to meet with one of the big radio honchos."

"He told you this?" Maggie was immediately hurt that Mac had been in contact with Lola but not her.

Lola smiled. "Don't worry, Mags. I haven't become Mac's little confidante."

"Then how do you know about this?" A sense of foreboding slowly crept into her system as she realized the significance of what Lola was telling her.

"I have a lot of contacts in this business," Lola explained. "And when I overheard that Frank Copla had called Mac at the station this morning, I got right on the phone myself. You know who Frank Copla is, don't you?"

Maggie nodded. It had happened. The worst had happened.

"Well, I'm pretty chummy with Copla's promotion director," Lola continued. "He gave me the lowdown. Copla offered Mac the prime spot on his station. Morning superjock."

Maggie sank down on the sofa. "That's great for Mac. That's what he most wanted." Even more than he wanted me, she thought. She placed her hand on her chest. It felt as if there was a hole where her heart should have been. "Do you know when he starts?"

Lola shook her head. "That's the hitch, Maggie. My friend called back later today. It seems Copla stomped into the promo department in a rage and ordered them to delay all plans announcing the return of Mad Dog MacNair. Mac turned down his offer, Maggie. And do you want to know why?"

"He's holding out for more money?"

"Now that would make sense, wouldn't it? But no. He's holding out for his Magnolia Blossom."

Maggie stared at her, wide-eyed. "I don't get it."

"Sweetie, neither do I," Lola replied. "But it seems Mac can't find it in his heart to part with his partner. My friend told me that even though Copla is furious with Mac now, he still wants him. But not *you*, Maggie."

Maggie put her hand to her chest again. Her heart was there all right, pounding furiously. What further proof did she need that Mac did indeed love her? "You're here because you want me to convince Mac to accept that offer, aren't you, Lola?"

She sat down on the sofa with Maggie and looked at her earnestly. "That's right. You're the only one who can, Maggie. And this is such a great opportunity for him. Don't let him throw it away for the sake of—"

"Love?" Maggie smiled softly. "Why not? I know that sounds selfish but it isn't, really. Mac knows what he's doing. He was miserable when he was a New York jock and it seems he's finally realized what will make him happy. He wants to stay in Rutland with me and continue our show on PEU. What's so awful about that?"

"Everything, as far as I'm concerned," Lola replied bluntly. "Not only is Mac wasting his talent at PEU. But you two may not even have a job on the station for long."

"What?" Maggie leaped to her feet. "You mean we're being fired because of what happened this morning?"

"No. That was great radio. We've been getting calls all day from fans and reporters. You and Mac are the hottest item in chilly Vermont right now. So that's not the problem."

"What is? We've doubled the ratings since we took over that time slot. And ad revenues are up, aren't they, Lola?"

"You bet. PEU is finally showing a healthy profit. But it's still small potatoes for a conglomerate as big as the one I work for. I got the word from Stanmore Senior today. The corporation is dumping all the radio stations they acquired during the last fiscal period. Profits are too unpredictable, they say. What surprised Stanmore most was that the station he let his son manage turned out to be the most successful one."

"So who's going to buy PEU?" Maggie felt as if she were crassly discussing the sale of a loved one.

"Hey, do I have a crystal ball? Your guess is as good as mine, Mags. And who knows what the new owners will want? If they change the format, a show like yours and Mac's may not fit into the scheme of things. Do you want Mac to give up everything all for the sake of...love." Lola pronounced it as if it were a foreign word she was unfamiliar with.

Maggie thought for a moment. "No," she finally replied. "I can't let him do that."

"Thatta girl, Maggie. I knew that once we had this discussion you would see reason and help Mac to do the same."

"Why do you have such a deep interest in his welfare, Lola?"

"Because he's one of the few true gentlemen I've ever known. And he's been my friend when I've needed one. That's why."

Maggie nodded in understanding. "Thanks for coming to explain the situation, Lola. I won't let Mac make this sacrifice for my sake."

"I appreciate how hard it's going to be for you to break up your act with him."

Maggie put on a brave smile. "Just the hardest thing I've ever done, that's all."

After Lola left, Maggie's first inclination was to drive to Rutland and wait for Mac at his apartment. But then it occurred to her that he might be on his way to Jasper to see her and they would miss each other. She left a message on his answering machine and waited.

Her emotions were topsy-turvy. One moment she was elated. He loved her! He was willing to give up his goal for her! For *her*! Her heart soared and she felt like dancing. The next moment, her heart changed direction and plunged. She was going to lose him as her radio partner. They would work out some arrangement when he went to New York. But it would never be the same between them. He would get engrossed in his work and she would have no part in it anymore. Would they drift apart, become strangers?

When the doorbell rang Maggie froze for a moment, then went to answer it, resolved to hide her misgivings from Mac.

Mac waited on the other side of the door, praying that Maggie would let him in. She had every right to be angry with him. He heard the handle turn and he braced himself. He would have to talk fast—faster than he'd ever talked in his life. His career didn't depend on it now. But his very survival did.

Maggie threw open the door and the hall light behind her lit her hair like a halo.

"Please don't slam it back in my face," Mac pleaded. "Hear me out, first. I know I don't deserve it but—"

"Come in out of the cold, Madison," she said softly, her smile a warm blessing upon him.

Confused and relieved by her welcoming reception, Mac followed her as she seemed to float up the stairs. When she reached the top she beckoned him to follow her down the long, dimly lit hall. Her pastel nightgown seemed to glow and Mac had the weird sensation that she was a mirage that had sprung from his very soul. But when they entered her room she turned to him suddenly, wrapped her arms around him and gave him a long deep kiss. She was real enough, Mac thought. She was also the woman of his dreams.

"Will I ever figure you out, Maggie?" he asked. "You never cease to amaze me."

She kept her arms draped around his shoulders. "You're probably wondering why I'm even speaking to you, let alone kissing you."

"The thought crossed my mind."

"I know what you did for me today, Madison. Lola found out and told me. But you're being very foolish." She kissed him again to reward such foolishness. "I want you to take that job. In fact, I insist that you do."

"Sorry. That bridge is already burned," he said.

"No, it isn't, Mac. Copla still wants you. So now you can have it both ways. You now have my undying regard and appreciation for your grand gesture. And you can have the job, too!"

"But I don't want it, honey. You're missing the major point here. I don't want to work on radio ever again without you as my partner." He paused to take a kiss from her. "What we have now is perfect. I hope we'll be doing our show at PEU when we're both oldsters in rocking chairs."

Maggie smiled at the image of them rocking away to rock and roll, the Ma and Pa Disc Jockeys of Rutland. But her smile quickly faded. "Our station is going to be sold, Mac. We may be out of jobs by next month. That's why it's so important that you take the one in New York."

"But what would *you* do then, Maggie?"

"Oh, I'll find something soon enough," she assured him. "I have an impressive background now. I've worked with a legend in his own time, the infamous Mad Dog MacNair!" Her voice cracked a little. She hoped Mac hadn't noticed. "Besides, if I can't find another job in front of the mike it's no big deal. The truth is I'm getting bored with it."

"The truth is you're lying, Maggie." Mac tapped her nose. "Your heart starts pumping the moment you're on the air. I can hear it through my headphones, honey. We're alike that way. And as much as our hearts belong to radio, they belong to each other. We can't split up and go our separate ways now. It's physically and mentally impossible."

"Oh, Mac, don't make this more difficult than it already is for me," she begged, leaning against him, breathing in his familiar, wonderful scent. "Take the job in New York, dammit! We'll work things out."

"Oh, I know we'll work things out, Maggie. But together. As partners. I don't want to be a solo act anymore, honey. I want to be a team."

She drew away from him to look up at his face. "You really mean that, don't you?"

Mac took her hand and guided her to the bed. He sat down and pulled her onto his lap. "You said today that you wouldn't marry me if your life depended on it, Maggie, and the whole world heard you. Or at least our special part of it did. But what I'm asking you now is this." He pressed his lips to her temple. "Would you marry me if *my* life depended on it? Because it does, my love. You've become so much a part of me that I can't live without you."

She closed her eyes and the tears slid down her cheeks. "When did you realize this, Madison?"

He laughed, his breath warm on her ear. "When I bought you all those toothbrushes. It seemed so right that we should always have our toothbrushes hanging side by side.

"And then, when I was leaving the drugstore, I spotted this gum-ball machine. The kind with tacky prizes inside. One of the prizes was a plastic engagement ring with a big glass stone. I went through five bucks in change before that ring finally slid down the shoot. Before I left for work yesterday morning I placed it on the pillow for you with a note saying that I'd get you a real one whenever you wanted. That's why I wanted you to come back to my place so badly, Maggie. That's why I went crazy when Lamar showed up and ruined the surprise. Ruined everything for me."

"Oh, Madison, you take the cake." She wept openly and the tears felt as soothing as spring rain on her cheeks.

"I've been carrying that ring around all day," he confessed. He shifted her weight on his lap and dug into his pocket for it. "Will you accept it now, my love?"

"Yes, I'll accept it," Maggie said in a choked voice. He slipped the gaudy bauble on her finger and smiling through her tears, she raised her hand to admire it. "It's perfect," she declared.

Mac kissed her palm. "We'll go shopping for one that's a little less ostentatious tomorrow," he said. "You understand that you've just committed yourself to a lifelong contract with me, don't you, honey?"

"Of course. That's the deal," she assured him.

Mac sighed and held her close. "I feel such a sense of peace now. A peace I've been searching for all my life. We're so right together, Maggie. It doesn't matter what happens to us in this crazy business we're in. All that matters is that we'll always have each other."

"You won't get any argument from me about that," Maggie said.

"Well, that's a switch!"

Laughing, Mac fell across the bed and pulled her on top of him. They kissed with the utmost tenderness, savoring their happiness. Then they undressed each other slowly and celebrated their love. They got little sleep during the night but when they awoke they were refreshed. They were each other's source of vitality.

"Having company while I get dressed for work is great," Mac said to Maggie as he walked around the room naked, picking his clothes off the floor. "The loneliest time of the day for me used to be these hours before dawn. I felt like I was the only person awake in the universe."

"Me, too," Maggie said from the bed where she watched him. "But we may not have to be getting up so early in the very near future if WPEU gets sold."

"There're always other jobs at other stations, honey."

"I know. But I really like it around here."

"Me, too, although I never thought I'd say it." Mac paused. "Hold everything, honey," he said, dropping his shirt. "I just got a brainstorm."

"For the show?"

"No. For our future. Let's buy the station, Maggie."

"Be serious, Madison. It would cost a fortune."

"I've never been more serious in my life. I'm going to buy you PEU as a wedding present, honey."

"Good Lord, Madison. Don't tell me you're not only sexy and handsome and funny, but *rich*, too!" She still thought he was joking.

"I may not be rich but I'm no pauper, honey. I managed to salt away a few of the big bucks I made in New York," he informed her. "Besides, we'll get investors. We're pretty famous in this area now. Even small investors will be welcome. Our fans can have a piece of the action." He began pacing as he always did when a great idea took hold of him. "Yeah! Why shouldn't the people who support a radio station profit for a change? And you *know* it's going to be profitable once we take charge, don't you, honey? We understand radio better than any faceless corporation could."

"Hmm, maybe it could work." As usual, Maggie was getting drawn into Mac's enthusiasm.

"Of course it will work if we want it to." Mac went back and forth past Maggie as he paced, deep in thought and oblivious to the fact that he was stark naked. "Stan should continue to be station manager, don't you think, honey? He's done a surprisingly good job. And what about Lola? You think she'd stay on to head sales? New York's no good for her. She needs a healthier climate. Her and Stan?" Mac shrugged his broad shoulders. "Who knows. Could work out. And what about Clyde Cobb, Maggie? It's time he got promoted. He's got more knowledge about radio in his little finger than all those corporate bozos put together. We'll have to rework the format, of course. Maybe hire a program director. And then we can—" He stopped and looked at Maggie. "You haven't been saying much, honey."

"You haven't given me much of a chance to, love."

"Well? What do you think? Do you believe we can do it, Maggie."

"Yes. I believe in the idea. And I believe in you, Madison. Sure we can do it." Her golden eyes glowed. "And we're *going* to do it."

Satisfied, he resumed his pacing and Maggie was glad. She'd always liked the way he moved.

"So how does this hit you, Maggie? We get married on the air. Our fans would love it."

She laughed. "Oh, Mac, you are incorrigible!"

"Okay, okay, bad idea. But listen to this one. Mad Dog and Magnolia take a trip down the Amazon and..."

*   *   *   *   *

Silhouette Special Edition.

presents

★ LOVE AND GLORY ★

from
Lindsay McKenna

Introducing a gripping new series celebrating our men—and women—in uniform. Meet the Trayherns, a military family as proud and colorful as the American flag, a family fighting the shadow of dishonor, a family determined to triumph—with **LOVE AND GLORY!**

June: **A QUESTION OF HONOR** (SE #529) leads the fast-paced excitement. When Coast Guard officer Noah Trayhern offers Kit Anderson a safe house, he unwittingly endangers his own guarded emotions.

July: **NO SURRENDER** (SE #535) Navy pilot Alyssa Trayhern's assignment with arrogant jet jockey Clay Cantrell threatens her career—and her heart—with a crash landing!

August: **RETURN OF A HERO** (SE #541) Strike up the band to welcome home a man whose top-secret reappearance will make headline news . . . with a delicate, daring woman by his side.

Silhouette Romance

AWARD OF EXCELLENCE

LONG, TALL TEXANS

Diana Palmer brings you the second Award of Excellence title

SUTTON'S WAY

In Diana Palmer's bestselling Long, Tall Texans trilogy, you had a mesmerizing glimpse of Quinn Sutton—a mean, lean Wyoming wildcat of a man, with a disposition to match.

Now, in September, Quinn's back with a story of his own. Set in the Wyoming wilderness, he learns a few things about women from snowbound beauty Amanda Callaway—and a lot more about love.

He's a Texan at heart . . . who soon has a Wyoming wedding in mind!

The Award of Excellence is given to one specially selected title per month. Spend September discovering *Sutton's Way* #670 . . . only in Silhouette Romance.

RS670-1R

Go Wild With Desire....

THIS SEPTEMBER
Silhouette Desire
Fires Your Imagination With
A HOT NEW LOOK!

Slip between
the striking new covers
to find six sensuous
contemporary love stories
every month from

SILHOUETTE

Desire

DNCS-1

Silhouette Intimate Moments®

COMING IN OCTOBER!
A FRESH LOOK FOR
Silhouette Intimate Moments!

Silhouette Intimate Moments has always brought you the perfect combination of love and excitement, and now they're about to get a new cover design that's just as exciting as the stories inside.

Over the years we've brought you stories that combined romance with something a little bit different, like adventure or suspense. We've brought you longtime favorite authors like Nora Roberts and Linda Howard. We've brought you exciting new talents like Patricia Gardner Evans and Marilyn Pappano. Now let us bring you a new cover design guaranteed to catch your eye just as our heroes and heroines catch your heart.

Look for it in October—
Only from Silhouette Intimate Moments!

IMNC-1